Once a Week

A. A. Milne

Once a Week

The present edition is a reproduction of previous publication of this classic work. Minor typographical errors may have been corrected without note; however, for an authentic reading experience the spelling, punctuation, and capitalization have been retained from the original text.

ISBN: 978-1-63637-479-6

TO

MY COLLABORATOR
WHO BUYS THE INK AND PAPER
LAUGHS
AND, IN FACT, DOES ALL THE REALLY DIFFICULT
PART OF THE BUSINESS
THIS BOOK IS GRATEFULLY DEDICATED
IN MEMORY OF A WINTER'S MORNING
IN SWITZERLAND

CONTENTS

THE HEIR

I

HE INTRODUCES HIMSELF

"In less refined circles than ours," I said to Myra, "your behaviour would be described as swank. Really, to judge from the airs you put on, you might be the child's mother."

"He's jealous because he's not an aunt himself. Isn't he, ducksey darling?"

"I do wish you wouldn't keep dragging the baby into the conversation; we can make it go quite well as a duologue. As to being jealous—why, it's absurd. True, I'm not an aunt, but in a very short time I shall be an uncle by marriage, which sounds to me much superior. That is," I added, "if you're still equal to it."

Myra blew me a kiss over the cradle.

"Another thing you've forgotten," I went on, "is that I'm down for a place as a godfather. Archie tells me that it isn't settled yet, but that there's a good deal of talk about it in the clubs. Who's the other going to be? Not Thomas, I suppose? That would be making the thing rather a farce."

"Hasn't Dahlia broken it to you?" said Myra anxiously.

"Simpson?" I asked, in an awed whisper.

Myra nodded. "And, of course, Thomas," she said.

"Heavens! Not three of us? What a jolly crowd we shall be. Thomas can play our best ball. We might——"

"But of course there are only going to be two godfathers," she said, and leant over the cradle again.

I held up my three end fingers. "Thomas," I said, pointing to the smallest, "me," I explained, pointing to the next, "and Simpson, the tall gentleman in glasses. One, two, three."

"Oh, baby," sighed Myra, "what a very slow uncle by marriage you're going to have!"

I stood and gazed at my three fingers for some time.

"I've got it," I said at last, and I pulled down the middle one. "The rumour in the clubs was unauthorized. I don't get a place after all."

"Don't say you mind," pleaded Myra. "You see, Dahlia thought

1

that as you were practically one of the family already, an uncle-elect by marriage, and as she didn't want to choose between Thomas and Samuel——"

"Say no more. I was only afraid that she might have something against my moral character. Child," I went on, rising and addressing the unresponsive infant, "England has lost a godfather this day, but the world has gained a——what? I don't know. I want my tea."

Myra gave the baby a last kiss and got up.

"Can I trust him with you while I go and see about Dahlia?"

"I'm not sure. It depends how I feel. I may change him with some poor baby in the village. Run away, aunt, and leave us men to ourselves. We have several matters to discuss."

When the child and I were alone together, I knelt by his cradle and surveyed his features earnestly. I wanted to see what it was he had to offer Myra which I could not give her. "This," I said to myself, "is the face which has come between her and me," for it was unfortunately true that I could no longer claim Myra's undivided attention. But the more I looked at him the more mysterious the whole thing became to me.

"Not a bad kid?" said a voice behind me.

I turned and saw Archie.

"Yours, I believe," I said, and I waved him to the cradle.

Archie bent down and tickled the baby's chin, making appropriate noises the while—one of the things a father has to learn to do.

"Who do you think he's like?" he asked proudly.

"The late Mr. Gladstone," I said, after deep thought.

"Wrong. Hallo, here's Dahlia coming out. I hope, for your sake, that the baby's all right. If she finds he's caught measles or anything, you'll get into trouble."

By a stroke of bad luck the child began to cry as soon as he saw the ladies. Myra rushed up to him.

"Poor little darling," she said soothingly. "Did his uncle by marriage frighten him, then?"

"Don't listen to her, Dahlia," I said. "I haven't done anything to him. We were chatting together quite amicably until he suddenly caught sight of Myra and burst into tears."

"He's got a little pain," said Dahlia gently taking him up and patting him.

"I think the trouble is mental," suggested Archie. "He looks to me as if he had something on his conscience. Did he say anything to you about it when you were alone?"

2

"He didn't say much," I confessed, "but he seemed to be keeping something back. I think he wants a bit of a run, really."

"Poor little lamb," said Dahlia. "There, he's better now, thank you." She looked up at Archie and me. "I don't believe you two love him a bit."

Archie smiled at his wife and went over to the tea-table to pour out. I sat on the grass and tried to analyse my feelings to my nephew by marriage.

"As an acquaintance," I said, "he is charming; I know no one who is better company. If I cannot speak of his more solid qualities, it is only because I do not know him well enough. But to say whether I love him or not is difficult; I could tell you better after our first quarrel. However, there is one thing I must confess. I am rather jealous of him."

"You envy his life of idleness?"

"No, I envy him the amount of attention he gets from Myra. The love she wastes on him which might be better employed on me is a heartrending thing to witness. As her betrothed I should expect to occupy the premier place in her affections, but, really, I sometimes think that if the baby and I both fell into the sea she would jump in and save the baby first."

"Don't talk about his falling into the sea," said Dahlia, with a shudder; "I can't a-bear it."

"I think it will be all right," said Archie, "I was touching wood all the time."

"What a silly godfather he nearly had!" whispered Myra at the cradle. "It quite makes you smile, doesn't it, baby? Oh, Dahlia, he's just like Archie when he smiles!"

"Oh, yes, he's the living image of Archie," said Dahlia confidently.

I looked closely at Archie and then at the baby.

"I should always know them apart," I said at last. "That," and I pointed to the one at the tea-table, "is Archie, and this," and I pointed to the one in the cradle, "is the baby. But then I've such a wonderful memory for faces."

"Baby," said Myra, "I'm afraid you're going to know some very foolish people."

II

HE MEETS HIS GODFATHERS

Thomas and Simpson arrived by the twelve-thirty train, and Myra and I drove down in the wagonette to meet them. Myra handled the ribbons ("handled the ribbons"—we must have that again) while I sat on the box-seat and pointed out any traction-engines and things in the road. I am very good at this.

"I suppose," I said, "there will be some sort of ceremony at the station? The station-master will read an address while his little daughter presents a bouquet of flowers. You don't often get two godfathers travelling by the same train. Look out," I said, as we swung round a corner, "there's an ant coming."

"What did you say? I'm so sorry, but I listen awfully badly when I'm driving."

"As soon as I hit upon anything really good I'll write it down. So far I have been throwing off the merest trifles. When we are married, Myra——"

"Go on; I love that."

"When we are married we shan't be able to afford horses, so we'll keep a couple of bicycles, and you'll be able to hear everything I say. How jolly for you."

"All right," said Myra quietly.

There was no formal ceremony on the platform, but I did not seem to feel the want of it when I saw Simpson stepping from the train with an enormous Teddy-bear under his arm.

"Hallo, dear old chap," he said, "here we are! You're looking at my bear. I quite forgot it until I'd strapped up my bags, so I had to bring it like this. It squeaks," he added, as if that explained it. "Listen," and the piercing roar of the bear resounded through the station.

"Very fine. Hallo, Thomas!"

"Hallo!" said Thomas, and went to look after his luggage.

"I hope he'll like it," Simpson went on. "Its legs move up and down." He put them into several positions, and then squeaked it again. "Jolly, isn't it?"

"Ripping," I agreed. "Who's it for?"

He looked at me in astonishment for a moment.

"My dear old chap, for the baby."

"Oh, I see. That's awfully nice of you. He'll love it." I wondered if Simpson had ever seen a month-old baby. "What's its name?"

"I've been calling it Duncan in the train, but, of course, he will want to choose his own name for it."

"Well, you must talk it over with him to-night after the ladies have gone to bed. How about your luggage? We mustn't keep Myra waiting."

"Hallo, Thomas!" said Myra, as we came out. "Hallo, Samuel! Hooray!"

"Hallo, Myra!" said Thomas. "All right?"

"Myra, this is Duncan," said Simpson, and the shrill roar of the bear rang out once more.

Myra, her mouth firm, but smiles in her eyes, looked down lovingly at him. Sometimes I think that she would like to be Simpson's mother. Perhaps, when we are married, we might adopt him.

"For baby?" she said, stroking it with her whip. "But he won't be allowed to take it into church with him, you know. No, Thomas, I won't have the luggage next to me; I want some one to talk to. You come."

Inside the wagonette Simpson squeaked his bear at intervals, while I tried to prepare him for his coming introduction to his godson. Having known the baby for nearly a week, and being to some extent in Myra's confidence, I felt quite the family man beside Simpson.

"You must try not to be disappointed with his looks," I said. "Anyway, don't let Dahlia think you are. And if you want to do the right thing say that he's just like Archie. Archie doesn't mind this for some reason."

"Is he tall for his age?"

"Samuel, pull yourself together. He isn't tall at all. If he is anything he is long, but how long only those can say who have seen him in his bath. You do realize that he is only a month old?"

"My dear old boy, of course. One can't expect much from him. I suppose he isn't even toddling about yet?"

"No—no. Not actually toddling."

"Well, we can teach him later on. And I'm going to have a lot of fun with him. I shall show him my watch—babies always love that."

There was a sudden laugh from the front, which changed just a little too late into a cough. The fact is I had bet Myra a new golf-ball that Simpson would show the baby his watch within two minutes of meeting him. Of course, it wasn't a certainty yet, but I thought there would be no harm in mentioning the make of ball I preferred. So I changed the conversation subtly to golf.

5

Amidst loud roars from the bear we drove up to the house and were greeted by Archie.

"Hallo, Thomas! how are you? Hallo, Simpson! Good heavens! I know that face. Introduce me, Samuel."

"This is Duncan. I brought him down for your boy to play with."

"Duncan, of course. The boy will love it. He's tired of me already. He proposes to meet his godfathers at four p.m. precisely. So you'll have nearly three hours to think of something genial to say to him."

We spent the last of the three hours playing tennis, and at four p.m. precisely the introduction took place. By great good luck Duncan was absent; Simpson would have wasted his whole two minutes in making it squeak.

"Baby," said Dahlia, "this is your Uncle Thomas."

"Hallo!" said Thomas, gently kissing the baby's hand. "Good old boy," and he felt for his pipe.

"Baby," said Dahlia, "this is your Uncle Samuel."

As he leant over the child I whipped out my watch and murmured, "Go!" 4 hrs. 1 min. 25 sec. I wished Myra had not taken my "two minutes" so literally, but I felt that the golf-ball was safe.

Simpson looked at the baby as if fascinated, and the baby stared back at him. It was a new experience for both of them.

"He's just like Archie," he said at last, remembering my advice. "Only smaller," he added.

4 hrs. 2 min. 7 sec.

"I can see you, baby," he said. "Goo-goo."

Myra came and rested her chin on my shoulder. Silently I pointed to the finishing place on my watch, and she gave a little gurgle of excitement. There was only one minute left.

"I wonder what you're thinking about," said Simpson to the baby. "Is it my glasses you want to play with?"

"Help!" I murmured. "This will never do."

"He just looks and looks. Ah! but his Uncle Samuel knows what baby wants to see." (I squeezed Myra's arm. 4 hrs. 3 mins. 10 secs. There was just time.) "I wonder if it's anything in his uncle's waistcoat?"

"No!" whispered Myra to me in agony. "Certainly not."

"He shall see it if he wants to," said Simpson soothingly, and put his hand to his waistcoat pocket. I smiled triumphantly at Myra. He had five seconds to get the watch out—plenty of time.

"Bother!" said Simpson. "I left it upstairs."

III

HE CHOOSES A NAME

The afternoon being wet we gathered round the billiard-room fire and went into committee.

"The question before the House," said Archie, "is what shall the baby be called, and why. Dahlia and I have practically decided on his names, but it would amuse us to hear your inferior suggestions and point out how ridiculous they are."

Godfather Simpson looked across in amazement at Godfather Thomas.

"Really, you are taking a good deal upon yourself, Archie," he said coldly. "It is entirely a matter for my colleague and myself to decide whether the ground is fit for—to decide, I should say, what the child is to be called. Unless this is quite understood we shall hand in our resignations."

"We've been giving a lot of thought to it," said Thomas, opening his eyes for a moment. "And our time is valuable." He arranged the cushions at his back and closed his eyes again.

"Well, as a matter of fact, the competition isn't quite closed," said Archie. "Entries can still be received."

"We haven't really decided at all," put in Dahlia gently. "It is so difficult."

"In that case," said Samuel, "Thomas and I will continue to act. It is my pleasant duty to inform you that we had a long consultation yesterday, and finally agreed to call him—er—Samuel Thomas."

"Thomas Samuel," said Thomas sleepily.

"How did you think of those names?" I asked. "It must have taken you a tremendous time."

"With a name like Samuel Thomas Mannering," went on Simpson ["Thomas Samuel Mannering," murmured Thomas], "your child might achieve almost anything. In private life you would probably call him Sam."

"Tom," said a tired voice.

"Or, more familiarly, Sammy."

"Tommy," came in a whisper from the sofa.

"What do you think of it?" asked Dahlia.

"I mustn't say," said Archie; "they're my guests. But I'll tell you privately some time."

7

There was silence for a little, and then a thought occurred to me.

"You know, Archie," I said, "limited as their ideas are, you're rather in their power. Because I was looking through the service in church on Sunday, and there comes a point when the clergyman says to the godfathers, 'Name this child.' Well, there you are, you know. They've got you. You may have fixed on Montmorency Plantagenet, but they've only to say 'Bert,' and the thing is done."

"You all forget," said Myra, coming over to sit on the arm of my chair, "that there's a godmother too. I shall forbid the Berts."

"Well, that makes it worse. You'll have Myra saying 'Montmorency Plantagenet,' and Samuel saying 'Samuel Thomas,' and Thomas saying 'Thomas Samuel.'"

"It will sound rather well," said Archie, singing it over to himself. "Thomas, you take the tenor part, of course: 'Thomas Samuel, Thomas Samuel, Thom-as Sam-u-el.' We must have a rehearsal."

For five minutes Myra, Thomas, and Simpson chanted in harmony, being assisted after the first minute by Archie, who took the alto part of "Solomon Joel." He explained that as this was what he and his wife really wanted the child christened ("Montmorency Plantagenet" being only an invention of the godmother's) it would probably be necessary for him to join in too.

"Stop!" cried Dahlia, when she could bear it no longer; "you'll wake baby."

There was an immediate hush.

"Samuel," said Archie in a whisper, "if you wake the baby I'll kill you."

The question of his name was still not quite settled, and once more we gave ourselves up to thought.

"Seeing that he's the very newest little Rabbit," said Myra, "I do think he might be called after some very great cricketer."

"That was the idea in christening him 'Samuel,'" said Archie.

"Gaukrodger Carkeek Butt Bajana Mannering," I suggested— "something like that?"

"Silly; I meant 'Charles,' after Fry."

"'Schofield,' after Haigh," murmured Thomas.

"'Warren,' after Bardsley, would be more appropriate to a Rabbit," said Simpson, beaming round at us. There was, however, no laughter. We had all just thought of it ourselves.

"The important thing in christening a future first-class cricketer," said Simpson, "is to get the initials right. What could be better than 'W. G.' as a nickname for Grace? But if 'W. G.'s' initials had been 'Z. Z.,' where would you have been?"

8

"Here," said Archie.

The shock of this reply so upset Simpson that his glasses fell off. He picked them out of the fender and resumed his theme.

"Now, if the baby were christened 'Samuel Thomas' his initials would be 'S. T.,' which are perfect. And the same as Coleridge's."

"Is that Coleridge the wicket-keeper, or the fast bowler?"

Simpson opened his mouth to explain, and then, just in time, decided not to.

"I forgot to say," said Archie, "that anyhow he's going to be called Blair, after his mamma."

"If his name's Blair Mannering," I said at once, "he'll have to write a book. You can't waste a name like that. The Crimson Spot, by Blair Mannering. Mr. Blair Mannering, the well-known author of The Gash. Our new serial, The Stain on the Bath Mat, has been specially written for us by Mr. and Mrs. Blair Mannering. It's simply asking for it."

"Don't talk about his wife yet, please," smiled Dahlia. "Let me have him a little while."

"Well, he can be a writer and a cricketer. Why not? There are others. I need only mention my friend, S. Simpson."

"But the darling still wants another name," said Myra. "Let's call him John to-day, and William to-morrow, and Henry the next day, and so on until we find out what suits him best."

"Let's all go upstairs now and call him Samuel," said Samuel.

"Thomas," said Thomas.

We looked at Dahlia. She got up and moved to the door. In single file we followed her on tip-toe to the nursery. The baby was fast asleep.

"Thomas," we all said in a whisper, "Thomas, Thomas."

There was no reply.

"Samuel!"

Dead silence.

"I think," said Dahlia, "we'll call him Peter."

IV

HE IS CHRISTENED

On the morning of the christening, as I was on my way to the bathroom, I met Simpson coming out of it. There are people who have never seen Simpson in his dressing-gown; people also who have never waited for the sun to rise in glory above the snow-capped peaks of the Alps; who have never stood on Waterloo Bridge and watched St. Paul's come through the mist of an October morning. Well, well, one cannot see everything.

"Hallo, old chap!" he said. "I was just coming to talk to you. I want your advice."

"A glass of hot water the last thing at night," I said, "no sugar or milk, a Turkish bath once a week and plenty of exercise. You'll get it down in no time."

"Don't be an ass. I mean about the christening. I've been to a wedding, of course, but that isn't quite the same thing."

"A moment, while I turn on the tap." I turned it on and came back to him. "Now then, I'm at your service."

"Well, what's the—er—usual costume for a christening?"

"Leave that to the mother," I said. "She'll see that the baby's dressed properly."

"I mean for a godfather."

Dahlia has conveniently placed a sofa outside the bathroom door. I dropped into it and surveyed the dressing-gown thoughtfully.

"Go like that," I said at last.

"What I want to know is whether it's a top-hat affair or not?"

"Have you brought a top-hat?"

"Of course."

"Then you must certainly—— I say! Come out of it, Myra!"

I jumped up from the sofa, but it was too late. She had stolen my bath.

"Well, of all the cheek——"

The door opened and Myra's head appeared round the corner.

"Hush! you'll wake the baby," she said. "Oh, Samuel, what a dream! Why haven't I seen it before?"

"You have, Myra. I've often dressed up in it."

"Then I suppose it looks different with a sponge. Because——"

"Really!" I said as I took hold of Simpson and led him firmly

10

away; "if the baby knew that you carried on like this of a morning he'd be shocked."

Thomas is always late for breakfast. Simpson on this occasion was delayed by his elaborate toilet. They came in last together, by opposite doors, and stood staring at each other. Simpson wore a frock-coat, dashing double-breasted waistcoat, perfectly creased trousers, and a magnificent cravat; Thomas had on flannels and an old blazer.

"By Jove!" said Archie, seeing Simpson first, "you are a——" and then he caught sight of Thomas. "Hul-lo!" His eyes went from one to the other, and at last settled on the toast. He went on with his breakfast. "The two noble godfathers," he murmured.

Meanwhile the two godfathers continued to gaze at each other as if fascinated. At last Simpson spoke.

"We can't both be right," he said slowly to himself.

Thomas woke up.

"Is it the christening to-day? I quite forgot."

"It is, Thomas. The boat-race is to-morrow."

"Well, I can change afterwards. You don't expect me to wear anything like that?" he said, pointing to Simpson.

"Don't change," said Archie. "Both go as you are. Mick and Mack, the Comedy Duo. Simpson does the talking while Thomas falls over the pews."

Simpson collected his breakfast and sat down next to Myra.

"Am I all right?" he asked her doubtfully.

"Your tie's up at the back of your neck," I said.

"Because if Dahlia would prefer it," he went on, ignoring me, "I could easily wear a plain dark tweed."

"You're beautiful, Samuel," said Myra. "I hope you'll look as nice at my wedding."

"You don't think I shall be mistaken for the father?" he asked anxiously.

"By Peter? Well, that is just possible. Perhaps if——"

"I think you're right," said Simpson, and after breakfast he changed into the plain dark tweed.

As the hour approached we began to collect in the hall, Simpson reading the service to himself for the twentieth time.

"Do we have to say anything?" asked Thomas, as he lit his third pipe.

Simpson looked at him in horror.

"Say anything? Of course we do! Haven't you studied it? Here, you'll just have time to read it through."

"Too late now. Better leave it to the inspiration of the

moment," I suggested. "Does anybody know if there's a collection, because if so I shall have to go and get some money."

"There will be a collection for the baby afterwards," said Archie. "I hope you've all been saving up."

"Here he comes!" said Simpson, and Peter Blair Mannering came down the stairs with Dahlia and Myra.

"Good morning, everybody," said Dahlia.

"Good morning. Say 'Good morning,' baby."

"He's rather nervous," said Myra. "He says he's never been christened before, and what's it like?"

"I expect he'll be all right with two such handsome godfathers," said Dahlia.

"Isn't Mr. Simpson looking well?" said Myra in a society voice. "And do you know, dear, that's the third suit I've seen him in to-day."

"Well, are we all ready?"

"You're quite sure about his name?" said Archie to his wife. "This is your last chance, you know. Say the word to Thomas before it's too late."

"I think Peter is rather silly," I said.

"Why Blair?" said Myra. "I ask you."

Dahlia smiled sweetly at us and led the way with P. B. Mannering to the car. We followed ... and Simpson on the seat next the driver read the service to himself for the last time.

"I feel very proud," said Archie as we came out of the church. "I'm not only a father, but my son has a name. And now I needn't call him 'er' any more."

"He was a good boy, wasn't he?" said Myra.

"Thomas, say at once that your godson was a good boy."

But Thomas was quiet. He looked years older.

"I've never read the service before," he said. "I didn't quite know what we were in for. It seems that Simpson and I have undertaken a heavy responsibility; we are practically answerable for the child's education. We are supposed to examine him every few years and find out if he is being taught properly."

"You can bowl to him later on if you like."

"No, no. It means more than that." He turned to Dahlia. "I think," he said, "Simpson and I will walk home. We must begin at once to discuss the lines on which we shall educate our child."

V

HE SEES LIFE

There was no one in sight. If 'twere done well, 'twere well done quickly. I gripped the perambulator, took a last look round, and then suddenly rushed it across the drive and down a side path, not stopping until we were well concealed from the house. Panting, I dropped into a seat, having knocked several seconds off the quarter-mile record for babies under one.

"Hallo!" said Myra.

"Dash it, are there people everywhere to-day? I can't get a moment to myself. 'O solitude, where——'"

"What are you going to do with baby?"

"Peter and I are going for a walk." My eyes rested on her for more than a moment. She was looking at me over an armful of flowers ... and—well—"You can come too if you like," I said.

"I've got an awful lot to do," she smiled doubtfully.

"Oh, if you'd rather count the washing."

She sat down next to me.

"Where's Dahlia?"

"I don't know. We meant to have left a note for her, but we came away in rather a hurry. 'Back at twelve. Peter.'"

"'I am quite happy. Pursuit is useless,'" suggested Myra. "Poor Dahlia, she'll be frightened when she sees the perambulator gone."

"My dear, what could happen to it? Is this Russia?"

"Oh, what happens to perambulators in Russia?" asked Myra eagerly.

"They spell them differently," I said, after a little thought. "Anyhow, Dahlia's all right."

"Well, I'll just take these flowers in and then I'll come back. If you and Peter will have me?"

"I think so," I said.

Myra went in and left me to my reflections, which were mainly that Peter had the prettiest aunt in England, and that the world was very good. But my pleased and fatuous smile over these thoughts was disturbed by her announcement on her return.

"Dahlia says," she began, "that we may have Peter for an hour, but he must come in at once if he cries."

I got up in disgust.

"You've spoilt my morning," I said.

"Oh, no!"

"I had a little secret from Dahlia, or rather Peter and I had a little secret together; at least, you and I and Peter had a secret. Anyhow, it was a secret. And I was feeling very wicked and happy—Peter and I both were; and we were going to let you feel wicked too. And now Dahlia knows all about the desperate deed we were planning, and, to make it worse, all she says is, 'Certainly! By all means! Only don't get his feet wet.' Peter," I said, as I bent over the sleeping innocent, "we are betrayed."

"Miss Mannering will now relate her experiences," said Myra. "I went into the hall to put down the flowers, and just as I was coming out I saw Dahlia in the corner with a book. And she said, 'Tell your young man——'"

"How vulgar!" I interrupted.

"'Do be careful with my baby.' And I said in great surprise, 'What baby?' And she said, 'He was very kindly running him up and down the drive just now. Peter loves it, but don't let them go on too long or there may be an accident.' And then she gave a few more instructions, and—here we are."

"Peter," I said to the somnolent one, "you can't deceive a woman. Also men are pigs. Wake up, and we will apologize to your aunt for doubting her. Sorry, Myra."

Myra pinned a flower in my coat and forgave me, and we walked off together with the perambulator.

"Peter is seeing a bit of life this morning," I said. "What shall we show him now?"

"Thomas and Samuel are playing golf," said Myra casually.

I looked at her doubtfully.

"Is that quite suitable?"

"I think if we didn't let him stay too long it would be all right. Dahlia wouldn't like him to be overexcited."

"Well, he can't be introduced to the game too early. Come on, Peter." And we pushed into more open country.

The 9-hole course which Simpson planned a year ago is not yet used for the Open Championship, though it is certainly better than it was last summer. But it is short and narrow and dog-legged, and, particularly when Simpson is playing on it, dangerous.

"We are now in the zone of fire," I said. "Samuel's repainted ninepenny may whiz past us at any moment. Perhaps I had better go first." I tied my handkerchief to Myra's sunshade and led the way with the white flag.

A ball came over the barn and rolled towards us, just reaching one of the wheels. I gave a yell.

"Hallo!" bellowed Simpson from behind the barn.

"You're firing on the ambulance," I shouted.

He hurried up, followed leisurely by Thomas.

"I say," he said excitedly, "have I hurt him?"

"You have not even waked him. He has the special gift of—was it Wellington or Napoleon?—that of being able to sleep through the heaviest battle."

"Hallo!" said Thomas. "Good old boy! What's he been learning to-day?" he added, with godfatherly interest.

"We're showing him life to-day. He has come to see Simpson play golf."

"Doesn't he ever sit up?" asked Simpson, looking at him with interest. "I don't see how he's going to see anything if he's always on his back. Unless it were something in the air."

"Don't you ever get the ball in the air?" said Myra innocently.

"What will his Uncle Samuel show him if he does sit up?" I asked. "Let's decide first if it's going to be anything worth watching. Which hole are you for? The third?"

"The eighth. My last shot had a bit of a slice."

"A slice! It had about the whole joint. I doubt," I said to Myra, "if we shall do much good here; let's push on."

But Myra had put down the hood and taken some of the clothes off Peter. Peter stirred slightly. He seemed to know that something was going on. Then suddenly he woke up, just in time to see Simpson miss the ball completely. Instantly he gave a cry.

"Now you've done it," said Myra. "He's got to go in. And I'm afraid he'll go away with quite a wrong idea of the game."

But I was not thinking of the baby. Although I am to be his uncle by marriage I had forgotten him.

"If that's about Simpson's form to-day," I said to Myra, "you and I could still take them on and beat them."

Myra looked up eagerly.

"What about Peter?" she asked; but she didn't ask it very firmly.

"We promised Dahlia to take him in directly he cried," I said. "She'd be very upset if she thought she couldn't trust us. And we've got to go in for our clubs, anyway," I added.

Peter was sleeping peacefully again, but a promise is a promise. After all, we had done a good deal for his education that morning. We had shown him human nature at work, and the position of golf in the universe.

"We'll meet you on the first tee," said Myra to Thomas.

VI

HE SLEEPS

"It's sad to think that to-morrow we shall be in London," said Simpson, with a sigh.

"Rotten," agreed Thomas, and took another peach.

There was a moment's silence.

"We shall miss you," I said, after careful thought. I waited in vain for Dahlia to say something, and then added, "You must both come again next year."

"Thank you very much."

"Not at all." I hate these awkward pauses. If my host or hostess doesn't do anything to smooth them over, I always dash in. "It's been delightful to have you," I went on. "Are you sure you can't stay till Wednesday?"

"I'm so sorry," said Dahlia, "but you took me by surprise. I had simply no idea. Are you really going?"

"I'm afraid so."

"Are you really staying?" said Archie to me. "Help!"

"What about Peter?" asked Myra. "Isn't he too young to be taken from his godfathers?"

"We've been talking that over," said Simpson, "and I think it will be all right. We've mapped his future out very carefully and we shall unfold it to you when the coffee comes."

"Thomas is doing it with peach-stones," I said. "Have another, and make him a sailor, Thomas," and I passed the plate.

"Sailor indeed," said Dahlia. "He's going to be a soldier."

"It's too late. Thomas has begun another one. Well, he'll have to swallow the stone."

"A trifle hard on the Admiralty," said Archie. "It loses both Thomas and Peter at one gulp. My country, what of thee?"

However, when Thomas had peeled the peach, I cleverly solved the difficulty by taking it on to my plate while he was looking round for the sugar.

"No, no sugar, thanks," I said, and waved it away.

With the coffee and cigars Simpson unfolded his scheme of education for Peter.

"In the first place," he said, "it is important that even as a child he should always be addressed in rational English and not in that ridiculous baby-talk so common with young mothers."

"Oh dear," said Dahlia.

16

"My good Samuel," I broke in, "this comes well from you. Why, only yesterday I heard you talking to him. I think you called him his nunkey's ickle petsy wetsy lambkin."

"You misunderstood me," said Simpson quickly. "I was talking to you."

"Oh!" I said, rather taken aback. "Well—well, I'm not." I lit a cigar. "And I shall be annoyed if you call me so again."

"At the age of four," Simpson went on, "he shall receive his first lesson in cricket. Thomas will bowl to him——"

"I suppose that means that Thomas will have to be asked down here again," said Archie. "Bother! Still, it's not for four years."

"Thomas will bowl to him, Archie will keep wicket, and I shall field."

"And where do I come in?" I asked.

"You come in after Peter. Unless you would rather have your lesson first."

"That's the second time I've been sat on," I said to Myra, "Why is Simpson so unkind to me to-night?"

"I suppose he's jealous because you're staying on another week."

"Probably; still, I don't like it. Could you turn your back on him, do you think, to indicate our heavy displeasure?"

Myra moved her chair round and rested her elbow on the table.

"Go on, Samuel," said Dahlia. "You're lovely to-night. I suppose these are Thomas's ideas as well as your own?"

"His signature is duly appended to them."

"I didn't read 'em all," said Thomas.

"That's very rash of you," said Archie. "You don't know what you mightn't let yourself in for. You may have promised to pay the child threepence a week pocket-money."

"No, there's nothing like that," said Simpson, to Archie's evident disappointment. "Well, then, at the age of ten he goes to a preparatory school."

"Has he learnt to read yet?" asked Dahlia. "I didn't hear anything about it."

"He can read at six. I forgot to say that I am giving him a book which I shall expect him to read aloud to Thomas and me on his sixth birthday."

"Thomas has got another invitation," said Archie. "Dash it!"

"At fourteen he goes to a public school. The final decision as to which public school he goes to will be left to you, but, of course, we shall expect to be consulted on the subject."

17

"I'll write and tell you what we decide on," said Archie hastily; "there'll be no need for you to come down and be told aloud."

"So far we have not arranged anything for him beyond the age of fourteen. I now propose to read out a few general rules about his upbringing which we must insist on being observed."

"The great question whether Simpson is kicked out of the house to-night, or leaves unobtrusively by the milk train to-morrow morning, is about to be settled," I murmured.

"'Rule One.—He must be brought up to be ambidextrous.' It will be very useful," explained Simpson, "when he fields cover for England."

"Or when he wants to shake hands with two people at once," said Archie.

"'Rule Two.—He must be taught from the first to speak French and German fluently.' He'll thank you for that later on when he goes abroad."

"Or when he goes to the National Liberal Club," said Archie.

"'Rule Three.—He should be surrounded as far as possible with beautiful things.' Beautiful toys, beautiful wall-paper, beautiful scenery——"

"Beautiful godfathers?" I asked doubtfully.

Simpson ignored me and went on hurriedly with the rest of his rules.

"Well," said Archie, at the end of them, "they're all fairly futile, but if you like to write them out neatly and frame them in gold I don't mind hanging them up in the bathroom. Has anybody else got anything fatuous to say before the ladies leave us?"

I filled my glass.

"I've really got a lot to say," I began, "because I consider that I've been rather left out of things. If you come to think of it, I'm the only person here who isn't anything important, all the rest of you being godfathers, or godmothers, or mothers, or fathers, or something. However, I won't dwell on that now. But there's one thing I must say, and here it is." I raised my glass. "Peter Blair Mannering, and may he grow up to be a better man than any of us!"

Upstairs, in happy innocence of the tremendous task in front of him, the child slept. Poor baby!

We drank solemnly, but without much hope.

WINTER SPORT

I

AN INTRODUCTION

"I had better say at once," I announced as I turned over the wine list, "that I have come out here to enjoy myself, and enjoy myself I shall. Myra, what shall we drink?"

"You had three weeks' honeymoon in October," complained Thomas, "and you're taking another three weeks now. Don't you ever do any work?"

Myra and I smiled at each other. Coming from Thomas, who spends his busy day leaning up against the wireless installation at the Admiralty, the remark amused us.

"We'll have champagne," said Myra, "because it's our opening night. Archie, after you with the head-waiter."

It was due to Dahlia, really, that the Rabbits were hibernating at the Hôtel des Angéliques, Switzerland (central-heated throughout); for she had been ordered abroad, after an illness, to pull herself together a little, and her doctor had agreed with Archie that she might as well do it at a place where her husband could skate. On the point that Peter should come and skate too, however, Archie was firm. While admitting that he loved his infant son, he reminded Dahlia that she couldn't possibly get through Calais and Pontarlier without declaring Peter, and that the duty on this class of goods was remarkably heavy. Peter, therefore, was left behind. He had an army of nurses to look after him, and a stenographer to take down his more important remarks. With a daily bulletin and a record of his table-talk promised her, Dahlia was prepared to be content.

As for Myra and me, we might have hesitated to take another holiday so soon, had it not been for a letter I received one morning at breakfast.

"Simpson is going." I said. "He has purchased a pair of skis."

"That does it," said Myra decisively. And, gurgling happily to herself, she went out and bought a camera.

For Thomas I can find no excuses. At a moment of crisis he left his country's Navy in jeopardy and, the Admiralty yacht being otherwise engaged, booked a first return from Cook's. And so it was that at four o'clock one day we arrived together at the Hôtel des Angéliques, and some three hours later were settling down comfortably to dinner.

"I've had a busy time," said Archie. "I've hired a small bob, a luge and a pair of skis for myself, a pair of snow-shoes and some skates for Dahlia, a—a tricycle horse for Simpson, and I don't know what else. All in French."

"What is the French for a pair of snow-shoes?" asked Myra.

"I pointed to them in French. The undersized Robert I got at a bargain. The man who hired it last week broke his leg before his fortnight was up, and so there was a reduction of several centimes."

"I've been busy too," I said. "I've been watching Myra unpack, and telling her where not to put my things."

"I packed jolly well—except for the accident."

"An accident to the boot-oil," I explained. "If I get down to my last three shirts you will notice it."

We stopped eating for a moment in order to drink Dahlia's health. It was Dahlia's health which had sent us there.

"Who's your friend, Samuel?" said Archie, as Simpson caught somebody's eye at another table and nodded.

"A fellow I met in the lift," said Simpson casually.

"Samuel, beware of elevator acquaintances," said Myra in her most solemn manner.

"He's rather a good chap. He was at Peterhouse with a friend of mine. He was telling me quite a good story about a 'wine' my friend gave there once, when——"

"Did you tell him about your 'ginger-beers' at Giggleswick?" I interrupted.

"My dear old chap, he's rather a man to be in with. He knows the President."

"I thought nobody knew the President of the Swiss Republic," said Myra. "Like the Man in the Iron Mask."

"Not that President, Myra. The President of the Angéliques Sports Club."

"Never heard of it," we all said.

Simpson polished his glasses and prepared delightedly to give an explanation.

"The Sports Club runs everything here," he began. "It gives you prizes for fancy costumes and skating and so on."

"Introduce me to the President at once," cooed Myra, patting her hair and smoothing down her frock.

"Even if you were the Treasurer's brother," said Archie, "you wouldn't get a prize for skating, Simpson."

20

"You've never seen him do a rocking seventeen, sideways."

Simpson looked at us pityingly.

"There's a lot more in it than that," he said. "The President will introduce you to anybody. One might see—er—somebody one rather liked the look of, and—er—— Well, I mean in an hotel one wants to enter into the hotel life and—er—meet other people."

"Who is she?" said Myra.

"Anybody you want to marry must be submitted to Myra for approval first," I said. "We've told you so several times."

Simpson hastily disclaimed any intention of marrying anybody, and helped himself lavishly to champagne.

It so happened that I was the first of our party to meet the President, an honour which, perhaps, I hardly deserved. While Samuel was seeking tortuous introductions to him through friends of Peterhouse friends of his, the President and I fell into each other's arms in the most natural way.

It occurred like this. There was a dance after dinner; and Myra, not satisfied with my appearance, sent me upstairs to put some gloves on. (It is one of the penalties of marriage that one is always being sent upstairs.) With my hands properly shod I returned to the ball-room, and stood for a moment in a corner while I looked about for her. Suddenly I heard a voice at my side.

"Do you want a partner?" it said.

I turned, and knew that I was face to face with the President.

"Well——" I began.

"You are a new-comer, aren't you? I expect you don't know many people. If there is anybody you would like to dance with——"

I looked round the room. It was too good a chance to miss.

"I wonder," I said. "That girl over there—in the pink frock—just putting up her fan——"

He almost embraced me.

"I congratulate you on your taste," he said. "Excellent! Come with me."

He went over to the girl in the pink dress, I at his heels.

"Er—may I introduce?" he said. "Mr.—er—er—yes, this is Miss—er—yes. H'r'm." Evidently he didn't know her name.

"Thank you," I said to him. He nodded and left us. I turned to the girl in the pink frock. She was very pretty.

"May I have this dance?" I asked. "I've got my gloves on," I added.

She looked at me gravely, trying hard not to smile.

"You may," said Myra.

II

THE OPENING RUN

With a great effort Simpson strapped his foot securely into a ski and turned doubtfully to Thomas.

"Thomas," he said, "how do you know which foot is which?"

"It depends whose," said Thomas. He was busy tying a large rucksack of lunch on to himself, and was in no mood for Samuel's ball-room chatter.

"You've got one ski on one foot," I said. "Then the other ski goes on the foot you've got over. I should have thought you would have seen that."

"But I may have put the first one on wrong."

"You ought to know, after all these years, that you are certain to have done so," I said severely. Having had my own hired skis fixed on by the concierge I felt rather superior. Simpson, having bought his in London, was regarded darkly by that gentleman, and left to his own devices.

"Are we all ready?" asked Myra, who had kept us waiting for twenty minutes. "Archie, what about Dahlia?"

"Dahlia will join us at lunch. She is expecting a letter from Peter by the twelve o'clock post and refuses to start without it. Also she doesn't think she is up to ski-ing just yet. Also she wants to have a heart-to-heart talk with the girl in red, and break it to her that Thomas is engaged to several people in London already."

"Come on," growled Thomas, and he led the way up the hill. We followed him in single file.

It was a day of colour, straight from heaven. On either side the dazzling whiteness of the snow; above, the deep blue of the sky; in front of me the glorious apricot of Simpson's winter suiting. London seemed a hundred years away. It was impossible to work up the least interest in the Home Rule Bill, the Billiard Tournament, or the state of St. Paul's Cathedral.

"I feel extremely picturesque," said Archie. "If only we had a wolf or two after us, the illusion would be complete. The Boy Trappers, or Half-Hours among the Rocky Mountains."

"It is a pleasant thought, Archie," I said, "that in any wolf trouble the bachelors of the party would have to sacrifice themselves for us. Myra dear, the loss of Samuel in such circumstances would draw us very close together. There might be a loss of Thomas too, perhaps—for if there was not enough of Simpson to go round, if there was a hungry wolf left over, would Thomas hesitate?"

"No," said Thomas, "I should run like a hare."

Simpson said nothing. His face I could not see; but his back looked exactly like the back of a man who was trying to look as if he had been brought up on skis from a baby and was now taking a small party of enthusiastic novices out for their first lesson.

"What an awful shock it would be," I said, "if we found that Samuel really did know something about it after all; and, while we were tumbling about anyhow, he sailed gracefully down the steepest slopes. I should go straight back to Cricklewood."

"My dear chap, I've read a lot about it."

"Then we're quite safe."

"With all his faults," said Archie, "and they are many—Samuel is a gentleman. He would never take an unfair advantage of us. Hallo, here we are!"

We left the road and made our way across the snow to a little wooden hut which Archie had noticed the day before. Here we were to meet Dahlia for lunch; and here, accordingly, we left the rucksack and such garments as the heat of the sun suggested. Then, at the top of a long snow-slope, steep at first, more gentle later, we stood and wondered.

"Who's going first?" said Archie.

"What do you do?" asked Myra.

"You don't. It does it for you."

"But how do you stop?"

"Don't bother about that, dear," I said. "That will be arranged for you all right. Take two steps to the brink of the hill and pick yourself up at the bottom. Now then, Simpson! Be a man. The lady waits, Samuel. The—— Hallo! Hi! Help!" I cried, as I began to move off slowly. It was too late to do anything about it. "Good-bye," I called. And then things moved more quickly....

Very quickly....

Suddenly there came a moment when I realized that I wasn't keeping up with my feet....

I shouted to my skis to stop. It was no good. They went on....

I decided to stop without them....

The ensuing second went by too swiftly for me to understand rightly what happened. I fancy that, rising from my sitting position and travelling easily on my head, I caught my skis up again and passed them....

Then it was their turn. They overtook me....

But I was not to be beaten. Once more I obtained the lead. This time I took the inside berth, and kept it....

There seemed to be a lot more snow than I really wanted.... I struggled bravely with it....

And then the earthquake ceased, and suddenly I was in the outer air. My first ski-run, the most glorious run of modern times, was over.

"Ripping!" I shouted up the hill to them. "But there's rather a nasty bump at the bottom," I added kindly, as I set myself to the impossible business of getting up....

"Jove," said Archie, coming to rest a few yards off, "that's splendid!" He had fallen in a less striking way than myself, and he got to his feet without difficulty. "Why do you pose like that?" he asked, as he picked up his stick.

"I'm a fixture," I announced. "Myra," I said, as she turned a somersault and arrived beaming at my side, "I'm here for some time; you'll have to come out every morning with crumbs for me. In the afternoon you can bring a cheering book and read aloud to your husband. Sometimes I shall dictate little things to you. They will not be my best little things; for this position, with my feet so much higher than my head, is not the one in which inspiration comes to me most readily. The flow of blood to the brain impairs reflection. But no matter."

"Are you really stuck?" asked Myra in some anxiety. "I should hate to have a husband who lived by himself in the snow," she said thoughtfully.

"Let us look on the bright side," said Archie. "The snow will have melted by April, and he will then be able to return to you. Hallo, here's Thomas! Thomas will probably have some clever idea for restoring the family credit."

Thomas got up in a businesslike manner and climbed slowly back to us.

"Thomas," I said, "you see the position. Indeed," I added, "it is obvious. None of the people round me seems inclined—or, it may be, able—to help. There is a feeling that if Myra lives in the hotel alone while I remain here—possibly till April—people will talk. You know how ready they are. There is also the fact that I have only hired the skis for three weeks. Also—a minor point, but one that touches me rather—that I shall want my hair cut long before March is out. Thomas, imagine me to be a torpedo-destroyer on the Maplin Sands, and tell me what on earth to do."

"Take your skis off."

"Oh, brilliant!" said Myra.

"Take my skis off?" I cried. "Never! Is it not my duty to be the last to leave my skis? Can I abandon—— Hallo! is that Dahlia on the sky-line? Hooray, lunch! Archie, take my skis off, there's a good fellow. We mustn't keep Dahlia waiting."

III

A TYPICAL MORNING

"You take lunch out to-day—no?" said Josef, the head-waiter, in his invariable formula.

Myra and I were alone at breakfast, the first down. I was just putting some honey on to my seventh roll, and was not really in the mood for light conversation with Josef about lunch. By the way, I must say I prefer the good old English breakfast. With eggs and bacon and porridge you do know when you want to stop; with rolls and honey you hardly notice what you are doing, and there seems no reason why you should not go on for ever. Indeed, once ... but you would never believe me.

"We take lunch out to-day, yes, Josef. Lunch for—let me see—"

"Six?" suggested Myra.

"What are we all going to do? Archie said something about skating. I'm off that."

"But whatever we do we must lunch, and it's much nicer outdoors. Six, Josef."

Josef nodded and retired. I took my eighth roll.

"Do let's get off quickly to-day," I said. "There's always so much chat in the morning before we start."

"I've just got one swift letter to write," said Myra, as she got up, "and then I shall be pawing the ground."

Half an hour later I was in the lounge, booted, capped, gloved, and putteed—the complete St. Bernard. The lounge seemed to be entirely full of hot air and entirely empty of anybody I knew. I asked for letters; and, getting none, went out and looked at the thermometer. To my surprise I discovered that there were thirty-seven degrees of frost. A little alarmed, I tapped the thing impatiently. "Come, come," I said, "this is not the time for persiflage." However, it insisted on remaining at five degrees below zero. What I should have done about it I cannot say, but at that moment I remembered that it was a Centigrade thermometer with the freezing point in the wrong place. Slightly disappointed that there were only five degrees of frost (Centigrade) I returned to the lounge.

"Here you are at last," said Archie impatiently. "What are we all going to do?"

"Where's Dahlia?" asked Myra. "Let's wait till she comes and then we can all talk at once."

"Here she is. Dahlia, for Heaven's sake come and tell us the arrangements for the day. Start with the idea fixed in your mind that Myra and I have ordered lunch for six."

Dahlia shepherded us to a quiet corner of the lounge and we all sat down.

"By the way," said Simpson, "are there any letters for me?"

"No; it's your turn to write," said Archie.

"But, my dear chap, there must be one, because——"

"But you never acknowledged the bed-socks," I pointed out. "She can't write till you—— I mean, it was rather forward of her to send them at all; and if you haven't even——"

"Well," said Dahlia, "what does anybody want to do?"

Thomas was the first to answer the question. A girl in red came in from the breakfast-room and sat down near us. She looked up in our direction and met Thomas's eye.

"Good morning," said Thomas, with a smile, and he left us and moved across to her.

"That's the girl he danced with all last night," whispered Myra. "I can't think what's come over him. Is this our reserved Thomas—Thomas the taciturn, whom we know and love so well? I don't like the way she does her hair."

"She's a Miss Aylwyn," said Simpson in a loud voice. "I had one dance with her myself."

"The world," said Archie, "is full of people with whom Samuel has had one dance."

"Well, that washes Thomas out, anyway. He'll spend the day teaching her something. What are the rest of us going to do?"

There was a moment's silence.

"Oh, Archie," said Dahlia, "did you get those nails put in my boots?"

I looked at Myra ... and sighed.

"Sorry, dear," he said. "I'll take them down now. The man will do them in twenty minutes." He walked over to the lift at the same moment that Thomas returned to us.

"I say," began Thomas, a little awkwardly, "if you're arranging what to do, don't bother about me. I rather thought of—er—taking it quietly this morning. I think I overdid it a bit yesterday."

"We warned you at the time about the fourth hard-boiled egg," I said.

"I meant the ski-ing. We thought of—I thought of having lunch in the hotel, but, of course, you can have my rucksack to carry yours in. Er—I'll go and put it in for you."

He disappeared rather sheepishly in the direction of the dining-room.

"Now, Samuel," said Myra gently.

"Now what, Myra?"

"It's your turn. If you have a headache, tell us her name."

"My dear Myra, I want to ski to-day. Where shall we go? Let's go to the old slopes and practise the Christiania Turn."

"What you want to practise is the ordinary Hampstead Straight," I said. "A medium performance of yours yesterday, Samuel."

"But, my dear old chap," he said eagerly, "I told you it was the fault of my skis. They would stick to the snow. Oh, I say," he added, "that reminds me. I must go and buy some wax for them."

He dashed off. I looked at Myra ... and sighed.

"The nail-man won't be long," said Archie to Dahlia, on his return. "I'm to call for them in a quarter of an hour."

"Can't you wear some other boots, Dahlia, or your bedroom slippers or something? It's half-past eleven. We really must get off soon."

"But we haven't settled where we're going yet."

"Then for 'eving's sake let's do it. Myra and I thought we might go up above the wood at the back and explore. We can always ski down. It might be rather exciting."

"Remember," said Dahlia, "I'm not so expert as you are."

"Of course," said Myra, "we're the Oberland mixed champions."

"You know," said Archie, "I was talking to the man who's doing Dahlia's boots and he said the snow would be bad for ski-ing to-day."

"If he talked in French, no doubt you misunderstood him," I said, a little annoyed. "He was probably asking you to buy a pair of skates."

"Talking about that," said Archie, "why shouldn't we skate this morning, and have lunch at the hotel, and then get the bob out this afternoon?"

"Here you are," said Thomas, coming up with a heavy rucksack. "Lunch for six, so you'll have an extra one."

"I'd forgotten about lunch," said Archie. "Look here, just talk it over with Dahlia while I go and see about my skates. I don't suppose Josef will mind if we do stay in to lunch after all. What about Simpson?"

I looked at Myra ... and sighed.

"What about him?" I said.

Half an hour later two exhausted people—one of them with lunch for six on his back—began the ascent to the wood, trailing their skis behind them.

"Another moment," said Myra, "and I should have screamed."

IV

THOMAS, AND A TURN

Myra finished her orange, dried her hands daintily on my handkerchief, and spoke her mind.

"This is the third time," she said, "that Thomas has given us the slip. If he gets engaged to that girl in red I shall cry."

"There are," I said, idly throwing a crust at Simpson and missing him, "engagements and Swiss engagements—just as there are measles and German measles. It is well known that Swiss engagements don't count."

"We got engaged in Kent. A bit of luck."

"I have nothing against Miss Aylwyn——" I went on.

"Except the way she does her hair."

"—but she doesn't strike me as being the essential Rabbit. We cannot admit her to the—er—fold."

"The covey," suggested Myra.

"The warren. Anyhow, she—— Simpson, for goodness' sake stop fooling about with your bearded friend and tell us what you think of it all."

We were finishing lunch in the lee of a little chalet, high above the hotel, and Simpson had picked up an acquaintance with a goat, which he was apparently trying to conciliate with a piece of chocolate. The goat, however, seemed to want a piece of Simpson.

"My dear old chap, he won't go away. Here—shoo! shoo! I wish I knew what his name was."

"Ernest," said Myra.

"I can't think why you ever got into such a hirsute set,

28

Simpson. He probably wants your compass. Give it to him and let him withdraw."

Ernest, having decided that Simpson was not worth knowing, withdrew, and we resumed our conversation.

"When we elderly married folk have retired," I went on, "and you gay young bachelors sit up over a last cigar to discuss your conquests, has not Thomas unbent to you, Samuel, and told you of his hopes and fears?"

"He told me last night he was afraid he was going bald, and he said he hoped he wasn't."

"That's a bad sign," said Myra. "What did you say?"

"I said I thought he was."

With some difficulty I got up from my seat in the snow and buckled on my skis.

"Come on, let's forget Thomas for a bit. Samuel is now going to show us the Christiania Turn."

Simpson, all eagerness, began to prepare himself.

"I said I would, didn't I? I was doing it quite well yesterday. This is a perfect little slope for it. You understand the theory of it, don't you?"

"We hope to after the exhibition."

"Well, the great thing is to lean the opposite way to the way you think you ought to lean. That's what's so difficult."

"You understand, Myra? Samuel will lean the opposite way to what he thinks he ought to lean. Tell Ernest."

"But suppose you think you ought to lean the proper way, the way they do in Christiania," said Myra, "and you lean the opposite way, then what happens?"

"That is what Samuel will probably show us," I said.

Simpson was now ready.

"I am going to turn to the left," he said. "Watch carefully. Of course, I may not bring it off the first time."

"I can't help thinking you will," said Myra.

"It depends what you call bringing it off," I said. "We have every hope of—I mean we don't think our money will be wasted. Have you got the opera-glasses and the peppermints and the programme, darling? Then you may begin, Samuel."

Simpson started down the slope a little unsteadily. For one moment I feared that there might be an accident before the real accident, but he recovered himself nobly and sped to the bottom. Then a cloud of snow shot up, and for quite a long time there was no Simpson.

"I knew he wouldn't disappoint us," gurgled Myra.

We slid down to him and helped him up.

29

"You see the idea," he said. "I'm afraid I spoilt it a little at that end, but——"

"My dear Samuel, you improved it out of all knowledge."

"But that actually is the Christiania Turn."

"Oh, why don't we live in Christiania?" exclaimed Myra to me. "Couldn't we possibly afford it?"

"It must be a happy town," I agreed. "How the old streets must ring and ring again with jovial laughter."

"Shall I do it once more?"

"Can you?" said Myra, clasping her hands eagerly.

"Wait here," said Samuel, "and I'll do it quite close to you."

Myra unstrapped her camera.

Half an hour later, with several excellent films of the scene of the catastrophe, we started for home. It was more than a little steep, but the run down was accomplished without any serious trouble. Simpson went first to discover any hidden ditches (and to his credit be it said that he invariably discovered them); Myra, in the position of safety in the middle, profited by Samuel's frequent object-lessons; while I, at the back, was ready to help Myra up, if need arose, or to repel any avalanche which descended on us from above. On the level snow at the bottom we became more companionable.

"We still haven't settled the great Thomas question," said Myra. "What about to-morrow?"

"Why bother about to-morrow? Carpe diem. Latin."

"But the great tailing expedition is for to-morrow. The horses are ordered; everything is prepared. Only one thing remains to settle. Shall we have with us a grumpy but Aylwynless Thomas, or shall we let him bring her and spoil the party?"

"She can't spoil the party. I'm here to enjoy myself, and all Thomas's fiancées can't stop me. Let's have Thomas happy, anyway."

"She's really quite a nice girl," said Simpson. "I danced with her once."

"Right-o, then. I'll tell Dahlia to invite her."

We hurried on to the hotel; but as we passed the rink the President stopped me for a chat. He wanted me to recite at a concert that evening. Basely deserted by Myra and Samuel, I told him that I did not recite; and I took the opportunity of adding that personally I didn't think anybody else ought to. I had just persuaded him to my point of view when I noticed Thomas cutting remarkable figures on the ice. He picked himself up and skated to the side.

"Hallo!" he said. "Had a good day?"

"Splendid. What have you been doing?"

"Oh—skating."

"I say, about this tailing expedition to-morrow——"

"Er—yes, I was just going to talk about that."

"Well, it's all right. Myra is getting Dahlia to ask her to come with us."

"Good!" said Thomas, brightening up.

"You see, we shall only be seven, even with Miss Aylwyn, and——"

"Miss Aylwyn?" said Thomas in a hollow voice.

"Yes, isn't that the name of your friend in red?"

"Oh, that one. Oh, but that's quite—I mean," he went on hurriedly, "Miss Aylwyn is probably booked up for to-morrow. It's Miss Cardew who is so keen on tailing. That girl in green, you know."

For a moment I stared at him blankly. Then I left him and dashed after Myra.

V

A TAILING PARTY

The procession prepared to start in the following order:—

(1) A brace of sinister-looking horses.

(2) Gaspard, the Last of the Bandits; or "Why cause a lot of talk by pushing your rich uncle over the cliff, when you can have him stabbed quietly for one franc fifty?" (If ever I were in any vendetta business I should pick Gaspard first.)

(3) A sleigh full of lunch.

(4) A few well-known ladies and gentlemen (being the cream of the Hôtel des Angéliques) on luges; namely, reading from left to right (which is really the best method—unless you are translating Hebrew), Simpson, Archie, Dahlia, Myra, me, Miss Cardew, and Thomas.

While Gaspard was putting the finishing knots to the luges, I addressed a few remarks to Miss Cardew, fearing that she might be feeling a little lonely amongst us. I said that it was a lovely day, and did she think the snow would hold off till evening? Also had she ever done this sort of thing before? I forget what her answers were.

Thomas meanwhile was exchanging badinage on the hotel

steps with Miss Aylwyn. There must be something peculiar in the Swiss air, for in England Thomas is quite a respectable man ... and a godfather.

"I suppose we have asked the right one," said Myra doubtfully.

"His young affections are divided. There was a third girl in pink with whom he breakfasted a lot this morning. It is the old tradition of the sea, you know. A sailor—I mean an Admiralty civilian has a wife at every wireless station."

"Take your seats, please," said Archie. "The horses are sick of waiting."

We sat down. Archie took Dahlia's feet on his lap, Myra took mine, Miss Cardew took Thomas's. Simpson, alone in front, nursed a guide-book.

"En avant!" cried Simpson in his best French-taught-in-twelve-lessons accent.

Gaspard muttered an oath to his animals. They pulled bravely. The rope snapped—and they trotted gaily down the hill with Gaspard.

We hurried after them with the luges....

"It's a good joke," said Archie, after this had happened three times, "but, personally, I weary of it. Miss Cardew, I'm afraid we've brought you out under false pretences. Thomas didn't explain the thing to you adequately. He gave you to understand that there was more in it than this."

Gaspard, who seemed full of rope, produced a fourth piece and tied a knot that made even Simpson envious.

"Now, Samuel," I begged, "do keep the line taut this time. Why do you suppose we put your apricot suit right in the front? Is it, do you suppose, for the sunset effects at eleven o'clock in the morning, or is it that you may look after the rope properly?"

"I'm awfully sorry, Miss Cardew," said Simpson, feeling that somebody ought to apologize for something and knowing that Gaspard wouldn't, "but I expect it will be all right now."

We settled down again. Once more Gaspard cursed his horses, and once more they started off bravely. And this time we went with them.

"The idea all along," I explained to Miss Cardew.

"I rather suspected it," she said. Apparently she has a suspicious mind.

After the little descent at the start, we went uphill slowly for a couple of miles, and then more rapidly over the level. We had driven over the same road in a sleigh, coming from the station, and had been bitterly cold and extremely bored. Why our present position should be so much more enjoyable I didn't quite see.

32

"It's the expectation of an accident," said Archie. "At any moment somebody may fall off. Good."

"My dear old chap," said Simpson, turning round to take part in the conversation, "why anybody should fall off——"

We went suddenly round a corner, and quietly and without any fuss whatever Simpson left his luge and rolled on to the track. Luckily any possibility of a further accident was at once avoided. There was no panic at all. Archie kicked the body temporarily out of the way; after which Dahlia leant over and pushed it thoughtfully to the side of the road. Myra warded it off with a leg as she neared it; with both hands I helped it into the deep snow from which it had shown a tendency to emerge; Miss Cardew put a foot out at it for safety; and Thomas patted it gently on the head as the end of the "tail" went past....

As soon as we had recovered our powers of speech—all except Miss Cardew, who was in hysterics—we called upon Gaspard to stop. He indicated with the back of his neck that it would be dangerous to stop just then; and it was not until we were at the bottom of the hill, nearly a mile from the place where Simpson left us, that the procession halted, and gave itself up again to laughter.

"I hope he is not hurt," said Dahlia, wiping the tears from her eyes.

"He wouldn't spoil a good joke like that by getting hurt," said Myra confidently. "He's much too much of a sportsman."

"Why did he do it?" said Thomas.

"He suddenly remembered he hadn't packed his safety-razor. He's half-way back to the hotel by now."

Miss Cardew remained in hysterics.

Ten minutes later a brilliant sunset was observed approaching from the north. A little later it was seen to be a large dish of apricots and cream.

"He draws near," said Archie. "Now then, let's be stern with him."

At twenty yards' range Simpson began to talk. His trot had heated him slightly.

"I say," he said excitedly. "You——"

Myra shook her head at him.

"Not done, Samuel," she said reproachfully.

"Not what, Myra? What not——"

"You oughtn't to leave us like that without telling us."

"After all," said Archie, "we are all one party, and we are supposed to keep together. If you prefer to go about by yourself, that's all right; but if we go to the trouble of arranging something for the whole party——"

"You might have caused a very nasty accident," I pointed out. "If you were in a hurry, you had only to say a word to Gaspard and he would have stopped for you to alight. Now I begin to understand why you kept cutting the rope at the start."

"You have sent Miss Cardew into hysterics by your conduct," said Dahlia.

Miss Cardew gave another peal. Simpson looked at her in dismay.

"I say, Miss Cardew, I'm most awfully sorry. I really didn't—— I say, Dahlia," he went on confidentially, "oughtn't we to do something about this? Rub her feet with snow or—I mean, I know there's something you do when people have hysterics. It's rather serious if they go on. Don't you burn feathers under their nose?" He began to feel in his pockets. "I wonder if Gaspard's got a feather?"

With a great effort Miss Cardew pulled herself together. "It's all right, thank you," she said in a stifled voice.

"Then let's get on," said Archie.

We resumed our seats once more. Archie took Dahlia's feet on his lap. Myra took mine. Miss Cardew took Thomas's. Simpson clung tight to his luge with both hands.

"Right!" cried Archie.

Gaspard swore at his horses. They pulled bravely. The rope snapped—and they trotted gaily up the hill with Gaspard.

We hurried after them with the luges....

VI

A HAPPY ENDING

"For our last night they might at least have had a dance," said Myra, "even if there was no public presentation."

"As we had hoped," I admitted.

"What is a gymkhana, anyway?" asked Thomas.

"A few little competitions," said Archie. "One must cater for the chaperons sometimes. You are all entered for the Hat-making and the Feather-blowing—Dahlia thought it would amuse you."

"At Cambridge," I said reminiscently, "I once blew the feather

119 feet 7 inches. Unfortunately I stepped outside the circle. My official record is 2 feet."

"Did you ever trim a hat at Cambridge?" asked Myra. "Because you've got to do one for me to-night."

I had not expected this. My view of the competition had been that I should have to provide the face and that she would have to invent some suitable frame for it.

"I'm full of ideas," I lied.

Nine o'clock found a small row of us prepared to blow the feather. The presidential instructions were that we had to race our feather across a chalk-line at the end of the room, anybody touching his feather to be disqualified.

"In the air or on the floor?" asked Simpson earnestly.

"Just as you like," said the President kindly, and came round with the bag.

I selected Percy with care—a dear little feather about half an inch long and of a delicate whity-brown colour. I should have known him again anywhere.

"Go!" said the President. I was rather excited, with the result that my first blow was much too powerful for Percy. He shot up to the ceiling and, in spite of all I could do, seemed inclined to stay there. Anxiously I waited below with my mouth open; he came slowly down at last; and in my eagerness I played my second just a shade too soon. It missed him. My third (when I was ready for it) went harmlessly over his head. A frantic fourth and fifth helped him downwards ... and in another moment my beautiful Percy was on the floor. I dropped on my knees and played my sixth vigorously. He swirled to the left; I was after him like a shot ... and crashed into Thomas. We rolled over in a heap.

"Sorry!" we apologized as we got back on to our hands and knees.

Thomas went on blowing.

"Where's my feather?" I said.

Thomas was now two yards ahead, blowing like anything. A terrible suspicion darted through my mind.

"Thomas," I said, "you've got my feather."

He made no answer. I scrambled after him.

"That's Percy," I said. "I should know him anywhere. You're blowing Percy. It's very bad form to blow another man's feather. If it got about, you would be cut by the county. Give me back my feather, Thomas."

"How do you know it's your feather?" he said truculently. "Feathers are just alike."

"How do I know?" I asked in amazement. "A feather that I've

35

brought up from the egg? Of course I know Percy." I leant down to him. "P—percy," I whispered. He darted forward a good six inches. "You see," I said, "he knows his name."

"As a matter of fact," said Thomas, "his name's P—paul. Look, I'll show you."

"You needn't bother, Thomas," I said hastily. "This is mere trifling. I know that's my feather. I remember his profile distinctly."

"Then where's mine?"

"How do I know? You may have swallowed it. Go away and leave Percy and me to ourselves. You're only spoiling the knees of your trousers by staying here."

"Paul and I——" began Thomas.

He was interrupted by a burst of applause. Dahlia had cajoled her feather over the line first. Thomas rose and brushed himself. "You can 'ave him," he said.

"There!" I said, as I picked Percy up and placed him reverently in my waistcoat pocket. "That shows that he was mine. If he had been your own little Paul you would have loved him even in defeat. Oh, musical chairs now? Right-o." And at the President's touch I retired from the arena.

We had not entered for musical chairs. Personally I should have liked to, but it was felt that, if none of us did, then it would be more easy to stop Simpson doing so. For at musical chairs Simpson is—I am afraid there is only one word for it; it is a word that I hesitate to use, but the truth must prevail—Simpson is rough. He lets himself go. He plays all he knows. Whenever I take Simpson out anywhere I always whisper to my hostess, "Not musical chairs."

The last event of the evening was the hat-making competition. Each man of us was provided with five large sheets of coloured crinkly paper, a packet of pins, a pair of scissors, and a lady opposite to him.

"Have you any plans at all?" asked Myra.

"Heaps. Tell me, what sort of hat would you like? Something for the Park?" I doubled up a piece of blue paper and looked at it. "You know, if this is a success, Myra, I shall often make your hats for you."

Five minutes later I had what I believe is called a "foundation." Anyhow, it was something for Myra to put her head into.

"Our very latest Bond Street model," said Myra. "Only fifteen guineas—or three-and-ninepence if you buy it at our other establishment in Battersea."

"Now then, I can get going," I said, and I began to cut out a white feather. "Yes, your ladyship, this is from the genuine bird on our own ostrich farm in the Fulham Road. Plucked while the ingenuous biped had its head in the sand. I shall put that round the brim," and I pinned it round.

"What about a few roses?" said Myra, fingering the red paper.

"The roses are going there on the right." I pinned them on. "And a humming-bird and some violets next to them.... I say, I've got a lot of paper over. What about a nice piece of cabbage ... there ... and a bunch of asparagus ... and some tomatoes and a seagull's wing on the left. The back still looks rather bare—let's have some poppies."

"There's only three minutes more," said Myra, "and you haven't used all the paper yet."

"I've got about one William Allan Richardson and a couple of canaries over," I said, after examining my stock. "Let's put it inside as lining. There, Myra, my dear, I'm proud of you. I always say that in a nice quiet hat nobody looks prettier than you."

"Time!" said the President.

Anxious matrons prowled round us.

"We don't know any of the judges," I whispered. "This isn't fair."

The matrons conferred with the President. He cleared his throat. "The first prize," he said, "goes to——"

But I had swooned.

"Well," said Archie, "the Rabbits return to England with two cups won on the snowfields of Switzerland."

"Nobody need know," said Myra, "which winter-sport they were won at."

"Unless I have 'Ski-ing, First Prize' engraved on mine," I said, "as I had rather intended."

"Then I shall have 'Figure-Skating' on mine," said Dahlia.

"Two cups," reflected Archie, "and Thomas engaged to three charming girls. I think it has been worth it, you know."

A BAKER'S DOZEN

A TRAGEDY IN LITTLE

The great question of the day is, What will become of Sidney? Whenever I think of him now, the unbidden tear wells into my eye ... and wells down my cheek ... and wells on to my collar. My friends think I have a cold, and offer me lozenges; but it is Sidney who makes me weep. I fear that I am about to lose him.

He came into my life in the following way.

Some months ago I wanted to buy some silk stockings; not for myself, for I seldom wear them, but for a sister. The idea came suddenly to me that any woman with a brother and a birthday would simply love the one to give her silk stockings for the other. But, of course, they would have to be the right silk stockings—the fashionable shape for the year, the correct assortment of clocks, and so forth. Then as to material—could I be sure I was getting silk, and not silkette or something inferior? How maddening if, seeing that I was an unprotected man, they palmed off Jaeger on me! Clearly this was a case for outside assistance. So I called in Celia.

"This," I said to her, "is practically the only subject on which I am not an expert. At the same time I have a distinct feeling for silk stockings. If you can hurry me past all the embarrassing counters safely, and arrange for the lady behind the right one to show me the right line in silken hose, I will undertake to pick out half a dozen pairs that would melt any sister's heart."

Well, the affair went off perfectly. Celia took the matter into her own hands and behaved just as if I were buying them for her. The shop-assistant also behaved as if I were. Fortunately I kept my head when it came to giving the name and address. "No," I said firmly to Celia. "Not yours; my sister's." And I dragged her away to tea.

Now whether it was because Celia had particularly enjoyed her afternoon; or because she felt that a man who was as ignorant as I about silk stockings must lead a very lonely life; or because I had mentioned casually and erroneously that it was my own birthday that week, I cannot say; but on the following morning I received a little box, with a note on the outside which said in her handwriting, "Something for you. Be kind to him." And I opened it and found Sidney.

38

He was a Japanese dwarf-tree—the merest boy. At eighty or ninety, according to the photographs, he would be a stalwart fellow with thick bark on his trunk, and fir-cones or acorns (or whatever was his speciality) hanging all over him. Just at present he was barely ten. I had only eighty years to wait before he reached his prime.

Naturally I decided to lavish all my care upon his upbringing. I would water him after breakfast every morning, and (when I remembered it) at night. If there was any top-dressing he particularly fancied, he should have it. If he had any dead leaves to snip off, I would snip them.

It was at this moment that I discovered something else in the box—a card of instructions. I have not got it now, and I have forgotten the actual wording, but the spirit of it was this:

HINTS ON THE PROPER REARING AND BRINGING-UP OF A JAPANESE DWARF-TREE

The life of this tree is a precarious one, and if it is to be successfully brought to manhood the following rules must be carefully observed—

I. This tree requires, above all else, fresh air and exercise.

II. Whenever the sun is shining, the tree should be placed outside, in a position where it can absorb the rays.

III. Whenever the rain is raining, it should be placed outside, in a position where it can absorb the wet.

IV. It should be taken out for a trot at least once every day.

V. It simply loathes artificial light and artificial heat. If you keep it in your drawing-room, see that it is situated as far as possible from the chandelier and the gas-stove.

VI. It also detests noise. Do not place it on the top of the pianola.

VII. It loves moonlight. Leave it outside when you go to bed, in case the moon should come out.

VIII. On the other hand, it hates lightning. Cover it up with the canary's cloth when the lightning begins.

IX. If it shows signs of drooping, a course of massage will generally bring it round.

X. But in no case offer it buns.

Well, I read these instructions carefully, and saw at once that I should have to hand over the business of rearing Sidney to another.

I have my living to earn the same as anybody else, and I should never get any work done at all if I had constantly to be rushing home from the office on the plea that it was time for Master Sidney's sun-bath.

So I called up my housekeeper, and placed the matter before her.

I said: "Let me introduce you to Sidney. He is very dear to me; dearer to me than a—a brother. No, on second thoughts my brother is perhaps—well, anyhow, Sidney is very dear to me. I will show my trust in you by asking you to tend him for me. Here are a few notes about his health. Frankly he is delicate. But the doctors have hope. With care, they think, he may live to be a hundred-and-fifty. His future is in your hands."

My housekeeper thanked me for this mark of esteem and took the card of instructions away with her. I asked her for it a week afterwards and it appeared that, having committed the rules to memory, she had lost it. But that she follows the instructions I have no doubt; and certainly she and Sidney understand each other's ways exactly. Automatically she gives him his bath, his massage, his run in the park. When it rains or snows or shines, she knows exactly what to do with Sidney.

But as a consequence I see little of him. I suppose it must always be so; we parents must make these sacrifices for our children. Think of a mother only seeing her eldest-born for fifteen weeks a year through the long period of his schooling; and think of me, doomed to catch only the most casual glimpses of Sidney until he is ninety.

For, you know, I might almost say that I never see him at all now. As I go to my work I may, if I am lucky, get a fleeting glance of him on the tiles, where he sits drinking in the rain or sun. In the evening, when I return, he is either out in the moonlight or, if indoors, shunning the artificial light with the cloth over his head. Indeed, the only times when I really see him to talk to are when Celia comes to tea with me. Then my housekeeper hurries him in from his walk or his sun-bath, and puts him, brushed and manicured, on my desk; and Celia and I whisper fond nothings to him. I believe Celia thinks he lives there!

As I began by saying, I weep for Sidney's approaching end. For my housekeeper leaves this week. A new one takes her place. How will she treat my poor Sidney? The old card of instructions is lost; what can I give her in its place? The legend that Sidney's is a precious life—that he must have his morning bath, his run, his glass of hot water after meals! She would laugh at it. Besides, she may not be at all the sort of foster-mother for a Japanese dwarf-tree....

40

It will break my heart if Sidney dies now, for I had so looked forward to celebrating his ninetieth birthday with him. It will hurt Celia too. But her grief, of course, will be an inferior affair. In fact, a couple of pairs of silk stockings will help her to forget him altogether.

THE FINANCIER

I

This is how I became a West African mining magnate with a stake in the Empire.

During February I grew suddenly tired of waiting for the summer to begin. London in the summer is a pleasant place, and chiefly so because you can keep on buying evening papers to see what Kent is doing. In February life has no such excitements to offer. So I wrote to my solicitor about it.

"I want you" (I wrote) "to buy me fifty rubber shares, so that I can watch them go up and down." And I added "Brokerage 1/8" to show that I knew what I was talking about.

He replied tersely as follows:—

"Don't be a fool. If you have any money to invest I can get you a safe mortgage at five per cent. Let me know."

It's a funny thing how the minds of solicitors run upon mortgages. If they would only stop to think for a moment they would see that you couldn't possibly watch a safe mortgage go up and down. I left my solicitor alone and consulted Henry on the subject. In the intervals between golf and golf Henry dabbles in finance.

"You don't want anything gilt-edged, I gather?" he said. It's wonderful how they talk.

"I want it to go up and down," I explained patiently, and I indicated the required movement with my umbrella.

"What about a little flutter in oil?" he went on, just like a financier in a novel.

"I'll have a little flutter in raspberry jam if you like. Anything as long as I can rush every night for the last edition of the evening papers and say now and then, 'Good heavens, I'm ruined.'"

"Then you'd better try a gold-mine," said Henry bitterly, in the voice of one who had tried. "Take your choice," and he threw the paper over to me.

"I don't want a whole mine—only a vein or two. Yes, this is very interesting," I went on, as I got among the West Africans. "The scoring seems to be pretty low; I suppose it must have been a wet wicket. 'H.E. Reef, 1-3/4, 2'—he did a little better in the second innings. '1/2, Boffin River, 5/16, 7/16'—they followed on, you see, but they saved the innings defeat. By the way, which figure do I really keep my eye on when I want to watch them go up and down?"

"Both. One eye on each. And don't talk about Boffin River to me."

"Is it like that, Henry? I am sorry. I suppose it's too late now to offer you a safe mortgage at five per cent? I know a man who has some. Well, perhaps you're right."

On the next day I became a magnate. The Jaguar Mine was the one I fixed upon—for two reasons. First, the figure immediately after it was 1, which struck me as a good point from which to watch it go up and down. Secondly, I met a man at lunch who knew somebody who had actually seen the Jaguar Mine.

"He says that there's no doubt about there being lots there."

"Lots of what? Jaguars or gold?"

"Ah, he didn't say. Perhaps he meant jaguars."

Anyhow, it was an even chance, and I decided to risk it. In a week's time I was the owner of what we call in the City a "block" of Jaguars—bought from one Herbert Bellingham, who, I suppose, had been got at by his solicitor and compelled to return to something safe. I was a West African magnate.

My first two months as a magnate were a great success. With my heart in my mouth I would tear open the financial editions of the evening papers, to find one day that Jaguars had soared like a rocket to 1-1/16, the next that they had dropped like a stone to 1-1/32. There was one terrible afternoon when for some reason which will never be properly explained we sank to 15/16. I think the European situation had something to do with it, though this naturally is not admitted. Lord Rothschild, I fancy, suddenly threw all his Jaguars on the market; he sold and sold and sold, and only held his hand when, in desperation, the Tsar granted the concession for his new Southend to Siberia railway. Something like that. But he never recked how the private investor would suffer; and there was I, sitting at home and sending out madly for all the papers, until my rooms were littered with copies of The Times, The Financial News, Answers, The Feathered World, and Home Chat. Next day we were up to 31/32, and I was able to breathe again.

42

But I had other pleasures than these. Previously I had regarded the City with awe, but now I felt a glow of possession come over me whenever I approached it. Often in those first two months I used to lean against the Mansion House in a familiar sort of way; once I struck a match against the Royal Exchange. And what an impression of financial acumen I could make in a drawing-room by a careless reference to my "block of Jaguars"! Even those who misunderstood me and thought I spoke of my "flock of jaguars" were startled. Indeed life was very good just then.

But lately things have not been going well. At the beginning of April Jaguars settled down at 1-1/16. Though I stood for hours at the club tape, my hair standing up on end and my eyeballs starting from their sockets, Jaguars still came through steadily at 1-1/16. To give them a chance of doing something, I left them alone for a whole week—with what agony you can imagine. Then I looked again; a whole week and anything might have happened. Pauper or millionaire?—No, still 1-1/16.

Worse was to follow. Editors actually took to leaving out Jaguars altogether. I suppose they were sick of putting 1-1/16 in every edition. But how ridiculous it made my idea seem of watching them go up and down! How blank life became again!

And now what I dreaded most of all has happened. I have received a "Progress Report" from the mine. It gives the "total footage" for the month, special reference being made to "cross-cutting, winzing, and sinking." The amount of "tons crushed" is announced. There is serious talk of "ore" being "extracted"; indeed there has already been a most alarming "yield in fine gold." In short, it can no longer be hushed up that the property may at any moment be "placed on a dividend-paying basis."

Probably I shall be getting a safe five per cent!

"Dash it all," as I said to my solicitor this morning, "I might just as well have bought a rotten mortgage."

THE FINANCIER

II

(Eighteen months later)

It is nearly two years ago that I began speculating in West African mines. You may remember what a stir my entry into the financial world created; how Sir Isaac Isaacstein went mad and shot himself; how Sir Samuel Samuelstein went mad and shot his typist; and how Sir Moses Mosestein went mad and shot his typewriter, permanently damaging the letter "s." There was panic in the City on that February day in 1912 when I bought Jaguars and set the market rocking.

I bought Jaguars partly for the rise and partly for the thrill. In describing my speculation to you eighteen months ago I dwelt chiefly on the thrill part; I alleged that I wanted to see them go up and down. It would have been more accurate to have said that I wanted to see them go up. It was because I was sure they were going up that, with the united support of my solicitor, my stockbroker, my land agent, my doctor, my architect and my vicar (most of them hired for the occasion), I bought fifty shares in the Jaguar mine of West Africa.

When I bought Jaguars they were at 1—1-1/16. This means that—— No, on second thoughts I won't. There was a time when, in the pride of my new knowledge, I should have insisted on explaining to you what it meant, but I am getting blasé now; besides, you probably know. It is enough that I bought them, and bought them on the distinct understanding from my financial adviser that by the end of the month they would be up to 2. In that case I should have made rather more than forty pounds in a few days, simply by assembling together my solicitor, stockbroker, land-agent, etc., etc., in London, and without going to West Africa at all. A wonderful thought.

At the end of a month Jaguars were steady at 1-1/16; and I had received a report from the mine to the effect that down below they were simply hacking gold out as fast as they could hack, and up at the top were very busy rinsing and washing and sponging and drying it. The next month the situation was the same: Jaguars in London very steady at 1-1/16, Jaguar diggers in West Africa very steady at gold-digging. And at the end of the third month I realized not only that I was not going to have any thrills at all, but (even worse) that I was not going to make any money at all. I had been deceived.

That was where, eighteen months ago, I left the story of my City life. A good deal has happened since then; as a result of which I am once more eagerly watching the price of Jaguars.

A month or two after I had written about them, Jaguars began to go down. They did it (as they have done everything since I have known them) stupidly. If they had dropped in a single night to 3/4, I should at least have had my thrill. I should have suffered in a single night the loss of some pounds, and I could have borne it dramatically; either with the sternness of the silent Saxon, or else with the volubility of the volatile—I can't think of anybody beginning with a "V." But, alas! Jaguars never dropped at all. They subsided. They subsided slowly back to 1—so slowly that you could hardly observe them going. A week later they were 63/64, which, of course, is practically the same as 1. A month afterwards they were 31/32, and it is a debatable point whether that is less or more than 63/64. Anyhow, by the time I had worked it out and decided that it was slightly less, they were at 61/64, and one had the same trouble all over again. At 61/64 I left them for a time; and when I next read the financial column they were at 15/16, which still seemed to be fairly near to 1. And even when at last, after many months, I found them down to 7/8 I was not seriously alarmed, but felt that it was due to some little local trouble (as that the manager had fallen down the main shaft and was preventing the gold being shot out properly), and that, when the obstruction had been removed, Jaguars would go up to 1 again.

But they didn't. They continued to subside. When they had subsided to 1/2 I woke up. My dream of financial glory was over. I had lost my money and my faith in the City; well, let them go. With an effort I washed Jaguars out of my mind. Henceforward they were nothing to me.

And then, months after, Andrew came on the scene. At lunch one day he happened to mention that he had been talking to his broker.

"Do you often talk to your broker?" I asked in admiration. It sounded so magnificent.

"Often."

"I haven't got a broker to talk to. When you next chat to yours, I wish you'd lead the conversation round to Jaguars and see what he says."

"Why, have you got some?"

"Yes, but they're no good. Have a cigarette, won't you?"

Next morning to my amazement I got a telegram from Andrew. "Can get you ten shillings for Jaguars. Wire if you will sell, and how many."

It was really a shock to me. When I had asked Andrew to mention Jaguars to his broker it was solely in the hope of hearing some humorous City comment on their futility—one of those crisp jests for which the Stock Exchange is famous. I had no idea that his broker might like to buy them from me.

I wired back: "Sell fifty, quick."

Next day he told me he had sold them.

"That's all right," I said cheerfully; "they're his. He can watch them go up and down. When do I get my twenty-five pounds?" To save twenty-five pounds from the wreck was wonderful.

"Not for a month; and, of course, you don't deliver the shares till then."

"What do you mean, 'deliver the shares'?" I asked in alarm. "I haven't got the gold-mine here; it's in Africa or somewhere. Must I go out and——"

"But you've got a certificate for them."

My heart sank.

"Have I?" I whispered. "Good Lord, I wonder where it is."

I went home and looked. I looked for two days; I searched drawers and desks and letter-books and safes and ice-tanks and trouser-presses—every place in which a certificate might hide. It was no good. I went back to Andrew. I was calm.

"About these Jaguars," I said casually. "I don't quite understand my position. What have I promised to do? And can they put me in prison if I don't do it?"

"You've promised to sell fifty Jaguars to a man called Stevens by the middle of next month. That's all."

"I see," I said, and I went home again.

And I suppose you see too. I've got to sell fifty Jaguars to a man called Stevens by the middle of next month. Although I really have fifty fully matured ones of my own, there's nothing to prove it, and they are so suspicious in the City that they will never take my bare word. So I shall have to buy fifty new Jaguars for this man called Stevens—and buy them by the middle of next month.

And this is why I am still eagerly watching the price of Jaguars. Yesterday they were 5/8. I am hoping that by the middle of next month they will be down to 1/2 again. But I find it difficult to remember sometimes which way I want them to go. This afternoon, for instance, when I saw they had risen to 11/16 I was quite excited for a moment; I went out and bought some cigars on the strength of it. Then I remembered; and I came home and almost decided to sell the pianola. It is very confusing. You must see how very confusing it is.

THE DOUBLE

I was having lunch in one of those places where you stand and eat sandwiches until you are tired, and then try to count up how many you have had. As the charm of these sandwiches is that they all taste exactly alike, it is difficult to recall each individual as it went down; one feels, too, after the last sandwich, that one's mind would more willingly dwell upon other matters. Personally I detest the whole business—the place, the sandwiches, the method of scoring—but it is convenient and quick, and I cannot keep away. On this afternoon I was giving the foie gras plate a turn. I know a man who will never touch foie gras because of the cruelty involved in the preparation of it. I excuse myself on the ground that my own sufferings in eating these sandwiches are much greater than those of any goose in providing them.

There was a grey-haired man in the corner who kept looking at me. I seemed to myself to be behaving with sufficient propriety, and there was nothing in my clothes or appearance to invite comment; for in the working quarter of London a high standard of beauty is not insisted upon. On the next occasion when I caught his eye I frowned at him, and a moment later I found myself trying to stare him down. After two minutes it was I who retired in confusion to my glass.

As I prepared to go—for to be watched at meals makes me nervous, and leads me sometimes to eat the card with "Foie Gras" on it in mistake for the sandwich—he came up to me and raised his hat.

"You must excuse me, sir, for staring at you," he said, "but has any one ever told you that you are exactly like A. E. Barrett?"

I drew myself up and rested my left hand lightly on my hip. I thought he said David Garrick.

"The very image of him," he went on, "when first I met him."

Something told me that in spite of his grey hair he was not talking of David Garrick after all.

"Like who?" I said in some disappointment.

"A. E. Barrett."

I tried to think of a reply, both graceful and witty. The only one I could think of was, "Oh?"

"It's extraordinary. If your hair were just a little longer the likeness would be perfect."

I thought of offering to go away now and come back in a month's time. Anyway, it would be an excuse for going now.

"I first knew him at Cambridge," he explained. "We were up together in the 'seventies."

"Ah, I was up in the nineteen hundreds," I said. "I just missed you both."

"Well, didn't they ever tell you at Cambridge that you were the image of A. E. Barrett?"

I tried to think. They had told me lots of things at Cambridge, but I couldn't remember any talk about A. E. Barrett.

"I should have thought every one would have noticed it," he said.

I had something graceful for him this time all right.

"Probably," I said, "those who were unfortunate enough to know me had not the honour of knowing A. E. Barrett."

"But everybody knew A. E. Barrett. You've heard of him, of course?"

The dreadful moment had arrived. I knew it would.

"Of course," I said.

"A charming fellow."

"Very brainy," I agreed.

"Well, just ask any of your artist friends if they don't notice the likeness. The nose, the eyes, the expression—wonderful! But I must be going. Perhaps I shall see you here again some day. Good afternoon"; and he raised his hat and left me.

You can understand that I was considerably disturbed. First, why had I never heard of A. E. Barrett? Secondly, what sort of looking fellow was he? Thirdly, with all this talk about A. E. Barrett, however many sandwiches had I eaten? The last question seemed the most impossible to answer, so I said "eight," to be on the safe side, and went back to work.

In the evening I called upon Peter. My acquaintance of the afternoon had assumed too readily that I should allow myself to be on friendly terms with artists; but Peter's wife illustrates books, and they both talk in a disparaging way of our greatest Academicians.

"Who," I began at once, as I shook hands, "did I remind you of as I came in at the door?"

Peter was silent. Mrs. Peter, feeling that some answer was called for, said, "The cat."

"No, no. Now I'll come in again." I went out and returned dramatically. "Now then, tell me frankly, doesn't that remind you of A. E. Barrett entering his studio?"

"Who is A. E. Barrett?"

I was amazed at their ignorance.

"He's the well-known artist. Surely you've heard of him?"

"I seem to know the name," lied Peter. "What did he paint?"

"'Sunrise on the Alps,' 'A Corner of the West,' 'The Long Day Wanes'—I don't know. Something. The usual thing."

"And are you supposed to be like him?"

"I am. Particularly when eating sandwiches."

"Is it worth while getting you some, in order to observe the likeness?" asked Mrs. Peter.

"If you've never seen A. E. Barrett I fear you'd miss the likeness, even in the most favourable circumstances. Anyhow, you must have heard of him—dear old A. E.!"

They were utterly ignorant of him, so I sat down and told them what I knew; which, put shortly, was that he was a very remarkable-looking fellow.

I have not been to the sandwich-place since. Detesting the sandwiches as I do, I find A. E. Barrett a good excuse for keeping away. For, upon the day after that when he came into my life, I had a sudden cold fear that the thing was a plant. How, in what way, I cannot imagine. That I am to be sold a Guide to Cambridge at the next meeting; that an A. E. Barrett hair-restorer is about to be placed on the market; that an offer will be made to enlarge my photograph (or Barrett's) free of charge if I buy the frame—no, I cannot think what it can be.

Yet, after all, why should it be a plant? We Barretts are not the sort of men to be mixed up with fraud. Impetuous the Barrett type may be, obstinate, jealous—so much you see in our features. But dishonest? Never!

Still, as I did honestly detest those last eight sandwiches, I shall stay away.

A BREATH OF LIFE

This is the story of a comedy which nearly became a tragedy. In its way it is rather a pathetic story.

The comedy was called The Wooing of Winifred. It was written by an author whose name I forget; produced by the well-known and (as his press-agent has often told us) popular actor-manager, Mr. Levinski; and played by (among others) that very charming young man, Prosper Vane—known locally as Alfred Briggs until he took to the stage. Prosper played the young hero, Dick Seaton, who was actually wooing Winifred. Mr. Levinski himself took the part of a middle-aged man of the world with a slight embonpoint; down in the programme as Sir Geoffrey Throssell but fortunately still Mr. Levinski. His opening words, as he came on, were, "Ah, Dick, I have a note for you somewhere," which gave the audience an interval in which to welcome him, while he felt in all his pockets for the letter. One can bow quite easily while feeling in one's pockets, and it is much more natural than stopping in the middle of an important speech in order to acknowledge any cheers. The realization of this, by a dramatist, is what is called "stagecraft." In this case the audience could tell at once that the "technique" of the author (whose name unfortunately I forget) was going to be all right.

But perhaps I had better describe the whole play as shortly as possible. The theme—as one guessed from the title, even before the curtain rose—was the wooing of Winifred. In the First Act Dick proposed to Winifred and was refused by her, not from lack of love, but for fear lest she might spoil his career, he being one of those big-hearted men with a hip-pocket to whom the open spaces of the world call loudly; whereupon Mr. Levinski took Winifred on one side and told the audience how, when he had been a young man, some good woman had refused him for a similar reason and had been miserable ever since. Accordingly in the Second Act Winifred withdrew her refusal and offered to marry Dick, who declined to take advantage of her offer for fear that she was willing to marry him from pity rather than from love; whereupon Mr. Levinski took Dick on one side and told the audience how, when he had been a young man, he had refused to marry some good woman (a different one) for a similar reason, and had been broken-hearted ever afterwards. In the Third Act it really seemed as though they were coming together at last; for at the beginning of it Mr. Levinski took them both aside and told the audience a parable about a butterfly and a snap-dragon, which was both pretty and helpful, and caused several middle-aged ladies in the first and second rows of the upper circle to say, "What a nice man Mr. Levinski must be at home, dear!"—the purport of the allegory being to show that both Dick and Winifred were being very silly, as indeed by this time everybody but the author was aware. Unfortunately at that moment a footman entered with a telegram for Miss Winifred, which announced that she had been left fifty thousand pounds by a dead uncle in Australia; and, although Mr. Levinski seized this fresh opportunity to tell the audience how in similar circumstances Pride, to his lasting remorse, had kept him and some good woman (a third one) apart, nevertheless Dick held back once more, for fear lest he should be thought to be marrying her for her money. The curtain comes down as he says, "Good-bye ... good ber-eye." But there is a Fourth Act, and in the Fourth Act Mr. Levinski has a splendid time. He tells the audience two parables—one about a dahlia and a sheep, which I couldn't quite follow—and three reminiscences of life in India; he brings together finally and for ever these hesitating lovers; and, best of all, he has a magnificent love-scene of his own with a pretty widow, in which we see, for the first time in the play, how love should really be made—not boy-and-girl pretty-pretty love, but the deep emotion felt (and with occasional lapses of memory explained) by a middle-aged man with a slight embonpoint who has knocked about the world a bit and knows life. Mr. Levinski, I need not say, was at his best in this Act.

I met Prosper Vane at the club some ten days before the first night, and asked him how rehearsals were going.

"Oh, all right," he said. "But it's a rotten play. I've got such a dashed silly part."

"From what you told me," I said, "it sounded rather good."

"It's so dashed unnatural. For three whole acts this girl and I are in love with each other, and we know we're in love with each other, and yet we simply fool about. She's a dashed pretty girl, too, my boy. In real life I'd jolly soon——"

"My dear Alfred," I protested, "you're not going to fall in love with the girl you have to fall in love with on the stage? I thought actors never did that."

"They do sometimes; it's a dashed good advertisement. Anyway, it's a silly part, and I'm fed up with it."

"Yes, but do be reasonable. If Dick got engaged at once to Winifred what would happen to Levinski? He'd have nothing to do."

Prosper Vane grunted. As he seemed disinclined for further conversation I left him.

The opening night came, and the usual distinguished and fashionable audience (including myself), such as habitually attends Mr. Levinski's first nights, settled down to enjoy itself. Two acts went well. At the end of each Mr. Levinski came before the curtain and bowed to us, and we had the honour of clapping him loud and long. Then the Third Act began....

Now this is how the Third Act ends:—

Exit Sir Geoffrey

Winifred (breaking the silence). Dick, you heard what he said. Don't let this silly money come between us. I have told you I love you, dear. Won't you—won't you speak to me?

51

Dick. Winifred, I—— (He gets up and walks round the room, his brow knotted, his right fist occasionally striking his left palm. Finally he comes to a stand in front of her.) Winifred, I—— (He raises his arms slowly at right angles to his body and lets them fall heavily down again.) I can't. (In a low, hoarse voice) I—can't! (He stands for a moment with bent head; then with a jerk he pulls himself together.) Good-bye! (His hands go out to her, but he draws them back as if frightened to touch her. Nobly) Good ber-eye.

[He squares his shoulders and stands looking at the audience with his chin in the air; then with a shrug of utter despair, which would bring tears into the eyes of any young thing in the pit, he turns and with bent head walks slowly out.

Curtain

That is how the Third Act ends. I went to the dress rehearsal, and so I know.

How the accident happened I do not know. I suppose Prosper was nervous; I am sure he was very much in love. Anyhow, this is how, on that famous first night, the Third Act ended:—

Exit Sir Geoffrey

Winifred (breaking the silence). Dick, you heard what he said. Don't let this silly money come between us. I have told you I love you, dear. Won't you—won't you speak to me?

Dick (jumping up). Winifred, I—— (with a great gulp) I LOVE YOU!!!

Whereupon he picked her up in his arms and carried her triumphantly off the stage ... and after a little natural hesitation the curtain came down.

Behind the scenes all was consternation. Mr. Levinski (absolutely furious) had a hasty consultation with the author (also furious), in the course of which they both saw that the Fourth Act as written was now an impossibility. Poor Prosper, who had almost immediately recovered his sanity, tremblingly suggested that Mr. Levinski should announce that, owing to the sudden illness of Mr. Vane, the Fourth Act could not be given. Mr. Levinski was kind enough to consider this suggestion not entirely stupid; his own idea having been (very regretfully) to leave out the two parables and three reminiscences from India and concentrate on the love-scene with the widow.

"Yes, yes," he said. "Your plan is better. I will say you are ill. It is true; you are mad. To-morrow we will play it as it was written."

"You can't," said the author gloomily. "The critics won't come till the Fourth Act, and they'll assume that the Third Act ended as it did to-night. The Fourth Act will seem all nonsense to them."

"True. And I was so good, so much myself, in that Act." He turned to Prosper. "You—fool!"

"Or there's another way," began the author. "We might——"

And then a gentleman in the gallery settled it from the front of the curtain. There was nothing in the programme to show that the play was in four acts. "The Time is the present day and the Scene is in Sir Geoffrey Throssell's town-house," was all it said. And the gentleman in the gallery, thinking it was all over, and being pleased with the play and particularly with the realism of the last moment of it, shouted "Author!" And suddenly everybody else cried "Author! Author!" The play was ended.

I said that this was the story of a comedy which nearly became a tragedy. But it turned out to be no tragedy at all. In the three acts to which Prosper Vane had condemned it the play appealed to both critics and public; for the Fourth Act (as he recognised so clearly) was unnecessary, and would have spoilt the balance of it entirely. Best of all, the shortening of the play demanded that some entertainment should be provided in front of it, and this enabled Mr. Levinski to introduce to the public Professor Wollabollacolla and Princess Collabollawolla, the famous exponents of the Bongo-Bongo, that fascinating Central African war dance which was soon to be the rage of society. But though, as a result, the takings of the Box Office surpassed all Mr. Levinski's previous records, our friend Prosper Vane received no practical acknowledgment of his services. He had to be content with the hand and heart of the lady who played Winifred, and the fact that Mr. Levinski was good enough to attend the wedding. There was, in fact, a photograph in all the papers of Mr. Levinski doing it.

"UNDER ENTIRELY NEW MANAGEMENT"

I know a fool of a dog who pretends that he is a Cocker Spaniel, and is convinced that the world revolves round him wonderingly. The sun rises so it may shine on his glossy morning coat; it sets so his master may know that it is time for the evening biscuit; if the rain falls it is that a fool of a dog may wipe on his mistress's skirt his muddy boots. His day is always exciting, always full of the same good things; his night a repetition of his day, more gloriously developed. If there be a sacred moment before the dawn when he lies awake and ponders on life, he tells himself confidently that it will go on for ever like this—a life planned nobly for himself, but one in which the master and mistress whom he protects must always find a place. And I think perhaps he would want a place for me, too, in that life, who am not his real master but yet one of the house. I hope he would.

What Chum doesn't know is this: his master and mistress are leaving him. They are going to a part of the world where a fool of a dog with no manners is a nuisance. If Chum could see all the good little London dogs, who at home sit languidly on their mistress's lap, and abroad take their view of life through a muff much bigger than themselves; if he could see the big obedient dogs who walk solemnly through the Park carrying their master's stick, never pausing in their impressive march unless it be to plunge into the Serpentine and rescue a drowning child, he would know what I mean. He would admit that a dog who cannot answer to his own name and pays but little more attention to "Down, idiot," and "Come here, fool," is not every place's dog. He would admit it, if he had time. But before I could have called his attention to half the good dogs I had marked out he would have sat down beaming in front of a motor-car ... and then he would never have known what now he will know so soon—that his master and mistress are leaving him.

It has been my business to find a new home for him. This is harder than you think. I can make him sound lovable, but I cannot make him sound good. Of course, I might leave out his doubtful qualities, and describe him merely as beautiful and affectionate; I might ... but I couldn't. I think Chum's habitual smile would get larger, he would wriggle the end of himself more ecstatically than ever if he heard himself summed up as beautiful and affectionate. Anyway, I couldn't do it, for I get carried away when I speak of him and I reveal all his bad qualities.

"I am afraid he is a snob," I confessed to one woman of whom

54

I had hopes. "He doesn't much care for what he calls the lower classes."

"Oh?" she said.

"Yes, he hates badly dressed people. Corduroy trousers tied up at the knee always excite him. I don't know if any of your family— no, I suppose not. But if he ever sees a man with his trousers tied up at the knee he goes for him. And he can't bear tradespeople; at least not the men. Washerwomen he loves. He rather likes the washing-basket too. Once, when he was left alone with it for a moment, he appeared shortly afterwards on the lawn with a pair of—well, I mean he had no business with them at all. We got them away after a bit of a chase, and then they had to go to the wash again. It seemed rather a pity when they'd only just come back. Of course, I smacked his head for him; but he looks so surprised and reproachful when he's done wrong that you never feel it's quite his fault."

"I doubt if I shall be able to take him after all," she said. "I've just remembered——"

I forget what it was she remembered, but it meant that I was still without a new home for Chum.

"What does he eat?" somebody else asked me. It seemed hopeful; I could see Chum already installed.

"Officially," I said, "he lives on puppy biscuits; he also has the toast-crusts after breakfast and an occasional bone. Privately, he is fond of bees. I have seen him eat as many as six bees in an afternoon. Sometimes he wanders down to the kitchen-garden and picks the gooseberries; he likes all fruit, but gooseberries are the things he can reach best. When there aren't any gooseberries about he has to be content with the hips and haws from the rose-trees. But really you needn't bother, he can eat anything. The only thing he doesn't like is whitening. We were just going to mark the lawn one day, and while we were busy pegging it out he wandered up and drank the whitening out of the marker. It is practically the only disappointment he has ever had. He looked at us, and you could see that his opinion of us had gone down. 'What did you put it there for, if you didn't mean me to drink it?' he said reproachfully. Then he turned and walked slowly and thoughtfully back to his kennel. He never came out till next morning."

"Really?" said my man. "Well, I shall have to think about it. I'll let you know."

Of course, I knew what he meant.

With a third dog-lover to whom I spoke the negotiations came to grief, not apparently because of any fault of Chum's, but because, if you will believe it, of my shortcomings. At least I can suppose nothing else. For this man had been enthusiastic about him. He had revelled in the tale of Chum's wickedness; he had adored him for being so conceited. He had practically said that he would take him.

"Do," I begged. "I'm sure he'd be happy with you. You see, he's not everybody's dog; I mean, I don't want any odd man whom I don't know to take him. It must be a friend of mine, so that I shall often be able to see Chum afterwards."

"So that—what?" he asked anxiously.

"So that I shall often be able to see Chum afterwards. Week-ends, you know, and so on. I couldn't bear to lose the silly old ass altogether."

He looked thoughtful; and, when I went on to speak about Chum's fondness for chickens, and his other lovable ways, he changed the subject altogether. He wrote afterwards that he was sorry he couldn't manage with a third dog. And I like to think he was not afraid of Chum—but only of me.

But I have found the right man at last. A day will come soon when I shall take Chum from his present home to his new one. That will be a great day for him. I can see him in the train, wiping his boots effusively on every new passenger, wriggling under the seat and out again from sheer joy of life; I can see him in the taxi, taking his one brief impression of a world that means nothing to him; I can see him in another train, joyous, eager, putting his paws on my collar from time to time and saying excitedly, "What a day this is!" And if he survives the journey; if I can keep him on the way from all the delightful deaths he longs to try; if I can get him safely to his new house, then I can see him——

Well, I wonder. What will they do to him? When I see him again, will he be a sober little dog, answering to his name, careful to keep his muddy feet off the visitor's trousers, grown up, obedient, following to heel round the garden, the faithful servant of his master? Or will he be the same old silly ass, no use to anybody, always dirty, always smiling, always in the way, a clumsy, blundering fool of a dog who knows you can't help loving him? I wonder....

Between ourselves, I don't think they can alter him now.... Oh, I hope they can't.

A FAREWELL TOUR

This is positively Chum's last appearance in print—for his own sake no less than for yours. He is conceited enough as it is, but if once he got to know that people are always writing about him in books his swagger would be unbearable. However, I have said good-bye to him now; I have no longer any rights in him. Yesterday I saw him off to his new home, and when we meet again it will be on a different footing. "Is that your dog?" I shall say to his master. "What is he? A Cocker? Jolly little fellows, aren't they? I had one myself once."

As Chum refused to do the journey across London by himself, I met him at Liverpool Street. He came up in a crate; the world must have seemed very small to him on the way. "Hallo, old ass," I said to him through the bars, and in the little space they gave him he wriggled his body with delight. "Thank Heaven there's one of 'em alive," he said.

"I think this is my dog," I said to the guard, and I told him my name.

He asked for my card.

"I'm afraid I haven't one with me," I explained. When policemen touch me on the shoulder and ask me to go quietly; when I drag old gentlemen from underneath motor-'buses, and they decide to adopt me on the spot; on all the important occasions when one really wants a card, I never have one with me.

"Can't give him up without proof of identity," said the guard, and Chum grinned at the idea of being thought so valuable.

I felt in my pockets for letters. There was only one, but it offered to lend me £10,000 on my note of hand alone. It was addressed to "Dear Sir," and though I pointed out to the guard that I was the "Sir," he still kept tight hold of Chum. Strange that one man should be prepared to trust me with £10,000, and another should be so chary of confiding to me a small black spaniel.

"Tell the gentleman who I am," I said imploringly through the bars. "Show him you know me."

"He's really all right," said Chum, looking at the guard with his great honest brown eyes. "He's been with us for years."

And then I had an inspiration. I turned down the inside pocket of my coat; and there, stitched into it, was the label of my tailor with my name written on it. I had often wondered why tailors did this; obviously they know how stupid guards can be.

"I suppose that's all right," said the guard reluctantly. Of course, I might have stolen the coat. I see his point.

"You—you wouldn't like a nice packing-case for yourself?" I said timidly. "You see, I thought I'd put Chum on the lead. I've got to take him to Paddington, and he must be tired of his shell by now. It isn't as if he were really an armadillo."

The guard thought he would like a shilling and a nice packing-case. Wood, he agreed, was always wood, particularly in winter, but there were times when you were not ready for it.

"How are you taking him?" he asked, getting to work with a chisel. "Underground?"

"Underground?" I cried in horror. "Take Chum on the Underground? Take—— Have you ever taken a large live conger-eel on the end of a string into a crowded carriage?"

The guard never had.

"Well, don't. Take him in a taxi instead. Don't waste him on other people."

The crate yawned slowly, and Chum emerged all over straw. We had an anxious moment, but the two of us got him down and put the lead on him. Then Chum and I went off for a taxi.

"Hooray," said Chum, wriggling all over, "isn't this splendid? I say, which way are you going? I'm going this way?... No, I mean the other way."

Somebody had left some of his milk-cans on the platform. Three times we went round one in opposite directions and unwound ourselves the wrong way. Then I hauled him in, took him struggling in my arms and got into a cab.

The journey to Paddington was full of interest. For a whole minute Chum stood quietly on the seat, rested his fore-paws on the open window and drank in London. Then he jumped down and went mad. He tried to hang me with the lead, and then in remorse tried to hang himself. He made a dash for the little window at the back; missed it and dived out of the window at the side; was hauled back and kissed me ecstatically in the eye with his sharpest tooth.... "And I thought the world was at an end," he said, "and there were no more people. Oh, I am an ass. I say, did you notice I'd had my hair cut? How do you like my new trousers? I must show you them." He jumped on to my lap. "No, I think you'll see them better on the ground," he said, and jumped down again. "Or no, perhaps you would get a better view if——" he jumped up hastily, "and yet I don't know——" he dived down, "though, of course, if you—— Oh lor! this is a day," and he put both paws lovingly on my collar.

Suddenly he was quiet again. The stillness, the absence of storm in the taxi was so unnatural that I began to miss it. "Buck up, old fool," I said, but he sat motionless by my side, plunged in thought. I tried to cheer him up. I pointed out King's Cross to him;

he wouldn't even bark at it. I called his attention to the poster outside the Euston Theatre of The Two Biffs; for all the regard he showed he might never even have heard of them. The monumental masonry by Portland Road failed to uplift him.

At Baker Street he woke up and grinned cheerily. "It's all right," he said, "I was trying to remember what happened to me this morning—something rather miserable, I thought, but I can't get hold of it. However, it's all right now. How are you?" And he went mad again.

At Paddington I bought a label at the bookstall and wrote it for him. He went round and round my leg looking for me. "Funny thing," he said as he began to unwind, "he was here a moment ago. I'll just go round once more. I rather think ... Ow! Oh, there you are!" I stepped off him, unravelled the lead and dragged him to the Parcels Office.

"I want to send this by the two o'clock train," I said to the man the other side of the counter.

"Send what?" he said.

I looked down. Chum was making himself very small and black in the shadow of the counter. He was completely hidden from the sight of anybody the other side of it.

"Come out," I said, "and show yourself."

"Not much," he said. "A parcel! I'm not going to be a jolly old parcel for anybody."

"It's only a way of speaking," I pleaded. "Actually you are travelling as a small black gentleman. You will go with the guard—a delightful man."

Chum came out reluctantly. The clerk leant over the counter and managed to see him.

"According to our regulations," he said, and I always dislike people who begin like that, "he has to be on a chain. A leather lead won't do."

Chum smiled all over himself. I don't know which pleased him more—the suggestion that he was a very large and fierce dog, or the impossibility now of his travelling with the guard, delightful man though he might be. He gave himself a shake and started for the door.

"Tut, tut, it's a great disappointment to me," he said, trying to look disappointed, but his back would wriggle. "This chain business—silly of us not to have known—well, well, we shall be wiser another time. Now let's go home."

Poor old Chum; I had known. From a large coat pocket I produced a chain.

"Dash it," said Chum, looking up at me pathetically, "you might almost want to get rid of me."

He was chained, and the label tied on to him. Forgive me that label, Chum; I think that was the worst offence of all. And why should I label one who was speaking so eloquently for himself; who said from the tip of his little black nose to the end of his stumpy black tail, "I'm a silly old ass, but there's nothing wrong in me, and they're sending me away!" But according to the regulations—one must obey the regulations, Chum.

I gave him to the guard—a delightful man. The guard and I chained him to a brake or something. Then the guard went away, and Chum and I had a little talk....

After that the train went off.

Good-bye, little dog.

THE TRUTH ABOUT HOME RAILS

Imagine us, if you can, sitting one on each side of the fire, I with my feet on the mantelpiece, Margery curled up in the blue arm-chair, both of us intent on the morning paper. To me, by good chance, has fallen the sporting page; to Margery the foreign, political, and financial intelligence of the day.

"What," said Margery, "does it mean when it says——" She stopped and spelt it over to herself again.

I put down my piece of the paper and prepared to explain. The desire for knowledge in the young cannot be too strongly encouraged, and I have always flattered myself that I can explain in perfectly simple language anything which a child wants to know. For instance, I once told Margery what "Miniature Rifle Shooting" meant; it was a head-line which she had come across in her paper. The explanation took some time, owing to Margery's preconceived idea that a bird entered into it somewhere; several times, when I thought the lesson was over, she said, "Well, what about the bird?" But I think I made it plain to her in the end, though maybe she has forgotten about it now.

"What," said Margery, "does it mean when it says 'Home Rails Firm'?"

I took up my paper again. The Cambridge fifteen, I was glad to see, were rapidly developing into a first-class team, and——

"'Home Rails Firm,'" repeated Margery, and looked up at me.

My mind worked rapidly, as it always does in a crisis.

"What did you say?" I asked in surprise.

"What does 'Home Rails Firm' mean?"

"Where does it say that?" I went on, still thinking at lightning speed.

"There. It said it yesterday too."

"Ah, yes." I made up my mind. "Well, that," I said—"I think that is something you must ask your father."

"I did ask him yesterday."

"Well, then——"

"He told me to ask Mummy."

Coward!

"You can be sure," I said firmly, "that what Mummy told you would be right," and I returned to my paper.

"Mummy told me to wait till you came."

Really, these parents! The way they shirk their responsibilities nowadays is disgusting.

"'Home Rails Firm,'" said Margery, and settled herself to listen.

It is good that children should be encouraged to take an interest in the affairs of the day, but I do think that a little girl might be taught by her father (or if more convenient, mother) which part of a newspaper to read. Had Margery asked me the difference between a bunker and a banker, had she demanded an explanation of "ultimatum" or "guillotine," I could have done something with it; but to let a child of six fill her head with ideas as to the firmness or otherwise of Home Rails is hardly nice. However, an explanation had to be given.

"Well, it's like this, Margery," I said at last. "Supposing—well, you see, supposing—that is to say, if I——" and then I stopped. I had a sort of feeling—intuition, they call it—that I was beginning in the wrong way.

"Go on," said Margery.

"Perhaps I had better put it this way. Supposing you were to—— Well, we'd better begin further back than that. You know what—— No, I don't suppose you do know that. Well, if I—that is to say, when a man—you know, it's rather difficult to explain this, Margery."

"Are you explaining it now?"

"I'm just going to begin."

"Thank you, Uncle."

I lit my pipe slowly, while I considered again how best to approach the matter.

"'Home Rails Firm,'" said Margery. "Isn't it a funny thing to say?"

It was. It was a very silly thing to say. Whoever said it first might have known what it would lead to.

"Perhaps I can explain it best like this, Margery," I said, beginning on a new tack. "I suppose you know what 'firm' means?"

"What does it mean?"

"Ah, well, if you don't know that," I said, rather pleased, "perhaps I had better explain that first. 'Firm' means that—that is to say, you call a thing firm if it—well, if it doesn't—that is to say, a thing is firm if it can't move."

"Like a house?"

"Well, something like that. This chair, for instance," and I put my hand on her chair, "is firm because you can't shake it. You see, it's quite—— Hallo, what's that?"

"Oh, you bad Uncle, you've knocked the castor off again," cried Margery, greatly excited at the incident.

"This is too much," I said bitterly. "Even the furniture is against me."

"Go on explaining," said Margery, rocking herself in the now wobbly chair.

I decided to leave "firm." It is not an easy word to explain at the best of times, and when everything you touch goes and breaks itself it becomes perfectly impossible.

"Well, so much for that," I said. "And now we come to 'rails.' You know what rails are?"

"Like I've got in the nursery?"

This was splendid. I had forgotten these for the moment.

"Exactly. The rails your train goes on. Well then, 'Home Rails' would be rails at home."

"Well, I've got them at home," said Margery in surprise. "I couldn't have them anywhere else."

"Quite so. Then 'Home Rails Firm' would mean that—er—home rails were—er—firm."

"But mine aren't, because they wobble. You know they do."

"Yes, but——"

"Well, why do they say 'Home Rails Firm' when they mean 'Home Rails Wobble'?"

"Ah, that's just it. The point is that when they say 'Home Rails Firm,' they don't mean that the rails themselves are firm. In fact, they don't mean at all what you think they mean. They mean something quite different."

"What do they mean?"

"I am just going to explain," I said stiffly.

62

"Or perhaps I had better put it this way," I said ten minutes later. "Supposing—— Oh, Margery, it is difficult to explain."

"I must know," said Margery.

"Why do you want to know so badly?"

"I want to know a million million times more than anything else in the whole world."

"Why?"

"So as I can tell Angela," said Margery.

I plunged into my explanation again. Angela is three, and I can quite see how important it is that she should be sound on the question.

THE KING'S SONS

"Tell me a story," said Margery.
"What sort of a story?"
"A fairy story, because it's Christmas-time."
"But you know all the fairy stories."
"Then tell me a new fairy story."
"Right," I said.

Once upon a time there was a King who had three sons. The eldest son was a very thoughtful youth. He always had a reason for everything he did, and sometimes he would say things like "Economically it is to the advantage of the State that——" or "The civic interests of the community demand that——" before doing something specially horrid. He didn't want to be unkind to anybody, but he took what he called a "large view" of things; and if you happened to ask for a third help of plum-pudding he took the large view that you would be sorry about it next morning—and so you didn't have your plum-pudding. He was called Prince Proper.

The second son was a very wise youth. You couldn't catch him anyhow. If you asked him whether he knew the story of the three wells, or "Why does a chicken cross the road?" or anything really amusing like that, he would always say, "Oh, I heard that years ago!"—and whenever you began "Adam and Eve and Pinchme" he would pinch you at once without waiting like a gentleman until you had got to the end of the verse. He was called Prince Clever.

And the third son was just wonderfully beautiful. He had the most marvellously pink cheeks and long golden hair that you have ever seen. I don't much care for that style myself, but in the country in which he lived it was admired more than I can tell you. He was called Prince Goldenlocks. I'll give you three guesses why.

Now the King had reigned a long time, so long that he was tired of being king, and he often used to wonder which of his sons ought to succeed him. Of course, nowadays they never wonder, and the eldest son becomes king at once, and quite right too; but in those days it was generally left to the sons to prove which among themselves was the most worthy. Sometimes they would all be sent out to find the magic Dragon's Tooth, and only one would come back alive, which would save a lot of trouble; or else, after a lot of discussion, they would be told to go and find beautiful Princesses for themselves, and the one which brought back the most beautiful Princess—but very often that would lead to another discussion. The best way of all was to call in a Fairy to help. A Fairy has all sorts of tricks for finding out about you, and her favourite plan is to pretend to be something else and see what you do.

So the King called in a Fairy and said, "To-morrow I am sending out my three sons into the world to seek their fortune. I want you to test them for me and find out which is the most fitted to succeed to my throne. If it should happen to be Prince Goldenlocks—but, of course, I don't want to influence you in any way."

"Leave it to me," said the Fairy. "You agree, no doubt, that the quality most desirable in a king is love and kindliness——"

"Y-yes," said the King doubtfully.

"I was sure of it. Well, I have a way of putting this quality to the test which has never yet failed." And with that she vanished. She could have gone out at the door quite easily, but she preferred to vanish.

I expect you know what her way was. You have read about it often in your fairy books. On the next day, as Prince Proper was coming along the road, she appeared suddenly in front of him in the shape of a poor old woman.

"Please give me something to buy a crust of bread, pretty gentleman," she pleaded. "I'm starving."

Prince Proper looked at her sternly.

"Economically," he said, "it is to the advantage of the State that the submerged classes should be a charge on the State itself and not on individuals. The civic interests of the community demand that promiscuous charity should be sternly discouraged. Surely you see that for yourself?"

The Fairy didn't quite. The language had taken her by

surprise. In all her previous adventures of this kind, two of the young Princes had refused her roughly, and the third had shared his last piece of bread with her. This adventure was going all wrong.

"Let me explain it to you more fully," went on Proper, and for an hour and twenty-seven minutes he did so. Then he went on his way, leaving a dazed Fairy behind him.

By and by Prince Clever came along. Suddenly he saw a poor old woman in front of him.

"Please give me something to buy a crust of bread," she pleaded. "I'm starving."

Prince Clever burst into a roar of laughter.

"You don't catch me," he said. "I've read about this a hundred times. You're not an old woman at all; you're a Fairy."

"W-what do you mean?" she stammered.

"This is a silly test of Father's. Well, you can tell him he's got one son who's clever enough to see through him." And he went on his way.

By and by Prince Goldenlocks came along. I need not say that he did all that you would expect of a third and youngest son who had pink cheeks, long golden hair, and (as I ought to have said before) a very loving nature. He shared his last piece of bread with the poor old woman....

(Surely he will get the throne!)

But the Fairy was an honest Fairy. She did understand Proper's point of view; she had to admit that, if Clever saw through her deception, it was honourable of him to have said so. And though, of course, her loving heart was all for Prince Goldenlocks, she felt that it would not be fair to award the throne to him without a further trial. So she did another thing that she was very fond of doing. She changed herself into a pretty little dove and—right in front of Prince Proper—she flew with a hawk in pursuit of her. "Now we shall see," she said to herself, "which of the three youths has the softest heart."

You can guess what Proper said.

"Life," he said, "is one constant battle. Nature," he said, "is ruthless, and the weakest must go to the wall. If I kill the hawk," he said, "I am kind to the dove, but am I," he said, and I think there was a good deal in this—"am I kind to the caterpillar or whatever it is that the dove eats?" Of course, you know, there is that to be thought of. Anyhow, after soliloquizing for forty-seven minutes Prince Proper went on his way; and by and by Prince Clever came along.

You can guess what Clever said.

"My whiskers!" he said, "this is older than the last. I knew this in my cradle." With one of those nasty sarcastic laughs that I hate so much he went on his way; and by and by Prince Goldenlocks came along.

(Now then, Goldenlocks, the throne is almost yours!)

You can guess what Goldenlocks said.

"Poor little dove," he said. "But I can save its life."

Rapidly he fitted an arrow to his bow and with careful aim let fly at the pursuing hawk....

I say again that Prince Goldenlocks was the most beautiful youth you have ever seen in your life, and he had a very loving nature. But he was a poor shot.

He hit the dove....

"Is that all?" said Margery.
"That's all," I said. "Good night."

DISAPPOINTMENT

My young friend Bobby (now in the early thirteens) has been making his plans for the Christmas holidays. He communicated them to me in a letter from school:—

"I am going to write an opera in the holidays with a boy called Short, a very great and confident friend of mine here. I am doing the words and Short is doing the music. We have already got the title; it is called 'Disappointment.'"

Last week, on his return to town, he came to see me at my club, and when the waiter had brought in drinks, and Bobby had refused a cigar, I lighted up and prepared to talk shop. His recent discovery that I write too leads him to treat me with more respect than formerly.

"Now then," I said, "tell me about it. How's it going on?"

"Oo, I haven't done much yet," said Bobby. "But I've got the plot."

"Let's have it."

Bobby unfolded it rapidly.

"Well, you see, there's a chap called Tommy—he's the hero—and he's just come back from Oxford, and he's awfully good-looking and decent and all that, and he's in love with Felicia, you see, and there's another chap called Reynolds, and, you see, Felicia's really

66

the same as Phyllis, who's going to marry Samuel, and that's the disappointment, because Tommy wants to marry her, you see."

"I see. That ought to be all right. You could almost get two operas out of that."

"Oo, do you think so?"

"Well, it depends how much Reynolds comes in. You didn't tell me what happened to him. Does he marry anybody?"

"Oo, no. He comes in because I want somebody to tell the audience about Tommy when Tommy isn't there."

(How well Bobby has caught the dramatic idea.)

"I see. He ought to be very useful."

"You see, the First Act's in a very grand restaurant, and Tommy comes in to have dinner, and he explains to Reynolds how he met Felicia on a boat, and she'd lost her umbrella, and he said, 'Is this your umbrella?' and it was, and they began to talk to each other, and then he was in love with her. And then he goes out, and then Reynolds tells the audience what an awfully decent chap Tommy is."

"Why does he go out?"

"Well, you see, Reynolds couldn't tell everybody what an awfully decent chap Tommy is if Tommy was there."

(Of course he couldn't.)

"And where's Felicia all this time?"

"Oo, she doesn't come on: She's in the country with Samuel. You see, the Second Act is a grand country wedding, and Samuel and Phyllis are married, and Tommy is one of the guests, and he's very unhappy, but he tries not to show it, and he shoots himself."

"Reynolds is there too, I suppose?"

"Oo, I don't know yet."

(He'll have to be, of course. He'll be wanted to tell the audience how unhappy Tommy is.)

"And how does it end?" I asked.

"Well, you see, when the wedding's over, Tommy sings a song about Felicia, and it ends up, 'Felicia, Felicia, Felicia,' getting higher each time—Short has to do that part, of course, but I've told him about it—and then the curtain comes down."

"I see. And has Short written any of the music yet?"

"He's got some of the notes. You see, I've only just got the plot, and I've written about two pages. I'm writing it in an exercise-book."

A shadow passed suddenly across the author's brow.

"And the sickening thing," he said, as he leant back in his chair and sipped his ginger-beer, "is that on the cover of it I've spelt Disappointment with two 's's.'"

(The troubles of this literary life!)

67

"Sickening," I agreed.

If there is one form of theft utterly unforgivable it is the theft by a writer of another writer's undeveloped ideas. Borrow the plot of Sir J. M. Barrie's last play, and you do him no harm; you only write yourself down a plagiarist. But listen to the scenario of his next play (if he is kind enough to read it to you) and write it up before he has time to develop it himself, and you do him a grievous wrong; for you fix the charge of plagiarism on him. Surely, you say, no author could sink so low as this.

And yet, when I got home, the plot of "Disappointment" (with one "s") so took hold of me that I did the unforgivable thing; I went to my desk and wrote the opera. I make no excuses for myself. I only point out that Bobby's opera, as performed at Covent Garden in Italian, with Short's music conducted by Richter, is not likely to be belittled by anything that I may write here. I have only written in order that I may get the scenario—which had begun to haunt me— off my chest. Bobby, I know, will understand and forgive; Short I have not yet had the pleasure of meeting, but I believe he is smaller than Bobby.

Act I

Scene—A grand restaurant. Enter Tommy, a very handsome man, just back from Oxford.

Tommy sings:

> Felicia, I love you,
> By all the stars above you
> I swear you shall be mine!—
> And now I'm going to dine.

[He sits down and orders a bottle of ginger-beer and some meringues.

Waiter. Your dinner, Sir.
Tommy. Thank you. And would you ask Mr. Reynolds to come in, if you see him? *(To the audience)* A week ago I was crossing the Channel—*(enter Reynolds)*— Oh, here you are, Reynolds! I was just saying that a week ago I was crossing the Channel when I saw the most beautiful girl I have ever seen who had lost her umbrella. I said, "Excuse me, but is this your umbrella?" She said,

"Yes." Reynolds, I sat down and fell in love with her. Her name was Felicia. And now I must go and see about something.

[*Exit.*

Reynolds. Poor Tommy! An awfully decent chap if ever there was one. But he will never marry Felicia, because I happen to know her real name is Phyllis, and she is engaged to Samuel.

(Recitative.)

She is engaged to Samuel. Poor Tommy,
He does not know she's fond of Samuel.
He will be disappointed when he knows.

Curtain

Act II

Scene—A beautiful country wedding

Tommy (in pew nearest door, to Reynolds). Who's the bride?
Reynolds. Phyllis. She's marrying Samuel.

Enter Bride.

Tommy. Heavens, it's Felicia!
Reynolds (to audience). Poor Tommy! How disappointed he must be! (Aloud) Yes, Felicia and Phyllis are really the same girl. She's engaged to Samuel.
Tommy. Then I cannot marry her!
Reynolds. No.

Tommy sings:

Good-bye, Felicia, good-bye,
I'm awfully disappointed, I
Am now, in fact, about to die,
Felicia, Felicia, Felicia!

[*Shoots himself.*

Curtain

That is how I see it. But no doubt Bobby and Short, when they really get to work, will make something better of it. It is an engaging theme, but, of course, the title wants to be spelt properly.

AMONG THE ANIMALS

Jeremy was looking at a card which his wife had just passed across the table to him.

"'Lady Bendish. At Home,'" he read. "'Pets.' Is this for us?"

"Of course," said Mrs. Jeremy.

"Then I think 'Pets' is rather familiar. 'Mr. and Mrs. J. P. Smith' would have been more correct."

"Don't be silly, Jeremy. It means it's a Pet party. You have to bring some sort of pet with you, and there are prizes for the prettiest, and the most intelligent, and the most companionable, and so on." She looked at the fox-terrier curled up in front of the fire-place. "We could take Rags, of course."

"Or Baby," said Jeremy. "We'll enter her in the Fat Class."

But when the day arrived Jeremy had another idea. He came in from the garden with an important look on his face, and joined his wife in the hall.

"Come on," he said. "Let's start."

"But where's Rags?"

"Rags isn't coming. I'm taking Hereward instead." He opened his cigarette-case and disclosed a small green animal. "Hereward," he said.

"Why, Jeremy," cried his wife, "it's—why, it's blight from the rose-tree!"

"It isn't just blight, dear; it's one particular blight. A blight. Hereward, the Last of the Blights." He wandered round the hall. "Where's the lead?" he asked.

"Jeremy, don't be absurd."

"My dear, I must have something to lead him up for his prize on. During the parade he can sit on my shoulder informally, but when we come to the prize-giving, 'Mr. J. P. Smith's blight, Hereward,' must be led on properly." He pulled open a drawer. "Oh, here we are. I'd better take the chain; he might bite through the leather one."

They arrived a little late, to find a lawn full of people and animals; and one glance was sufficient to tell Jeremy that in some of the classes at least his pet would have many dangerous rivals.

"If there's a prize for the biggest," he said to his wife, "my blight has practically lost it already. Adams has brought a cart-horse. Hullo, Adams," he went on, "how are you? Don't come too close or Hereward may do your animal a mischief."

"Who's Hereward?"

Jeremy opened his cigarette-case.

"Hereward," he said. "Not the woodbine; that's quite wild. The blight. He's much more domesticated, but there are moments when he gets out of hand and becomes unmanageable. He gave me the slip coming here, and I had to chase him through the churchyard; that's why we're late."

"Does he take meals with the family?" asked Adams with a grin.

"No, no; he has them alone in the garden. You ought to see him having his bath. George, our gardener, looks after him. George gives him a special bath of soapy water every day. Hereward simply loves it. George squirts on him, and Hereward lies on his back and kicks his legs in the air. It's really quite pretty to watch them."

He nodded to Adams, and wandered through the crowd with Mrs. Jeremy. The collection of animals was remarkable; they varied in size from Adams's cart-horse to Jeremy's blight; in playfulness from the Vicar's kitten to Miss Trehearne's chrysalis; and in ability for performing tricks from the Major's poodle to Dr. Bunton's egg of the Cabbage White.

"There ought to be a race for them all," said Mrs. Jeremy. "A handicap, of course."

"Hereward is very fast over a short distance," said Jeremy, "but he wants encouragement. If he were given ninety-nine yards, two feet, and eleven inches in a hundred, and you were to stand in front of him with a William Allan Richardson, I think we might pull it off. But, of course, he's a bad starter. Hullo, there's Miss Bendish."

Miss Bendish, hurrying along, gave them a word as she went past.

"They're going to have the inspection directly," she said, "and give the prizes. Is your animal quite ready?"

"I should like to brush him up a bit," said Jeremy. "Is there a tent or anywhere where I could prepare him? His eyebrows get so matted if he's left to himself for long." He took out a cigarette and lit it.

"There's a tent, but you'll have to hurry up."

"Oh, well, it doesn't really matter," said Jeremy, as he walked along with her. "Hereward's natural beauty and agility will take him through."

On the south lawn the pets and their owners were assembling. Jeremy took the leash out of his pocket and opened his cigarette-case.

"Good heavens!" he cried. "Hereward has escaped! Quick! Shut the gates!" He saw Adams near and hurried up to him. "My blight has escaped," he said breathlessly, holding up the now useless leash. "He gnawed through the chain and got away. I'm afraid he may be running amok among the guests. Supposing he were to leap upon Sir Thomas from behind and savage him—it's too terrible." He moved anxiously on. "Have you seen my blight?" he asked Miss Trehearne. "He has escaped, and we are rather anxious. If he were to get the Vicar down and begin to worry him——" He murmured something about "once getting the taste for blood" and hurried off. The guests were assembled, and the judges walked down the line and inspected their different animals. They were almost at the end of it when Jeremy sprinted up and took his place by the last beast.

"It's all right," he panted to his wife, "I've got him. Silly of me to mislay him, but he's so confoundedly shy." He held out his finger as the judges approached, and introduced them to the small green pet perching on the knuckle. "A blight," he said. "Hereward, the Chief Blight. Been in the family for years. A dear old friend."

Jeremy went home a proud man. "Mr. J. P. Smith's blight, Hereward," had taken first prize in the All-round class.

"Yes," he admitted to his wife at dinner, "there is something on my mind." He looked at the handsome cigarette-box on the table in front of him and sighed.

"What is it, dear? You enjoyed yourself this afternoon, you know you did, and Hereward won you that beautiful cigarette-box. You ought to be proud."

"That's the trouble. Hereward didn't win it."

"But they said—they read it out, and——"

"Yes, but they didn't know. It was really Elspeth who won it."

"Elspeth?"

"Yes, dear." Jeremy sighed again. "When Hereward escaped and I went back for him, I didn't find him as I—er—pretended. So I went to the rose garden and—and borrowed Elspeth. Fortunately no one noticed it was a lady blight ... they all took it for Hereward.... But it was really Elspeth—and belonged to Lady Bendish."

He helped himself to a cigarette from the box.

"It's an interesting point," he said. "I shall go and confess to-morrow to Sir Thomas, and see what he thinks about it. If he wants the box back, well and good."

He refilled his glass.

"After all," he said, "the real blow is losing Hereward. Elspeth—Elspeth is very dear to me, but she can never be quite the same."

A TRAGEDY OF THE SEA

William Bales—as nice a young man as ever wore a cummerbund on an esplanade—was in despair. For half an hour he and Miss Spratt had been sitting in silence on the pier, and it was still William's turn to say something. Miss Spratt's last remark had been, "Oh, Mr. Bales, you do say things!" and William felt that his next observation must at all costs live up to the standard set for it. Three or four times he had opened his mouth to speak, and then on second thoughts had rejected the intended utterance as unworthy. At the end of half an hour his mind was still working fruitlessly. He knew that the longer he waited the more brilliant he would have to be, and he told himself that even Bernard Shaw or one of those clever writing fellows would have been hard put to it now.

William was at odds with the world. He was a romantic young man who had once been told that he nearly looked like Lewis Waller when he frowned, and he had resolved that his holiday this year should be a very dashing affair indeed. He had chosen the sea in the hopes that some old gentleman would fall off the pier and let himself be saved by—and, later on, photographed with—William Bales, who in a subsequent interview would modestly refuse to take any credit for the gallant rescue. As his holiday had progressed he had felt the need for some such old gentleman more and more; for only thus, he realised, could he capture the heart of the wayward Miss Spratt. But so far it had been a dull season; in a whole fortnight nobody had gone out of his way to oblige William, and to-morrow he must return to the City as unknown and as unloved as when he left it.

"Got to go back to-morrow," he said at last. As an impromptu it would have served, but as the result of half an hour's earnest thought he felt that it did not do him justice.

"So you said before," remarked Miss Spratt.

"Well, it's still true."

"Talking about it won't help it," said Miss Spratt.

William sighed and looked round the pier. There was an old gentleman fishing at the end of it, his back turned invitingly to William. In half an hour he had caught one small fish (which he had had to return as under the age limit) and a bunch of seaweed. William felt that there was a wasted life; a life, however, which a sudden kick and a heroic rescue by W. Bales might yet do something to justify. At the Paddington Baths, a month ago, he had won a plate-diving competition; and though there is a difference between diving for plates and diving for old gentlemen he was prepared to waive it. One kick and then ... Fame! And, not only Fame, but the admiration of Angelina Spratt.

It was perhaps as well for the old gentleman—who was really quite worthy, and an hour later caught a full-sized whiting—that Miss Spratt spoke at this moment.

"Well, you're good company, I must say," she observed to William.

"It's so hot," said William.

"You can't say I asked to come here."

"Let's go on the beach," said William desperately. "We can find a shady cave or something." Fate was against him; there was to be no rescue that day.

"I'm sure I'm agreeable," said Miss Spratt.

They walked in silence along the beach, and, rounding a corner of the cliffs, they came presently to a cave. In earlier days W. Bales could have done desperate deeds against smugglers there, with Miss Spratt looking on. Alas for this unromantic age! It was now a place for picnics, and a crumpled sheet of newspaper on the sand showed that there had been one there that very afternoon.

They sat in a corner of the cave, out of the sun, out of sight of the sea, and William prepared to renew his efforts as a conversationalist. In the hope of collecting a few ideas as to what the London clubs were talking about he picked up the discarded newspaper, and saw with disgust that it was the local Herald. But just as he threw it down, a line in it caught his eye and remained in his mind:

"High tide to-day—3.30."

William's heart leapt. He looked at his watch; it was 2.30. In one hour the waves would be dashing remorselessly into the cave, would be leaping up the cliff, what time he and Miss Spratt——

Suppose they were caught by the tide....

Meanwhile the lady, despairing of entertainment, had removed her hat.

"Really," she said, "I'm that sleepy—— I suppose the tide's safe, Mr. Bales?"

It was William's chance.

"Quite, quite safe," he said earnestly. "It's going down hard."

"Well then, I almost think——" She closed her eyes. "Wake me up when you've thought of something really funny, Mr. Bales."

William was left alone with Romance.

He went out of the cave and looked round. The sea was still some way out, but it came up quickly on this coast. In an hour ... in an hour....

He scanned the cliffs, and saw the ledge whither he would drag her. She would cling to him crying, calling him her rescuer....

What should he do then? Should he leave her and swim for help? Or should he scale the mighty cliff?

He returned to the cave and, gazing romantically at the sleeping Miss Spratt, conjured up the scene. It would go like this, he thought.

Miss Spratt (*wakened by the spray dashing over her face*). Oh, Mr. Bales! We're cut off by the tide! Save me!

W. Bales (*lightly*). Tut-tut, there's no danger. It's nothing. (*Aside*) Great Heavens! Death stares us in the face!

Miss Spratt (*throwing her arms around his neck*). William, save me; I cannot swim!

W. Bales (*with Waller face*). Trust me, Angelina. I will fight my way round yon point and obtain help. (*Aside*) An Englishman can only die once.

Miss Spratt. Don't leave me!

W. Bales. Fear not, sweetheart. See, there is a ledge where you will be beyond the reach of the hungry tide. I will carry you thither in my arms and will then——

At this point in his day-dream William took another look at the sleeping Miss Spratt, felt his biceps doubtfully, and went on——

W. Bales. I will help you to climb thither, and will then swim for help.

Miss Spratt. My hero!

Again and again William reviewed the scene to himself. It was perfect. His photograph would be in the papers; Miss Spratt would worship him; he would be a hero in his City office. The actual danger was slight, for at the worst she could shelter in the far end of the cave; but he would not let her know this. He would do the thing heroically—drag her to the ledge on the cliff, and then swim round the point to obtain help.

The thought struck him that he could conduct the scene better

75

in his shirt-sleeves. He removed his coat, and then went out of the cave to reconnoitre the ledge.

Miss Spratt awoke with a start and looked at her watch. It was 4.15. The cave was empty save for a crumpled page of newspaper. She glanced at this idly and saw that it was the local Herald ... eight days old.

Far away on the horizon William Bales was throwing stones bitterly at the still retreating sea.

OLD FRIENDS

"It was very nice of you to invite me to give you lunch," I said, "and if only the waiter would bring the toast I should be perfectly happy. I can't say more."

"Why not?" said Miss Middleton, looking up. "Oh, I see."

"And now," I said, when I had finished my business with a sardine, "tell me all about it. I know something serious must have brought you up to London. What is it? Have you run away from home?"

Miss Middleton nodded. "Sir Henery," she added dramatically, "waits for me in his yacht at Dover. My parents would not hear of the marriage, and immured me in the spare room. They tried to turn me against my love, and told wicked stories about him, vowing that he smoked five non-throat cigarettes in a day. Er—would you pass the pepper, please?"

"Go on," I begged. "Never mind the pepper."

"But, of course, I really came to see you," said Miss Middleton briskly. "I want you to do something for me."

"I knew it."

"Oh, do say you'd love to."

I drained my glass and felt very brave.

"I'd love to," I said doubtfully. "At least, if I were sure that——" I lowered my voice: "Look here—have I got to write to anybody?"

"No," said Miss Middleton.

"Let me know the worst. Have I—er—have I got to give advice to anybody?"

"No."

There was one other point that had to be settled. I leant across the table anxiously.

"Have I got to ring anybody up on the telephone?" I asked in a hoarse whisper.

"Oh, nothing like that at all," said Miss Middleton.

"Dash it," I cried, "then of course I'll do anything for you. What is it? Somebody you want killed? I could kill a mayor to-day."

Miss Middleton was silent for a moment while allowing herself to be helped to fish. When the waiters had moved away, "We are having a jumble sale," she announced.

I shook my head at her.

"Your life," I said, "is one constant round of gaiety."

"And I thought as I was coming to London I'd mention it to you. Because you're always saying you don't know what to do with your old things."

"I'm not always saying it. I may have mentioned it once or twice when the conversation was flagging."

"Well, mention it now, and then I'll mention my jumble sale."

I thought it over for a moment.

"It will mean brown paper and string," I said hopelessly, "and I don't know where to get them."

"I'll buy some after lunch for you. You shall hold my hand while I buy it."

"And then I should have to post it, and I'm rotten at posting things."

"But you needn't post it, because you can meet me at the station with it, and I'll take it home."

"I don't think it's quite etiquette for a young girl to travel alone with a big brown-paper parcel. What would Mrs. Middleton say if she knew?"

"Mother?" cried Miss Middleton. "But, of course, it's her idea. You didn't think it was mine?" she said reproachfully.

"The shock of it unnerved me for a moment. Of course, I see now that it is Mrs. Middleton's jumble sale entirely." I sighed and helped myself to salt. "How do I begin?"

"You drive me to my dressmaker and leave me there and go on to your rooms. And then you collect a few really old things that you don't want and tie them up and meet me at the 4.40. I'm afraid," she said frankly, "it is a rotten way of spending an afternoon; but I promised mother."

"I'll do it," I said.

My parcel and I arrived promptly to time. Miss Middleton didn't.

"Don't say I've caught the wrong train," she said breathlessly, when at last she appeared. "It does go at 4.40, doesn't it?"

"It does," I said, "and it did."

"Then my watch must be slow."

"Send it to the jumble sale," I advised. "Look here—we've a long time to wait for the next train; let's undress my parcel in the waiting-room, and I'll point out the things that really want watching. Some are absolutely unique."

It was an odd collection of very dear friends, Miss Middleton's final reminder having been that nothing was too old for a jumble sale.

"Lot One," I said. "A photograph of my house cricket eleven, framed in oak. Very interesting. The lad on the extreme right is now a clergyman."

"Oh, which is you?" said Miss Middleton eagerly.

I was too much wrapped up in my parcel to answer. "Lot Two," I went on. "A pink-and-white football shirt; would work up into a dressy blouse for adult, or a smart overcoat for child. Lot Three. A knitted waistcoat; could be used as bath-mat. Lot Four. Pair of bedroom slippers in holes. This bit is the slipper; the rest is the hole. Lot Five. Now this is something really good. Truthful Jane—my first prize at my Kindergarten."

"Mother is in luck. It's just the sort of things she wants," said Miss Middleton.

"Her taste is excellent. Lot Six. A pair of old grey flannel trousers. Lot Seven. Lot Seven forward. Where are you?" I began to go through the things again. "Er—I'm afraid Lot Seven has already gone."

"What about Lot Eight?"

"There doesn't seem to be a Lot Eight either. It's very funny; I'm sure I started with more than this. Some of the things must have eaten each other on the way."

"Oh, but this is heaps. Can you really spare them all?"

"I should feel honoured if Mrs. Middleton would accept them," I said with a bow. "Don't forget to tell her that in the photograph the lad on the extreme right——" I picked up the photograph and examined it more carefully. "I say, I look rather jolly, don't you think? I wonder if I have another copy of this anywhere." I gazed at it wistfully. "That was my first year for the house, you know."

"Don't give it away," said Miss Middleton suddenly. "Keep it."

"Shall I? I don't want to deprive—— Well, I think I will if you don't mind." My eyes wandered to the shirt. "I've had some fun in that in my time," I said thoughtfully. "The first time I wore it——"

"You really oughtn't to give away your old colours, you know."

"Oh, but if Mrs. Middleton," I began doubtfully—"at least, don't you—what?—oh, all right, perhaps I won't." I put the shirt on

78

one side with the photograph, and picked up the dear old comfy bedroom slippers. I considered them for a minute and then I sighed deeply. As I looked up I caught Miss Middleton's eye.... I think she had been smiling.

"About the slippers," she said gravely.

"Good-bye," I said to Miss Middleton. "It's been jolly to see you." I grasped my parcel firmly as the train began to move. "I'm always glad to help Mrs. Middleton, and if ever I can do so again be sure to let me know."

"I will," said Miss Middleton.

The train went out of the station, and my parcel and I looked about for a cab.

GETTING MARRIED

I

THE DAY

Probably you thought that getting married was quite a simple business. So did I. We were both wrong; it is the very dickens. Of course, I am not going to draw back now. As I keep telling Celia, her Ronald is a man of powerful fibre, and when he says he will do a thing he does it—eventually. She shall have her wedding all right; I have sworn it. But I do wish that there weren't so many things to be arranged first.

The fact that we had to fix a day was broken to me one afternoon when Celia was showing me to some relatives of hers in the Addison Road. I got entangled with an elderly cousin on the hearth-rug; and though I know nothing about motor-bicycles I talked about them for several hours under the impression that they were his subject. It turned out afterwards that he was equally ignorant of them, but thought they were mine. Perhaps we shall get on better at a second meeting. However, just when we were both thoroughly sick of each other, Celia broke off her gay chat with an aunt to say to me:

"By the way, Ronald, we did settle on the eleventh, didn't we?"

I looked at her blankly, my mind naturally full of motor-bicycles.

"The wedding," smiled Celia.

"Right-o," I said with enthusiasm. I was glad to be assured that I should not go on talking about motor-bicycles for ever, and that on the eleventh, anyhow, there would be a short interruption for the ceremony. Feeling almost friendly to the cousin, I plunged into his favourite subject again.

On the way home Celia returned to the matter.

"Or you would rather it was the twelfth?" she asked.

"I've never heard a word about this before," I said. "It all comes as a surprise to me."

"Why, I'm always asking you."

"Well, it's very forward of you, and I don't know what young people are coming to nowadays. Celia, what's the good of my talking to your cousin for three hours about motor-bicycling? Surely one can get married just as well without that?"

"One can't get married without settling the day," said Celia, coming cleverly back to the point.

Well, I suppose one can't. But somehow I had expected to be spared all this bother. I think my idea was that Celia would say to me suddenly one evening, "By the way, Ronald, don't forget we're being married to-morrow," and I should have said "Where?" And on being told the time and place, I should have turned up pretty punctually; and after my best man had told me where to stand, and the clergyman had told me what to say, and my solicitor had told me where to sign my name, we should have driven from the church a happy married couple ... and in the carriage Celia would have told me where we were spending the honeymoon.

However, it was not to be so.

"All right, the eleventh," I said. "Any particular month?"

"No," smiled Celia, "just any month. Or, if you like, every month."

"The eleventh of June," I surmised. "It is probably the one day in the year on which my Uncle Thomas cannot come. But no matter. The eleventh let it be."

"Then that's settled. And at St. Miriam's?"

For some reason Celia has set her heart on St. Miriam's. Personally I have no feeling about it. St. Andrew's-by-the-Wardrobe or St. Bartholomew's-Without would suit me equally well.

"All right," I said, "St. Miriam's."

There, you might suppose, the matter would have ended; but no.

"Then you will see about it to-morrow?" said Celia persuasively.

I was appalled at the idea.

"Surely," I said, "this is for you, or your father, or—or somebody to arrange."

"Of course it's for the bridegroom," protested Celia.

"In theory, perhaps. But anyhow not the bridegroom personally. His best man ... or his solicitor ... or ... I mean, you're not suggesting that I myself—— Oh, well, if you insist. Still, I must say I don't see what's the good of having a best man and a solicitor if—— Oh, all right, Celia, I'll go to-morrow."

So I went. For half an hour I padded round St. Miriam's nervously, and then summoning up all my courage, I knocked my pipe out and entered.

"I want," I said jauntily to a sexton or a sacristan or something—"I want—er—a wedding." And I added, "For two."

He didn't seem as nervous as I was. He enquired quite calmly when I wanted it.

"The eleventh of June," I said. "It's probably the one day in the year on which my Uncle Thomas—— However, that wouldn't interest you. The point is that it's the eleventh."

The clerk consulted his wedding-book. Then he made the surprising announcement that the only day he could offer me in June was the seventeenth. I was amazed.

"I am a very old customer," I said reproachfully. "I mean, I have often been to your church in my time. Surely——"

"We've weddings fixed on all the other days."

"Yes, yes, but you could persuade somebody to change his day, couldn't you? Or if he is very much set on being married on the eleventh you might recommend some other church to him. I daresay you know of some good ones. You see, Celia—my—that is, we're particularly keen, for some reason, on St. Miriam's."

The clerk didn't appreciate my suggestion. He insisted that the seventeenth was the only day.

"Then will you have the seventeenth?" he asked.

"My dear fellow, I can't possibly say off-hand," I protested. "I am not alone in this. I have a friend with me. I will go back and tell her what you say. She may decide to withdraw her offer altogether."

I went back and told Celia.

"Bother," she said. "What shall we do?"

"There are other churches. There's your own, for example."

"Yes, but you know I don't like that. Why shouldn't we be married on the seventeenth?"

"I don't know at all. It seems an excellent day; it lets in my Uncle Thomas. Of course, it may exclude my Uncle William, but one can't have everything."

"Then will you go and fix it for the seventeenth to-morrow?"

"Can't I send my solicitor this time?" I asked. "Of course, if you particularly want me to go myself, I will. But really, dear, I seem to be living at St. Miriam's nowadays."

And even that wasn't the end of the business. For, just as I was leaving her, Celia broke it to me that St. Miriam's was neither in her parish nor in mine, and that, in order to qualify as a bridegroom, I should have to hire a room somewhere near.

"But I am very comfortable where I am," I assured her.

"You needn't live there, Ronald. You only want to leave a hat there, you know."

"Oh, very well," I sighed.

She came to the hall with me; and, having said good-bye to her, I repeated my lesson.

"The seventeenth, fix it up to-morrow, take a room near St. Miriam's, and leave a hat there. Good-bye."

"Good-bye.... And oh, Ronald!" She looked at me critically as I stood in the doorway. "You might leave that one," she said.

II

FURNISHING

"By the way," said Celia suddenly, "what have you done about the fixtures?"

"Nothing," I replied truthfully.

"Well, we must do something about them."

"Yes. My solicitor—he shall do something about them. Don't let's talk about them now. I've only got three hours more with you, and then I must dash back to my work."

I must say that any mention of fixtures has always bored me intensely. When it was a matter of getting a house to live in I was all energy. As soon as Celia had found it, I put my solicitor on to it; and within a month I had signed my name in two places, and was the owner of a highly residential flat in the best part of the neighbourhood. But my effort so exhausted me that I have felt utterly unable since to cope with the question of the curtain-rod in the bathroom or whatever it is that Celia means by fixtures. These things will arrange themselves somehow, I feel confident.

Meanwhile the decorators are hard at work. A thrill of pride inflates me when I think of the decorators at work. I don't know how they got there; I suppose I must have ordered them. Celia says that she ordered them and chose all the papers herself, and that all I did was to say that the papers she had chosen were very pretty; but this doesn't sound like me in the least. I am convinced that I was the man of action when it came to ordering decorators.

"And now," said Celia one day, "we can go and choose the electric-light fittings."

"Celia," I said in admiration, "you're a wonderful person. I should have forgotten all about them."

"Why, they're about the most important thing in the flat."

"Somehow I never regarded anybody as choosing them. I thought they just grew in the wall. From bulbs."

When we got into the shop Celia became businesslike at once.

"We'd better start with the hall," she told the man.

"Everybody else will have to," I said, "so we may as well."

"What sort of a light did you want there?" he asked.

"A strong one," I said; "so as to be able to watch our guests carefully when they pass the umbrella-stand."

Celia waved me away and explained that we wanted a hanging lantern. It appeared that this shop made a speciality not so much of the voltage as of the lamps enclosing it.

"How do you like that?" asked the man, pointing to a magnificent affair in brass. He wandered off to a switch, and turned it on.

"Dare you ask him the price?" I asked Celia. "It looks to me about a thousand pounds. If it is, say that you don't like the style. Don't let him think we can't afford it."

"Yes," said Celia, in a careless sort of way. "I'm not sure that I care about that. How much is it?"

"Two pounds."

I was not going to show my relief. "Without the light, of course?" I said disparagingly.

"How do you think it would look in the hall?" said Celia to me.

"I think our guests would be encouraged to proceed. They'd see that we were pretty good people."

"I don't like it. It's too ornate."

"Then show us something less ornate," I told the man sternly.

He showed us things less ornate. At the end of an hour Celia said she thought we'd better get on to another room, and come back to the hall afterwards. We decided to proceed to the drawing-room.

"We must go all out over these," said Celia; "I want these to be really beautiful."

At the end of another hour Celia said she thought we'd better get on to my workroom. My workroom, as the name implies, is the room to which I am to retire when I want complete quiet. Sometimes I shall go there after lunch ... and have it.

"We can come back to the drawing-room afterwards," she said. "It's really very important that we should get the right ones for that. Your room won't be so difficult, but, of course, you must have awfully nice ones."

I looked at my watch.

"It's a quarter to one," I said. "At 2.15 on the seventeenth of June we are due at St. Miriam's. If you think we shall have bought anything by then, let's go on. If, as seems to me, there is no hope at all, then let's have lunch to-day anyhow. After lunch we may be able to find some way out of the impasse."

After lunch I had an idea.

"This afternoon," I said, "we will begin to get some furniture together."

"But what about the electric fittings? We must finish off those."

"This is an experiment. I want to see if we can buy a chest of drawers. It may just be our day for it."

"And we settle the fittings to-morrow. Yes?"

"I don't know. We may not want them. It all depends on whether we can buy a chest of drawers this afternoon. If we can't, then I don't see how we can ever be married on the seventeenth of June. Somebody's got to be, because I've engaged the church. The question is whether it's going to be us. Let's go and buy a chest of drawers this afternoon, and see."

The old gentleman in the little shop Celia knew of was delighted to see us.

"Chestesses? Ah, you 'ave come to the right place." He led the way into the depths. "There now. There's a chest—real old, that is." He gave it a hearty smack. "You don't see a chest like that nowadays. They can't make 'em. Three pound ten. You couldn't have got that to-morrer. I'd have sold it for four pound to-morrer."

"I knew it was our day," I said.

"Real old, that is. Spanish me'ogany, all oak lined. That's right, sir, pull the drawers out and see for yourself. Let the lady see. There's no imitation there, lady. A real old chest, that is. Come in 'ere in a week and you'd have to pay five pounds for it. Me'ogany's going up, you see, that's how."

"Well?" I said to Celia.

"It's perfectly sweet. Hadn't we better see some more?"

We saw two more. Both of them Spanish me'ogany, oak lined, pull-the-drawers-out-and-see-for-yourself-lady. Half an hour passed rapidly.

"Well?" I said.

"I really don't know which I like best. Which do you?"

"The first; it's nearer the door."

"There's another shop just over the way. We'd better just look there too, and then we can come back to decide to-morrow."

We went out. I glanced at my watch. It was 3.30, and we were being married at 2.15 on the seventeenth of June.

"Wait a moment," I said, "I've forgotten my gloves."

I may be a slow starter, but I am very firm when roused. I went into the shop, wrote a cheque for the three chests of drawers, and told the man where to send them. When I returned, Celia was at the shop opposite, pulling the drawers out of a real old mahogany chest which was standing on the pavement outside.

"This is even better," she said. "It's perfectly adorable. I wonder if it's more expensive."

"I'll just ask," I said.

I went in and, without an unnecessary word, bought that chest too. Then I came back to Celia. It was 3.45, and on the seventeenth of June at 2.15—— Well, we had four chests of drawers towards it.

"Celia," I said, "we may just do it yet."

III

THE HONEYMOON

"I know I oughtn't to be dallying here," I said; "I ought to be doing something strenuous in preparation for the wedding. Counting the bells at St. Miriam's, or varnishing the floors in the flat, or—— Tell me what I ought to be doing, Celia, and I'll go on not doing it for a bit."

"There's the honeymoon," said Celia.

"I knew there was something."

"Do tell me what you're doing about it?"

"Thinking about it."

"You haven't written to any one about rooms yet?"

"Celia," I said reproachfully, "you seem to have forgotten why I am marrying you."

When Celia was browbeaten into her present engagement, she said frankly that she was only consenting to marry me because of my pianola, which she had always coveted. In return I pointed out that I was only asking her to marry me because I wanted somebody to write my letters. There opened before me, in that glad moment, a vista of invitations and accounts-rendered all answered promptly by Celia, instead of put off till next month by me. It was a wonderful vision to one who (very properly) detests letter-writing. And yet, here she was, even before the ceremony, expecting me to enter into a deliberate correspondence with all sorts of strange people who as yet had not come into my life at all. It was too much.

86

"We will get," I said, "your father to write some letters for us."

"But what's he got to do with it?"

"I don't want to complain of your father, Celia, but it seems to me that he is not doing his fair share. There ought to be a certain give-and-take in the matter. I find you a nice church to be married in—good. He finds you a nice place to honeymoon in—excellent. After all, you are still his daughter."

"All right," said Celia, "I'll ask father to do it. 'Dear Mrs. Bunn, my little boy wants to spend his holidays with you in June. I am writing to ask you if you will take care of him and see that he doesn't do anything dangerous. He has a nice disposition, but wants watching.'" She patted my head gently. "Something like that."

I got up and went to the writing-desk.

"I can see I shall have to do it myself," I sighed. "Give me the address and I'll begin."

"But we haven't quite settled where we're going yet, have we?"

I put the pen down thankfully and went back to the sofa.

"Good! Then I needn't write to-day, anyhow. It is wonderful, dear, how difficulties roll away when you face them. Almost at once we arrive at the conclusion that I needn't write to-day. Splendid! Well, where shall we go? This will want a lot of thought. Perhaps," I added, "I needn't write to-morrow."

"We had almost fixed on England, hadn't we?"

"Somebody was telling me that Lynton was very beautiful. I should like to go to Lynton."

"But every one goes to Lynton for their honeymoon."

"Then let's be original and go to Birmingham. 'The happy couple left for Birmingham, where the honeymoon will be spent.' Sensation."

"'The bride left the train at Ealing.' More sensation."

"I think the great thing," I said, trying to be businesslike, "is to fix the county first. If we fixed on Rutland, then the rest would probably be easy."

"The great thing," said Celia, "is to decide what we want. Sea, or river, or mountains, or—or golf."

At the word golf I coughed and looked out of the window.

Now I am very fond of Celia—I mean of golf, and—what I really mean, of course, is that I am very fond of both of them. But I do think that on a honeymoon Celia should come first. After all, I shall have plenty of other holidays for golf ... although, of course, three weeks in the summer without any golf at all—— Still, I think Celia should come first.

"Our trouble," I said to her, "is that neither of us has ever been on a honeymoon before, and so we've no idea what it will be like.

After all, why should we get bored with each other? Surely we don't depend on golf to amuse us?"

"All the same, I think your golf would amuse me," said Celia. "Besides, I want you to be as happy as you possibly can be."

"Yes, but supposing I was slicing my drives all the time, I should be miserable. I should be torn between the desire to go back to London and have a lesson with the professional and the desire to stay on honeymooning with you. One can't be happy in a quandary like that."

"Very well then, no golf. Settled?"

"Quite. Now then, let's decide about the scenery. What sort of soil do you prefer?"

When I left Celia that day we had agreed on this much: that we wouldn't bother about golf, and that the mountains, rivers, valleys, and so on should be left entirely to nature. All we were to enquire for was (in the words of an advertisement Celia had seen) "a perfect spot for a honeymoon."

In the course of the next day I heard of seven spots; varying from a spot in Surrey "dotted with firs," to a dot in the Pacific spotted with—I forget what, natives probably. Taken together they were the seven only possible spots for a honeymoon.

"We shall have to have seven honeymoons," I said to Celia when I had told her my news. "One honeymoon, one spot."

"Wait," she said. "I have heard of an ideal spot."

"Speaking as a spot expert, I don't think that's necessarily better than an only possible spot," I objected. "Still, tell me about it."

"Well, to begin with, it's close to the sea."

"So we can bathe when we're bored. Good."

"And it's got a river, if you want to fish——"

"I don't. I should hate to catch a fish who was perhaps on his honeymoon too. Still, I like the idea of a river."

"And quite a good mountain, and lovely walks, and, in fact, everything. Except a picture-palace, luckily."

"It sounds all right," I said doubtfully. "We might just spend the next day or two thinking about my seven spots, and then I might ... possibly ... feel strong enough to write."

"Oh, I nearly forgot. I have written, Ronald."

"You have?" I cried. "Then, my dear, what else matters? It's a perfect spot." I lay back in relief. "And there, thank 'evings, is another thing settled. Bless you."

"Yes. And, by the way, there is golf quite close too. But that," she smiled, "needn't prevent us going there."

"Of course not. We shall just ignore the course."

"Perhaps, so as to be on the safe side, you'd better leave your clubs behind."

"Perhaps I'd better," I said carelessly.

All the same I don't think I will. One never knows what may happen ... and at the outset of one's matrimonial career to have to go to the expense of an entirely new set of clubs would be a most regrettable business.

IV

SEASONABLE PRESENTS

"I suppose," I said, "it's too late to cancel this wedding now?"

"Well," said Celia, "the invitations are out, and the presents are pouring in, and mother's just ordered the most melting dress for herself that you ever saw. Besides, who's to live in the flat if we don't?"

"There's a good deal in what you say. Still, I am alarmed, seriously alarmed. Look here." I drew out a printed slip and flourished it before her.

"Not a writ? My poor Ronald!"

"Worse than that. This is the St. Miriam's bill of fare for weddings. Celia, I had no idea marriage was so expensive. I thought one rolled-gold ring would practically see it."

It was a formidable document. Starting with "full choir and organ" which came to a million pounds, and working down through "boys' voices only," and "red carpet" to "policemen for controlling traffic—per policeman, 5s.," it included altogether some two dozen ways of disposing of my savings.

"If we have the whole menu," I said, "I shall be ruined. You wouldn't like to have a ruined husband."

Celia took the list and went through it carefully.

"I might say 'Season,'" I suggested, "or 'Press.'"

"Well, to begin with," said Celia, "we needn't have a full choir."

"Need we have an organ or a choir at all? In thanking people for their kind presents you might add, 'By the way, do you sing?'

Then we could arrange to have all the warblers in the front. My best man or my solicitor could give the note."

"Boys' voices only," decided Celia. "Then what about bells?"

"I should like some nice bells. If the price is 'per bell' we might give an order for five good ones."

"Let's do without bells. You see, they don't begin to ring till we've left the church, so they won't be any good to us."

This seemed to me an extraordinary line to take.

"My dear child," I remonstrated, "the whole thing is being got up not for ourselves, but for our guests. We shall be much too preoccupied to appreciate any of the good things we provide—the texture of the red carpet or the quality of the singing. I dreamt last night that I quite forgot about the wedding-ring till 1.30 on the actual day, and the only cab I could find to take me to a jeweller's was drawn by a camel. Of course, it may not turn out to be as bad as that, but it will certainly be an anxious afternoon for both of us. And so we must consider the entertainment entirely from the point of view of our guests. Whether their craving is for champagne or bells, it must be satisfied."

"I'm sure they'll be better without bells. Because when the policemen call out 'Mr. Spifkins' carriage,' Mr. Spifkins mightn't hear if there were a lot of bells clashing about."

"Very well, no bells. But, mind you," I said sternly, "I shall insist on a clergyman."

We went through the rest of the menu, course by course.

"I know what I shall do," I said at last. "I shall call on my friend the Clerk again, and I shall speak to him quite frankly. I shall say, 'Here is a cheque for a thousand pounds. It is all I can afford— and, by the way, you'd better pay it in quickly or it will be dishonoured. Can you do us up a nice wedding for a thousand inclusive?'"

"Like the Christmas hampers at the stores."

"Exactly. A dozen boys' voices, a half-dozen of bells, ten yards of awning, and twenty-four oranges, or vergers, or whatever it is. We ought to get a nice parcel for a thousand pounds."

"Or," said Celia, "we might send the list round to our friends as suggestions for wedding presents. I'm sure Jane would love to give us a couple of policemen."

"We'd much better leave the whole thing to your father. I incline more and more to the opinion that it is his business to provide the wedding. I must ask my solicitor about it."

"He's providing the bride."

"Yes, but I think he might go further. I can't help feeling that the bells would come very well from him. 'Bride's father to bridegroom—A peal of bells.' People would think it was something in silver for the hall. It would do him a lot of good in business circles."

"And that reminds me," smiled Celia, "there's been some talk about a present from Miss Popley."

I have come to the conclusion that it is impossible to get married decently unless one's life is ordered on some sort of system. Mine never has been; and the result is that I make terrible mistakes—particularly in the case of Miss Popley. At the beginning of the business, when the news got round to Miss Popley, I received from her a sweet letter of congratulation. Knowing that she was rather particular in these matters I braced myself up and thanked her heartily by return of post. Three days later, when looking for a cheque I had lost, I accidentally came across her letter. "Help, help!" I cried. "This came days ago, and I haven't answered yet." I sat down at once and thanked her enthusiastically. Another week passed and I began to feel that I must really make an effort to catch my correspondence up; so I got out all my letters of congratulation of the last ten days and devoted an afternoon to answering them. I used much the same form of thanks in all of them ... with the exception of Miss Popley's, which was phrased particularly warmly.

So much for that. But Miss Popley is Celia's dear friend also. When I made out my list of guests I included Miss Popley; so, in her list, did Celia. The result was that Miss Popley received two invitations to the wedding.... Sometimes I fear she must think we are pursuing her.

"What does she say about a present?" I asked.

"She wants us to tell her what we want."

"What are we to say? If we said an elephant——"

"With a small card tied on to his ear, and 'Best wishes from Miss Popley' on it. It would look heavenly among the other presents."

"You see what I mean, Celia. Are we to suggest something worth a thousand pounds, or something worth ninepence? It's awfully kind of her, but it makes it jolly difficult for us."

"Something that might cost anything from ninepence to a thousand pounds," suggested Celia.

"Then that washes out the elephant."

"Can't you get the ninepenny ones now?"

"I suppose," I said, reverting to the subject which most weighed on me, "she wouldn't like to give the men's voices for the choir?"

"No, I think a clock," said Celia. "A clock can cost anything you like—or don't like."

91

"Right-o. And perhaps we'd better settle now. When it comes, how many times shall we write and thank her for it?"

Celia considered. "Four times, I think," she said.

Well, as Celia says, it's too late to draw back now. But I shall be glad when it's all over. As I began by saying, there's too much "arranging" and "settling" and "fixing" about the thing for me. In the necessary negotiations and preparations I fear I have not shone. And so I shall be truly glad when we have settled down in our flat ... and Celia can restore my confidence in myself once more by talking loudly to her domestic staff about "The Master."

HOME AFFAIRS

AN INSURANCE ACT

Of course, I had always known that a medical examination was a necessary preliminary to insurance, but in my own case I had expected the thing to be the merest formality. The doctor, having seen at a glance what a fine, strong, healthy fellow I was, would look casually at my tongue, apologise for having doubted it, enquire genially what my grandfather had died of, and show me to the door. This idea of mine was fostered by the excellent testimonial which I had written myself at the Company's bidding. "Are you suffering from any constitutional disease?—No. Have you ever had gout?—No. Are you deformed?—No. Are you of strictly sober and temperate habits?—No," I mean Yes. My replies had been a model of what an Assurance Company expects. Then why the need of a doctor?

However, they insisted.

The doctor began quietly enough. He asked, as I had anticipated, after the health of my relations. I said that they were very fit; and, not to be outdone in politeness, expressed the hope that his people, too, were keeping well in this trying weather. He wondered if I drank much. I said, "Oh, well, perhaps I will," with an apologetic smile, and looked round for the sideboard. Unfortunately he did not pursue the matter....

"And now," he said, after the hundredth question, "I should like to look at your chest."

I had seen it coming for some time. In vain I had tried to turn the conversation—to lead him back to the subject of drinks or my relations. It was no good. He was evidently determined to see my chest. Nothing could move him from his resolve.

Trembling, I prepared for the encounter. What terrible disease was he going to discover?

He began by tapping me briskly all over in a series of double knocks. For the most part one double-knock at any point appeared to satisfy him, but occasionally there would be no answer and he would knock again. At one spot he knocked four times before he could make himself heard.

"This," I said to myself at the third knock, "has torn it. I shall be ploughed," and I sent an urgent message to my chest, "For 'eving's sake do something, you fool! Can't you hear the gentleman?" I suppose that roused it, for at the next knock he passed on to an adjacent spot....

"Um," he said, when he had called everywhere, "um."

"I wonder what I've done," I thought to myself. "I don't believe he likes my chest."

Without a word he got out his stethoscope and began to listen to me. As luck would have it he struck something interesting almost at once, and for what seemed hours he stood there listening and listening to it. But it was boring for me, because I really had very little to do. I could have bitten him in the neck with some ease ... or I might have licked his ear. Beyond that, nothing seemed to offer.

I moistened my lips and spoke.

"Am I dying?" I asked in a broken voice.

"Don't talk," he said. "Just breathe naturally."

"I am dying," I thought, "and he is hiding it from me." It was a terrible reflection.

"Um," he said and moved on.

By and by he went and listened behind my back. It is very bad form to listen behind a person's back. I did not tell him so, however. I wanted him to like me.

"Yes," he said. "Now cough."

"I haven't a cough," I pointed out.

"Make the noise of coughing," he said severely.

Extremely nervous, I did my celebrated imitation of a man with an irritating cough.

"H'm! h'm! h'm! h'm!"

"Yes," said the doctor. "Go on."

"He likes it," I said to myself, "and he must obviously be an excellent judge. I shall devote more time to mimicry in future. H'm! h'm! h'm!..."

The doctor came round to where I could see him again.

"Now cough like this," he said. "Honk! honk!"

I gave my celebrated imitation of a sick rhinoceros gasping out its life. It went well. I got an encore.

"Um," he said gravely, "um." He put his stethoscope away and looked earnestly at me.

"Tell me the worst," I begged. "I'm not bothering about this stupid insurance business now. That's off, of course. But—how long have I? I must put my affairs in order. Can you promise me a week?"

He said nothing. He took my wrists in his hands and pressed them. It was evident that grief over-mastered him and that he was taking a silent farewell of me. I bowed my head. Then, determined to bear my death-sentence like a man, I said firmly, "So be it," and drew myself away from him.

However, he wouldn't let me go.

"Come, come," I said to him, "you must not give way"; and I made an effort to release one of my hands, meaning to pat him encouragingly on the shoulder.

He resisted....

I realized suddenly that I had mistaken his meaning, and that he was simply feeling my pulses.

"Um," he said, "um," and continued to finger my wrists.

Clenching my teeth, and with the veins starting out on my forehead, I worked my pulses as hard as I could.

"Ah," he said, as I finished tying my tie; and he got up from the desk where he had been making notes of my disastrous case, and came over to me. "There is just one thing more. Sit down."

I sat down.

"Now cross your knees."

I crossed my knees. He bent over me and gave me a sharp tap below the knee with the side of his hand.

My chest may have disappointed him.... He may have disliked my back.... Possibly I was a complete failure with my pulses.... But I knew the knee-trick.

This time he should not be disappointed.

I was taking no risks. Almost before his hand reached my knee, my foot shot out and took him fairly under the chin. His face suddenly disappeared.

"I haven't got that disease," I said cheerily.

BACHELOR RELICS

"Do you happen to want," I said to Henry, "an opera hat that doesn't op? At least it only works on one side."

"No," said Henry.

"To any one who buys my opera hat for a large sum I am giving away four square yards of linoleum, a revolving book-case, two curtain rods, a pair of spring-grip dumb-bells, and an extremely patent mouse-trap."

"No," said Henry again.

"The mouse-trap," I pleaded, "is unused. That is to say, no mouse has used it yet. My mouse-trap has never been blooded."

"I don't want it myself," said Henry, "but I know a man who does."

"Henry, you know everybody. For Heaven's sake introduce me to your friend. Why does he particularly want a mouse-trap?"

"He doesn't. He wants anything that's old. Old clothes, old carpets, anything that's old he'll buy."

He seemed to be exactly the man I wanted.

"Introduce me to your fellow clubman," I said firmly.

That evening I wrote to Henry's friend, Mr. Bennett. "Dear Sir," I wrote, "if you would call upon me to-morrow I should like to show you some really old things, all genuine antiques. In particular I would call your attention to an old opera hat of exquisite workmanship and a mouse-trap of chaste and handsome design. I have also a few yards of Queen Anne linoleum of a circular pattern which I think will please you. My James the First spring-grip dumb-bells and Louis Quatorze curtain-rods are well known to connoisseurs. A genuine old cork bedroom suite, comprising one bath-mat, will also be included in the sale. Yours faithfully."

On second thoughts I tore the letter up and sent Mr. Bennett a postcard asking him to favour the undersigned with a call at 10.30 prompt. And at 10.30 prompt he came.

I had expected to see a bearded patriarch with a hooked nose and three hats on his head, but Mr. Bennett turned out to be a very spruce gentleman, wearing (I was sorry to see) much better clothes than the opera hat I proposed to sell him. He became businesslike at once.

"Just tell me what you want to sell," he said, whipping out a pocket-book, "and I'll make a note of it. I take anything."

I looked round my spacious apartment and wondered what to begin with.

"The revolving book-case," I announced.

"I'm afraid there's very little sale for revolving book-cases now," he said, as he made a note of it.

"As a matter of fact," I pointed out, "this one doesn't revolve. It got stuck some years ago."

He didn't seem to think that this would increase the rush, but he made a note of it.

"Then the writing-desk."

"The what?"

"The Georgian bureau. A copy of an old twentieth-century escritoire."

"Walnut?" he said, tapping it.

"Possibly. The value of this Georgian writing-desk, however, lies not in the wood but in the literary associations."

"Ah! My customers don't bother much about that, but still—whose was it?"

"Mine," I said with dignity, placing my hand in the breast pocket of my coat. "I have written many charming things at that desk. My 'Ode to a Bell-push,' my 'Thoughts on Asia,' my——"

"Anything else in this room?" said Mr. Bennett. "Carpet, curtains——"

"Nothing else," I said coldly.

We went into the bedroom and, gazing on the linoleum, my enthusiasm returned to me.

"The linoleum," I said, with a wave of the hand.

"Very much worn," said Mr. Bennett.

I called his attention to the piece under the bed.

"Not under there," I said. "I never walk on that piece. It's as good as new."

He made a note. "What else?" he said.

I showed him round the collection. He saw the Louis Quatorze curtain-rods, the cork bedroom suite, the Cæsarian nail-brush (quite bald), the antique shaving-mirror with genuine crack—he saw it all. And then we went back into the other rooms and found some more things for him.

"Yes," he said, consulting his note-book. "And now how would you like me to buy these?"

"At a large price," I said. "If you have brought your cheque-book I'll lend you a pen."

"You want me to make you an offer? Otherwise I should sell them by auction for you, deducting ten per cent commission."

"Not by auction," I said impulsively. "I couldn't bear to know how much, or rather how little, my Georgian bureau fetched. It was there, as I think I told you, that I wrote my Guide to the Round Pond. Give me an inclusive price for the lot, and never, never let me know the details."

He named an inclusive price. It was something under a hundred and fifty pounds. I shouldn't have minded that if it had only been a little over ten pounds. But it wasn't.

"Right," I agreed. "And, oh, I was nearly forgetting. There's an old opera hat of exquisite workmanship, which——"

"Ah, now, clothes had much better be sold by auction. Make a pile of all you don't want and I'll send round a sack for them. I have an auction sale every Wednesday."

"Very well. Send round to-morrow. And you might—er—also send round a—er—cheque for—quite so. Well, then, good morning."

97

When he had gone I went into my bedroom and made a pile of my opera hat. It didn't look very impressive—hardly worth having a sack specially sent round for it. To keep it company I collected an assortment of clothes. It pained me to break up my wardrobe in this way, but I wanted the bidding for my opera hat to be brisk, and a few preliminary suits would warm the public up. Altogether it was a goodly pile when it was done. The opera hat perched on the top, half of it only at work.

To-day I received from Mr. Bennett a cheque, a catalogue, and an account. The catalogue was marked "Lots 172-179." Somehow I felt that my opera hat would be Lot 176. I turned to it in the account.

"Lot 176—Six shillings."

"It did well," I said. "Perhaps in my heart of hearts I hoped for seven and sixpence, but six shillings—yes, it was a good hat."

And then I turned to the catalogue.

"Lot 176—Frock-coat and vest, dress-coat and vest, ditto, pair of trousers and opera hat."

"And opera hat." Well, well. At least it had the position of honour at the end. My opera hat was starred.

LORDS TEMPORAL

We have eight clocks, called after the kind people who gave them to us. Let me introduce you: William, Edward, Muriel, Enid, Alphonse, Percy, Henrietta, and John—a large family.

"But how convenient," said Celia. "Exactly one for each room."

"Or two in each corner of the drawing-room. I don't suggest it; I just throw out the idea."

"Which is rejected. How shall we arrange which goes into which room? Let's pick up. I take William for the drawing-room; you take John for your workroom; I take——"

"Not John," I said gently. John is—— John overdoes it a trifle. There is too much of John; and he exposes his inside—which is not quite nice.

"Well, whichever you like. Come on, let's begin. William."

As it happened, I particularly wanted William. He has an absolutely noiseless tick, such as is suitable to a room in which work is to be done. I explained this to Celia.

"What you want for the drawing-room," I went on, "is a clock which ticks ostentatiously, so that your visitors may be reminded of the flight of time. Edward is a very loud breather. No guest could fail to notice Edward."

"William," said Celia firmly.

"William has a very delicate interior," I pleaded. "You could never attend to him properly. I have been thinking of William ever since we had him, and I feel that I understand his case."

"Very well," said Celia, with sudden generosity; "Edward. You have William; I have Alphonse for the dining-room; you have John for your bedroom; I have Enid for mine; you——"

"Not John," I said gently. To be frank, John is improper.

"Well, Percy, then."

"Yes, Percy. He is young and fair. He shall sit on the chest of drawers and sing to my sock-suspenders."

"Then Henrietta had better go in the spare room, and Muriel in Jane's."

"Muriel is much too good for Jane," I protested. "Besides, a servant wants an alarm clock to get her up in the morning."

"You forget that Muriel cuckoos. At six o'clock she will cuckoo exactly six times, and at the sixth 'oo' Jane brisks out of bed."

I still felt a little doubtful, because the early morning is a bad time for counting cuckoos, and I didn't see why Jane shouldn't brisk out at the seventh "oo" by mistake one day. However, Jane is in Celia's department, and if Celia was satisfied I was. Besides, the only other place for Muriel was the bathroom; and there is something about a cuckoo-clock in a bathroom which—well, one wants to be educated up to it.

"And that," said Celia gladly, "leaves the kitchen for John." John, as I think I have said, displays his inside in a lamentable way. There is too much of John.

"If Jane doesn't mind," I added. "She may have been strictly brought up."

"She'll love him. John lacks reserve, but he is a good time-keeper."

And so our eight friends were settled. But, alas, not for long. Our discussion had taken place on the eve of Jane's arrival; and when she turned up next day she brought with her, to our horror, a clock of her own—called, I think, Mother. At any rate, she was fond of it and refused to throw it away.

"And it's got an alarm, so it goes in her bedroom," said Celia, "and Muriel goes into the kitchen. Jane loves it, because she comes from the country, and the cuckoo reminds her of home. That still leaves John eating his head off."

"And, moreover, showing people what happens to it," I added severely. (I think I have already mentioned John's foible.)

"Well, there's only one thing for it; he must go under the spare-room bed."

I tried to imagine John under the spare-room bed.

"Suppose," I said, "we had a nervous visitor ... and she looked under the bed before getting into it ... and saw John.... It is a terrible thought, Celia."

However, that is where he is. It is a lonely life for him, but we shall wind him up every week, and he will think that he is being of service to us. Indeed, he probably imagines that our guests prefer to sleep under the bed.

Now, with John at last arranged for, our family should have been happy; but three days ago I discovered that it was William who was going to be the real trouble. To think of William, the pride of the flock, betraying us!

As you may remember, William lives with me. He presides over the room we call "the library" to visitors and "the master's room" to Jane. He smiles at me when I work. Ordinarily, when I want to know the time, I look at my watch; but the other morning I happened to glance at William. He said "twenty minutes past seven." As I am never at work as early as that, and as my watch said eleven-thirty, I guessed at once that William had stopped. In the evening—having by that time found the key—I went to wind him up. To my surprise he said "six-twenty-five." I put my ear to his chest and heard his gentle breathing. He was alive and going well. With a murmured apology I set him to the right time ... and by the morning he was three-quarters of an hour fast.

Unlike John, William is reticent to a degree. With great difficulty I found my way to his insides, and then found that he had practically none to speak of at all. Certainly he had no regulator.

"What shall we do?" I asked Celia.

"Leave him. And then, when you bring your guests in for a smoke, you can say, 'Oh, don't go yet; this clock is five hours and twenty-three minutes fast.'"

"Or six hours and thirty-seven minutes slow. I wonder which would sound better. Anyhow, he is much too beautiful to go under a bed."

So we are leaving him. And when I am in the mood for beauty I look at William's mahogany sides and am soothed into slumber again ... and when I want to adjust my watch (which always loses a little), I creep under the spare-room bed and consult John. John alone of all our family keeps the correct time, and it is a pity that he alone must live in retirement.

100

THE MISSING CARD

What I say is this: A man has his own work to do. He slaves at the office all day, earning a living for those dependent on him, and when he comes home he may reasonably expect not to be bothered with domestic business. I am sure you will agree with me. And you would go on to say, would you not, that, anyhow, the insuring of his servants might safely be left to his wife? Of course you would! Thank you very much.

I first spoke to Celia about the insuring of the staff some weeks ago. Our staff consists of Jane Parsons the cook, the first parlourmaid (Jane) and Parsons the upper housemaid. We call them collectively Jane.

"By the way," I said to Celia, "I suppose Jane is insured all right?"

"I was going to see about it to-morrow," said Celia.

I looked at her in surprise. It was just the sort of thing I might have said myself.

"I hope she won't be unkind about it," I went on. "If she objects to paying her share, tell her I am related to a solicitor. If she still objects, er—tell her we'll pay it ourselves."

"I think it will be all right. Fortunately, she has no head for figures."

This is true. Jane is an excellent cook, and well worth the £75 a year or whatever it is we pay her; but arithmetic gives her a headache. When Celia has finished dividing £75 by twelve, Jane is in a state of complete nervous exhaustion, and is only too thankful to take the nine-and-sixpence that Celia hands over to her, without asking any questions. Indeed, anything that the Government wished deducted from Jane's wages we could deduct with a minimum of friction—from income-tax to a dog-licence. A threepenny insurance would be child's play.

Three weeks later I said to Celia—

"Has an inspector been to see Jane's card yet?"

"Jane's card?" she asked blankly.

"The insurance card with the pretty stamps on."

"No.... No.... Luckily."

"You mean——"

"I was going to see about it to-morrow," said Celia.

I got up and paced the floor. "Really," I murmured, "really." I tried the various chairs in the room, and finally went and stood with my back to the fire-place. In short, I behaved like a justly incensed master-of-the-house.

"You know what happens," I said, when I was calm again, "if we neglect this duty which Parliament has laid upon us?"

"No."

"We go to prison. At least, one of us does. I'm not quite sure which."

"I hope it's you," said Celia.

"As a matter of fact I believe it is. However, we shall know when the inspector comes round."

"If it's you," she went on, "I shall send you in a file, with which you can cut through your chains and escape. It will be concealed in a loaf of bread, so that your gaolers shan't suspect."

"Probably I shouldn't suspect either, until I had bitten on it suddenly. Perhaps you'd better not bother. It would be simpler if you got Jane's card to-morrow instead."

"But of course I will. That is to say, I'll tell Jane to get it herself. It's her cinema evening out."

Once a week Jane leaves us and goes to a cinema. Her life is full of variety.

Ten days elapsed, and then one evening I said—— At least I didn't. Before I could get it out Celia interrupted:

"No, not yet. You see, there's been a hitch."

I curbed my anger and spoke calmly.

"What sort of a hitch?"

"Well, Jane forgot last Wednesday, and I forgot to remind her this Wednesday. But next Wednesday——"

"Why don't you do it yourself?"

"Well, if you'll tell me what to do I'll do it."

"Well—er—you just—you—I mean—well, they'll tell you at the post-office."

"That's exactly how I keep explaining it to Jane," said Celia.

I looked at her mournfully.

"What shall we do?" I asked. "I feel quite hopeless about it. It seems too late now to do anything with Jane. Let's get a new staff and begin again properly."

"Lose Jane?" cried Celia. "I'd sooner go to prison—I mean I'd sooner you went to prison. Why can't you be a man and do something?"

Celia doesn't seem to realize that I married her with the sole idea of getting free of all this sort of bother. As it is, I nearly die once a year in the attempt to fill up my income-tax form. Any traffic in insurance cards would, my doctor says, be absolutely fatal.

However, something had to be done. Last week I went into a neighbouring post-office in order to send a telegram. The post-office is an annexe of the grocer's where the sardines come from on Jane's cinema evening. Having sent the telegram, I took a sudden desperate resolve. I—I myself—would do something.

"I want," I said bravely, "an insurance stamp."

"Sixpenny or sevenpenny?" said the girl, trying to put me off my balance at the very beginning.

"What's the difference?" I asked. "You needn't say a penny, because that is obvious."

However, she had no wish to be funny.

"Sevenpenny for men-servants, sixpenny for women," she explained.

I wasn't going to give away our domestic arrangements to so near a neighbour.

"Three sixpenny and four sevenpenny," I said casually, flicking the dust off my shoes with a handkerchief. "Tut, tut, I was forgetting Thomas," I added. "Five sevenpenny."

I took the stamps home and showered them on Celia.

"You see," I said, "it's not really difficult."

"Oh, you angel! What do I do with them?"

"Stick them on Jane," I said grandly. "Dot them about the house. Stamp your letters with them—I can always get you plenty more."

"Didn't you get a card too?"

"N-no. No, I didn't. The fact is, it's your turn now, Celia. You get the card."

"Oh, all right. I—er—suppose you just ask for a—a card?"

"I suppose so. And—er—choose a doctor, and—er—decide on an approved society, and—er—explain why it is you hadn't got a card before, and—er—— Well, anyhow, it's your turn now, Celia."

"It's really still Jane's turn," said Celia, "only she's so stupid about it."

But she turned out to be not so stupid as we thought. For yesterday there came a ring at the bell. Feeling instinctively that it was the inspector, Celia and I got behind the sofa ... and emerged some minutes later to find Jane alone in the room.

"Somebody come to see about an insurance card or something," she said. "I said you were both out, and would he come to-morrow."

Technically I suppose we were both out. That is, we were not receiving.

"Thank you, Jane," I said stiffly. I turned to Celia. "There you are," I said. "To-morrow something must be done."

"I always said I'd do it to-morrow," said Celia.

"We want some more coal," said Celia suddenly at breakfast.

"Sorry," I said, engrossed in my paper, and I passed her the marmalade.

"More coal," she repeated.

I pushed across the toast.

Celia sighed and held up her hand.

"Please may I speak to you a moment?" she said, trying to snap her fingers. "Good; I've caught his eye. We want——"

"I'm awfully sorry. What is it?"

"We want some more coal. Never mind this once whether Inman beat Hobbs or not. Just help me."

"Celia, you've been reading the paper," I said in surprise. "I thought you only read the feuill—the serial story. How did you know Inman was playing Hobbs?"

"Well, Poulton or Carpentier or whoever it is. Look here, we're out of coal. What shall I do?"

"That's easy. Order some more. What do you do when you're out of nutmegs?"

"It depends if the nutmeg porters are striking."

"Striking! Good heavens, I never thought about that." I glanced hastily down the headlines of my paper. "Celia, this is serious. I shall have to think about this seriously. Will you order a fire in the library? I shall retire to the library and think this over."

"You can retire to the library, but you can't have a fire there. There's only just enough for the kitchen for two days."

"Then come and chaperon me in the kitchen. Don't leave me alone with Jane. You and I and Jane will assemble round the oven and discuss the matter. B-r-r-r. It's cold."

"Not the kitchen. I'll assemble with you round the electric light somewhere. Come on."

We went into the library and rallied round a wax vesta. It was a terribly cold morning.

"I can't think like this," I said, after fifteen seconds' reflection. "I'm going to the office. There's a fire there, anyway."

"You wouldn't like a nice secretary," said Celia timidly, "or an office girl, or somebody to lick the stamps?"

"I should never do any work if you came," I said, looking at her thoughtfully. "Do come."

"No, I shall be all right. I've got shopping to do this morning, and I'm going out to lunch, and I can pay some calls afterwards."

"Right. And you might find out what other people are doing,

the people you call on. And—er—if you should be left alone in the drawing-room a moment ... and the coal-box is at all adjacent.... You'll have your muff with you, you see, and—— Well, I leave that to you. Do what you can."

I had a good day at the office and have never been so loth to leave. I always felt I should get to like my work some time. I arrived home again about six. Celia was a trifle later, and I met her on the mat as she came in.

"Any luck?" I asked eagerly, feeling in her muff. "Dash it, Celia, there are nothing but hands here. Do you mean to say you didn't pick up anything at all?"

"Only information," she said, leading the way into the drawing-room. "Hallo, what's this? A fire!"

"A small involuntary contribution from the office. I brought it home under my hat. Well, what's the news?"

"That if we want any coal we shall have to fetch it ourselves. And we can get it in small amounts from greengrocers. Why greengrocers, I don't know."

"I suppose they have to have fires to force the cabbages. But what about the striking coal porters? If you do their job, won't they picket you or pickaxe you or something?"

"Oh, of course, I should hate to go alone. But I shall be all right if you come with me."

Celia's faith in me is very touching. I am not quite so confident about myself. No doubt I could protect her easily against five or six great brawny hulking porters ... armed with coal-hammers ... but I am seriously doubtful whether a dozen or so, aided with a little luck, mightn't get the better of me.

"Don't let us be rash," I said thoughtfully. "Don't let us infuriate them."

"You aren't afraid of a striker?" asked Celia in amazement.

"Of an ordinary striker, no. In a strike of bank-clerks, or—or chess-players, or professional skeletons, I should be a lion among the blacklegs; but there is something about the very word coal porter which—— You know, I really think this is a case where the British Army might help us. We have been very good to it."

The British Army, I should explain, has been walking out with Jane lately. When we go away for week-ends we let the British Army drop in to supper. Luckily it neither smokes nor drinks nor takes any great interest in books. It is a great relief, on your week-ends in the country, to know that the British Army is dropping in to supper, when otherwise you might only have suspected it. I may say that we are rather hoping to get a position in the Army Recruiting film on the strength of this hospitality.

"Let the British Army go," I said. "We've been very kind to him."

"I fancy Jane has left the service. I don't know why."

"Probably they quarrelled because she gave him caviare two nights running," I said. "Well, I suppose I shall have to go. But it will be no place for women. To-morrow afternoon I will sally forth alone to do it. But," I added, "I shall probably return with two coal porters clinging round my neck. Order tea for three."

Next evening, after a warm and busy day at the office, I put on my top-hat and tail-coat and went out. If there was any accident I was determined to be described in the papers as "the body of a well-dressed man"; to go down to history as "the remains of a shabbily dressed individual" would be too depressing. Beautifully clothed, I jumped into a taxi and drove to Celia's greengrocer. Celia herself was keeping warm by paying still more calls.

"I want," I said nervously, "a hundredweight of coal and a cauliflower." This was my own idea. I intended to place the cauliflower on the top of a sack, and so to deceive any too-inquisitive coal porter. "No, no," I should say, "not coal; nice cauliflowers for Sunday's dinner."

"Can't deliver the coal," said the greengrocer.

"I'm going to take it with me," I explained.

He went round to a yard at the back. I motioned my taxi along and followed him at the head of three small boys who had never seen a top-hat and a cauliflower so close together. We got the sack into position.

"Come, come," I said to the driver, "haven't you ever seen a dressing-case before? Give us a hand with it or I shall miss my train and be late for dinner."

He grinned and gave a hand. I paid the greengrocer, pressed the cauliflower into the hand of the smallest boy, and drove off....

It was absurdly easy.

There was no gore at all.

"There!" I said to Celia when she came back. "And when that's done I'll get you some more."

"Hooray! And yet," she went on, "I'm almost sorry. You see, I was working off my calls so nicely, and you'd been having some quite busy days at the office, hadn't you?"

THE ORDER OF THE BATH

"We must really do something about the bath," said Celia.

"We must," I agreed.

At present what we do is this. Punctually at six-thirty or nine, or whenever it is, Celia goes in to make herself clean and beautiful for the new day, while I amuse myself with a razor. After a quarter of an hour or so she gives a whistle to imply that the bathroom is now vacant, and I give another one to indicate that I have only cut myself once. I then go hopefully in and find that the bath is half full of water; whereupon I go back to my room and engage in Dr. Hugh de Sélincourt's physical exercises for the middle-aged. After these are over I take another look at the bath, discover that it is now three-eighths full, and return to my room and busy myself with Dr. Archibald Marshall's mental drill for busy men. By the time I have committed three Odes of Horace to memory, it may be low tide or it may not; if not, I sit on the edge of the bath with the daily paper and read about the latest strike—my mind occupied equally with wondering when the water is going out and when the bricklayers are. And the thought that Celia is now in the dining-room eating more than her share of the toast does not console me in the least.

"Yes," I said, "it's absurd to go on like this. You had better see about it to-day, Celia."

"I don't think—I mean, I think—you know, it's really your turn to do something for the bathroom."

"What do you mean, my turn? Didn't I buy the glass shelves for it? You'd never even heard of glass shelves."

"Well, who put them up after they'd been lying about for a month?" said Celia. "I did."

"And who bumped his head against them the next day? I did."

"Yes, but that wasn't really a useful thing to do. It's your turn to be useful."

"Celia, this is mutiny. All household matters are supposed to be looked after by you. I do the brain work; I earn the money; I cannot be bothered with these little domestic worries. I have said so before."

"I sort of thought you had."

You know, I am afraid that is true.

"After all," she went on, "the drinks are in your department."

"Hock, perhaps," I said; "soapy water, no. There is a difference."

"Not very much," said Celia.

By the end of another week I was getting seriously alarmed. I began to fear that unless I watched it very carefully I should be improving myself too much.

"While the water was running out this morning," I said to Celia, as I started my breakfast just about lunch-time, "I got Paradise Lost off by heart, and made five hundred and ninety-six revolutions with the back paws. And then it was time to shave myself again. What a life for a busy man!"

"I don't know if you know that it's no——"

"Begin again," I said.

"—that it's no good waiting for the last inch or two to go out by itself. Because it won't. You have to—to hoosh it out."

"I do. And I sit on the taps looking like a full moon and try to draw it out. But it's no good. We had a neap tide to-day and I had to hoosh four inches. Jolly."

Celia gave a sigh of resignation.

"All right," she said, "I'll go to the plumber to-day."

"Not the plumber," I begged. "On the contrary. The plumber is the man who stops the leaks. What we really want is an unplumber."

We fell into silence again.

"But how silly we are!" cried Celia suddenly. "Of course!"

"What's the matter now?"

"The bath is the landlord's business! Write and tell him."

"But—but what shall I say?" Somehow I knew Celia would put it on to me.

"Why, just—say. When you're paying the rent, you know."

"I—I see."

I retired to the library and thought it out. I hate writing business letters. The result is a mixture of formality and chattiness which seems to me all wrong.

My first letter to the landlord went like this:—

"Dear Sir,—I enclose cheque in payment of last quarter's rent. Our bath won't run out properly. Yours faithfully."

It is difficult to say just what is wrong with that letter, and yet it is obvious that something has happened to it. It isn't right. I tried again.

"Dear Sir,—Enclosed please find cheque in payment of enclosed account. I must ask you either to enlarge the exit to our bath or to supply an emergency door. At present my morning and evening baths are in serious danger of clashing. Yours faithfully."

My third attempt had more sting in it:—

"Dear Sir,—Unless you do something to our bath I cannot send you enclosed cheque in payment of enclosed account. Otherwise I would have. Yours faithfully."

At this point I whistled to Celia and laid the letters before her.

"You see what it is," I said. "I'm not quite getting the note."

"But you're so abrupt," she said. "You must remember that this is all coming quite as a surprise to him. You want to lead up to it more gradually."

"Ah, perhaps you're right. Let's try again."

I tried again, with this result:—

"Dear Sir,—In sending you a cheque in payment of last quarter's rent I feel I must tell you how comfortable we are here. The only inconvenience—and it is indeed a trifling one, dear Sir— which we have experienced is in connection with the bathroom. Elegantly appointed and spacious as this room is, commodious as we find the actual bath itself, yet we feel that in the matter of the waste-pipe the high standard of efficiency so discernible elsewhere is sadly lacking. Were I alone I should not complain; but unfortunately there are two of us; and, for the second one, the weariness of waiting while the waters of the first bath exude drop by drop is almost more than can be borne. I speak with knowledge, for it is I who——"

I tore the letter up and turned to Celia.

"I'm a fool," I said. "I've just thought of something which will save me all this rotten business every morning."

"I'm so glad. What is it?"

"Why, of course—in future I will go to the bath first."

And I do. It is a ridiculously simple solution, and I cannot think why it never occurred to me before.

A TRUNK CALL

Last Wednesday, being the anniversary of the Wednesday before, Celia gave me a present of a door-knocker. The knocker was in the shape of an elephant's head (not life-size); and by bumping the animal's trunk against his chin you could produce a small brass noise.

"It's for the library," she explained eagerly. "You're going to work there this morning, aren't you?"

"Yes, I shall be very busy," I said in my busy voice.

"Well, just put it up before you start, and then if I have to interrupt you for anything important, I can knock with it. Do say you love it."

"It's a dear, and so are you. Come along, let's put it up."

I got a small screw-driver, and with very little loss of blood managed to screw it into the door. Some people are born screwists, some are not. I am one of the nots.

"It's rather sideways," said Celia doubtfully.

"Osso erry," I said.

"What?"

I took my knuckle from my mouth.

"Not so very," I repeated.

"I wish it had been straight."

"So do I; but it's too late now. You have to leave these things very largely to the screw-driver. Besides, elephants often do have their heads sideways; I've noticed it at the Zoo."

"Well, never mind. I think it's very clever of you to do it at all. Now then, you go in, and I'll knock and see if you hear."

I went in and shut the door, Celia remaining outside. After five seconds, having heard nothing, but not wishing to disappoint her, I said, "Come in," in the voice of one who has been suddenly disturbed by a loud "rat-tat."

"I haven't knocked yet," said Celia from the other side of the door.

"Why not?"

"I was admiring him. He is jolly. Do come and look at him again."

I went out and looked at him again. He really gave an air to the library door.

"His face is rather dirty," said Celia. "I think he wants some brass polish and a—and a bun."

She ran off to the kitchen. I remained behind with Jumbo and had a little practice. The knock was not altogether convincing, owing to the fact that his chin was too receding for his trunk to get at it properly. I could hear it quite easily on my own side of the door, but I felt rather doubtful whether the sound would penetrate into the room. The natural noise of the elephant—roar, bark, whistle, or whatever it is—I have never heard, but I am told it is very terrible to denizens of the jungle. Jumbo's cry would not have alarmed an ant.

Celia came back with flannels and things and washed Jumbo's face.

"There!" she said. "Now his mother would love him again." Very confidently she propelled his trunk against his chin and added, "Come in."

"You can hear it quite plainly," I said quickly.

"It doesn't re—rever—reverberate—is that the word?" said Celia, "but it's quite a distinctive noise. I'm sure you'd hear it."

"I'm sure I should. Let's try."

"Not now. I'll try later on, when you aren't expecting it. Besides, you must begin your work. Good-bye. Work hard." She pushed me in and shut the door.

I began to work.

I work best on the sofa; I think most clearly in what appears to the hasty observer to be an attitude of rest. But I am not sure that Celia really understands this yet. Accordingly, when a knock comes at the door I jump to my feet, ruffle my hair, and stride up and down the room with one hand on my brow. "Come in," I call impatiently, and Celia finds me absolutely in the throes. If there should chance to be a second knock later on, I make a sprint for the writing-desk, seize pen and paper, upset the ink or not as it happens, and present to any one coming in at the door the most thoroughly engrossed back in London.

But that was in the good old days of knuckle-knocking. On this particular morning I had hardly written more than a couple of thousand words—I mean I had hardly got the cushions at the back of my head comfortably settled when Celia came in.

"Well?" she said eagerly.

I struggled out of the sofa.

"What is it?" I asked sternly.

"Did you hear it all right?"

"I didn't hear anything."

"Oh!" she said in great disappointment. "But perhaps you were asleep," she went on hopefully.

"Certainly not. I was working."

"Did I interrupt you?"

"You did rather; but it doesn't matter."

"Oh, well, I won't do it again—unless I really have to. Good-bye, and good luck."

She went out and I returned to my sofa. After an hour or so my mind began to get to work, and I got up and walked slowly up and down the room. The gentle exercise seemed to stimulate me. Seeing my new putter in the corner of the room, I took it up (my brain full of other things) and, dropping a golf ball on the carpet, began to practise. After five or ten minutes, my ideas being now quite clear, I was just about to substitute the pen for the putter when Celia came in.

"Oh!" she said. "Are—are you busy?"

I turned round from a difficult putt with the club in my hand.

"Very," I said. "What is it?"

"I don't want to disturb you if you're working——"

"I am."

111

"But I just wondered if you—if you liked artichokes."

I looked at her coldly.

"I will fill in your confession book another time," I said stiffly, and I sat down with dignity at my desk and dipped the putter in the ink.

"It's for dinner to-night," said Celia persuasively. "Do say. Because I don't want to eat them all by myself."

I saw that I should have to humour her.

"If it's a Jerusalem artichoke you mean, yes," I said; "the other sort, no. J. Arthur Choke I love."

"Right-o. Sorry for interrupting." And then as she went to the door, "You did hear Jumbo this time, didn't you?"

"I believe that's the only reason you came in for."

"Well, one of them."

"Are you coming in again?"

"Don't know," she smiled. "Depends if I can think of an excuse."

"Right," I said. "In that case——"

There was nothing else for it; I took up my pen and began to work.

But I have a suggestion to make to Celia. At present, although Jumbo is really mine, she is having all the fun with him. And as long as Jumbo is on the outside of the door there can never rise an occasion when I should want to use him. My idea is that I should unscrew Jumbo and put him on the inside of the door, so that I can knock when I come out.

And then when Celia wants to come in she will warn me in the old-fashioned way with her knuckles ... and I shall have time to do something about it.

OTHER PEOPLE'S HOUSES

THE PARTING GUEST

When nice people ask me to their houses for the week-end, I reply that I shall be delighted to come, but that pressure of work will prevent my staying beyond Tuesday. Sometimes, in spite of this, they try to kick me out on the Monday; and if I find that they are serious about it I may possibly consent to go by an evening train. In any case, it always seems to me a pity to have to leave a house just as you are beginning to know your way to the bathroom.

"Is the 9.25 too early for you?" said Charles on Sunday night à propos of nothing that I had said.

"Not if it's in the evening," I answered.

"It's in the morning."

"Then it's much too early. I never travel before breakfast. But why do you ask?"

"Well, I've got to ride over to Newtown to-morrow——"

"To-morrow?" I said in surprise. "Aren't we talking about Tuesday?"

It appeared that we weren't. It also came out that Charles and his wife, not anticipating the pleasure of my company beyond Monday, had arranged to ride over the downs to Newtown to inspect a horse. They would not be back until the evening.

"But that's all right, Charles," I said. "If you have a spare horse, a steady one which doesn't wobble when it canters, I will ride with you."

"There's only the old pony," said Charles, "and he will be wanted to drive you to the station."

"Not until Tuesday," I pointed out.

Charles ignored this remark altogether.

"You couldn't ride Joseph, anyway," he said.

"Then I might run beside you, holding on to your stirrup. My ancestors always went into battle like that. We are still good runners."

Charles turned over some more pages of his timetable.

"There is a 10.41," he announced.

"Just when I shall be getting to like you," I sighed.

"Molly and I have to be off by ten. If you caught the 10.41, you would want to leave here by a quarter past."

"I shouldn't want to leave," I said reproachfully; "I should go with the greatest regret."

"The 9.25, of course, gets you up to town much earlier."

"Some such idea, no doubt, would account for its starting before the 10.41. What have you at about 4.30?"

"If you don't mind changing at Plimton, there's a 10.5——"

I got up and lit my candle.

"Let's wait till to-morrow and see what the weather's like," I said sleepily. "I am not a proud man, but after what you've said, and if it's at all wet, I may actually be glad to catch an early train." And I marched upstairs to bed.

However, a wonderful blue sky next morning made any talk of London utterly offensive. My host and hostess had finished breakfast by the time I got down, and I was just beginning my own when the sound of the horses on the gravel brought me out.

"I'm sorry we've got to dash off like this," said Mrs. Charles, smiling at me from the back of Pompey. "Don't you be in any hurry to go. There are plenty of trains."

"Thank you. It would be a shame to leave the country on a morning like this, wouldn't it? I shall take a stroll over the hills before lunch, and sit about in the garden in the afternoon. There's a train at five, I think."

"We shan't be back by then, I'm afraid, so this will be good-bye."

I made my farewells, and Pompey, who was rather fresh, went off sideways down the drive. This left me alone with Charles.

"Good-bye, Charles," I said, patting him with one hand and his horse with the other. "Don't you bother about me. I shall be quite happy by myself."

He looked at me with a curious smile and was apparently about to say something, when Cæsar suddenly caught sight of my stockings. These, though in reality perfectly tasteful, might well come as a surprise to a young horse, and Cæsar bolted down the drive to tell Pompey about it. I waved to them all from the distance and returned to my breakfast.

After breakfast I lit a pipe and strolled outside. As I stood at the door drinking in the beauty of the morning I was the victim of a curious illusion. It seemed to me that outside the front door was the pony-cart—Joseph in the shafts, the gardener's boy holding the reins, and by the side of the boy my bag!

"We'll only just have time, sir," said the boy.

"But—but I'm going by the five train," I stammered.

"Well, sir, I shall be over at Newtown this afternoon—with the cart."

I did not like to ask him why, but I thought I knew. It was, I told myself, to fetch back the horse which Charles was going over to inspect, the horse to which I had to give up my room that night.

"Very well," I said. "Take the bag now and leave it in the cloak-room. I'll walk in later." What the etiquette was when your host gave you a hint by sending your bag to the station and going away himself, I did not know. But however many bags he packed and however many horses he inspected, I was not to be moved till the five o'clock train.

Half an hour after my bag was gone I made a discovery. It was that, when I started walking to the five o'clock train, I should have to start in pumps....

"My dear Charles," I wrote that night, "it was delightful to see you this week-end, and I only wish I could have stayed with you longer, but, as you know, I had to dash up to town by the five train to inspect a mule. I am sorry to say that a slight accident happened just before I left you. In the general way, when I catch an afternoon train, I like to pack my bag overnight, but on this occasion I did not begin until nine in the morning. This only left me eight hours, and the result was that in my hurry I packed my shoes by mistake, and had to borrow a pair of yours in which to walk to the station. I will bring them down with me next time I come."

I may say that they are unusually good shoes, and if Charles doesn't want me he must at least want them. So I am expecting another invitation by every post. When it arrives I shall reply that I shall be delighted to come, but that, alas! pressure of work will prevent my staying beyond Tuesday.

THE LANDSCAPE GARDENER

Really I know nothing about flowers. By a bit of luck, James, my gardener, whom I pay half a crown a week for combing the beds, knows nothing about them either; so my ignorance remains undiscovered. But in other people's gardens I have to make something of an effort to keep up appearances. Without flattering myself I may say that I have acquired a certain manner; I give the impression of the garden lover, or the man with shares in a seed company, or—or something.

For instance, at Creek Cottage, Mrs. Atherley will say to me,

"That's an Amphilobertus Gemini," pointing to something which I hadn't noticed behind a rake.

"I am not a bit surprised," I say calmly.

"And a Gladiophinium Banksii next to it."

"I suspected it," I confess in a hoarse whisper.

Towards flowers whose names I know I adopt a different tone.

"Aren't you surprised to see daffodils out so early?" says Mrs. Atherley with pride.

"There are lots out in London," I mention casually. "In the shops."

"So there are grapes," says Miss Atherley.

"I was not talking about grapes," I reply stiffly.

However, at Creek Cottage just now I can afford to be natural; for it is not gardening which comes under discussion these days, but landscape-gardening, and any one can be an authority on that. The Atherleys, fired by my tales of Sandringham, Chatsworth, Arundel, and other places where I am constantly spending the week-end, are readjusting their two-acre field. In future it will not be called "the garden," but "the grounds."

I was privileged to be shown over the grounds on my last visit to Creek Cottage.

"Here," said Mrs. Atherley, "we are having a plantation. It will keep the wind off; and we shall often sit here in the early days of summer. That's a weeping ash in the middle. There's another one over there. They'll be lovely, you know."

"What's that?" I asked, pointing to a bit of black stick on the left; which, even more than the other trees, gave the impression of having been left there by the gardener while he went for his lunch.

"That's a weeping willow."

"This is rather a tearful corner of the grounds," apologized Miss Atherley. "We'll show you something brighter directly. Look there—that's the oak in which King Charles lay hid. At least, it will be when it's grown a bit."

"Let's go on to the shrubbery," said Mrs. Atherley. "We are having a new grass path from here to the shrubbery. It's going to be called Henry's Walk."

Miss Atherley has a small brother called Henry. Also there were eight Kings of England called Henry. Many a time and oft one of those nine Henrys has paced up and down this grassy walk, his head bent, his hands clasped behind his back; while behind his furrowed brow, who shall say what world-schemes were hatching? Is it the thought of Wolsey which makes him frown—or is he wondering where he left his catapult? Ah! who can tell us? Let us leave a veil of mystery over it ... for the sake of the next visitor.

116

"The shrubbery," said Mrs. Atherley proudly, waving her hand at a couple of laurel bushes and a—I've forgotten its name now, but it is one of the few shrubs I really know.

"And if you're a gentleman," said Miss Atherley, "and want to get asked here again, you'll always call it the shrubbery."

"Really, I don't see what else you could call it," I said, wishing to be asked down again.

"The patch."

"True," I said. "I mean, Nonsense."

I was rather late for breakfast next morning; a pity on such a lovely spring day.

"I'm so sorry," I began, "but I was looking at the shrubbery from my window and I quite forgot the time."

"Good," said Miss Atherley.

"I must thank you for putting me in such a perfect room for it," I went on, warming to my subject. "One can actually see the shrubs—er—shrubbing. The plantation, too, seems a little thicker to me than yesterday."

"I expect it is."

"In fact, the tennis lawn——" I looked round anxiously. I had a sudden fear that it might be the new deer-park. "It still is the tennis lawn?" I asked.

"Yes. Why, what about it?"

"I was only going to say the tennis lawn had quite a lot of shadows on it. Oh, there's no doubt that the plantation is really asserting itself."

Eleven o'clock found me strolling in the grounds with Miss Atherley.

"You know," I said, as we paced Henry's Walk together, "the one thing the plantation wants is for a bird to nest in it. That is the hall-mark of a plantation."

"It's mother's birthday to-morrow. Wouldn't it be a lovely surprise for her?"

"It would, indeed. Unfortunately this is a matter in which you require the co-operation of a feathered friend."

"Couldn't you try to persuade a bird to build a nest in the weeping ash? Just for this once?"

"You're asking me a very difficult thing," I said doubtfully. "Anything else I would do cheerfully for you; but to dictate to a bird on such a very domestic affair—— No, I'm afraid I must refuse."

"It need only just begin to build one," pleaded Miss Atherley, "because mother's going up to town by your train to-morrow. As soon as she's out of the house the bird can go back anywhere else it likes better."

117

"I will put that to any bird I see to-day," I said, "but I am doubtful."

"Oh, well," sighed Miss Atherley, "never mind."

"What do you think?" cried Mrs. Atherley as she came in to breakfast next day. "There's a bird been nesting in the plantation!"

Miss Atherley looked at me in undisguised admiration. I looked quite surprised—I know I did.

"Well, well!" I said.

"You must come out afterwards and see the nest and tell me what bird it is. There are three eggs in it. I am afraid I don't know much about these things."

"I'm glad," I said thankfully. "I mean, I shall be glad to."

We went out eagerly after breakfast. On about the only tree in the plantation with a fork to it a nest balanced precariously. It had in it three pale-blue eggs splotched with light brown. It appeared to be a blackbird's nest with another egg or two to come.

"It's been very quick about it," said Miss Atherley.

"Of our feathered bipeds," I said, frowning at her, "the blackbird is notoriously the most hasty."

"Isn't it lovely?" said Mrs. Atherley.

She was still talking about it as she climbed into the trap which was to take us to the station.

"One moment," I said, "I've forgotten something." I dashed into the house and out by a side door, and then sprinted for the plantation. I took the nest from the weeping and over-weighted ash and put it carefully back in the hedge by the tennis-lawn. Then I returned more leisurely to the house.

If you ever want a job of landscape-gardening thoroughly well done, you can always rely upon me.

THE SAME OLD STORY

We stood in a circle round the parrot's cage and gazed with interest at its occupant. She (Evangeline) was balancing easily on one leg, while with the other leg and her beak she tried to peel a monkey-nut. There are some of us who hate to be watched at meals, particularly when dealing with the dessert, but Evangeline is not of our number.

"There," said Mrs. Atherley, "isn't she a beauty?"

I felt that, as the last to be introduced, I ought to say something.

"What do you say to a parrot?" I whispered to Miss Atherley.

"Have a banana," suggested Reggie.

"I believe you say, 'Scratch-a-poll,'" said Miss Atherley, "but I don't know why."

"Isn't that rather dangerous? Suppose it retorted 'Scratch your own,' I shouldn't know a bit how to go on."

"It can't talk," said Reggie. "It's quite a baby—only seven months old. But it's no good showing it your watch; you must think of some other way of amusing it."

"Break it to me, Reggie. Have I been asked down solely to amuse the parrot, or did any of you others want to see me?"

"Only the parrot," said Reggie.

Evangeline paid no attention to us. She continued to wrestle with the monkey-nut. I should say that she was a bird not easily amused.

"Can't it really talk at all?" I asked Mrs. Atherley.

"Not yet. You see, she's only just come over from South America, and isn't used to the climate yet."

"But that's just the person you'd expect to talk a lot about the weather. I believe you've been had. Write a little note to the poulterers and ask if you can change it. You've got a bad one by mistake."

"We got it as a bird," said Mrs. Atherley with dignity, "not as a gramophone."

The next morning Evangeline was as silent as ever. Miss Atherley and I surveyed it after breakfast. It was still grappling with a monkey-nut, but no doubt a different one.

"Isn't it ever going to talk?" I asked. "Really, I thought parrots were continually chatting."

"Yes, but they have to be taught—just like you teach a baby."

"Are you sure? I quite see that you have to teach them any special things you want them to say, but I thought they were all born with a few simple obvious remarks, like 'Poor Polly,' or—or 'Dash Lloyd George.'"

"I don't think so," said Miss Atherley. "Not the green ones."

At dinner that evening, Mr. Atherley being now with us, the question of Evangeline's education was seriously considered.

"The only proper method," began Mr. Atherley——"By the way," he said, turning to me, "you don't know anything about parrots, do you?"

"No," I said. "You can go on quite safely."

"The only proper method of teaching a parrot—I got this from

119

a man in the City this morning—is to give her a word at a time, and to go on repeating it over and over again until she's got hold of it."

"And after that the parrot goes on repeating it over and over again until you've got sick of it," said Reggie.

"Then we shall have to be very careful what word we choose," said Mrs. Atherley.

"What is your favourite word?"

"Well, really——"

"Animal, vegetable, or mineral?" asked Archie.

"This is quite impossible. Every word by itself seems so silly."

"Not 'home' and 'mother,'" I said reproachfully.

"You shall recite your little piece in the drawing-room afterwards," said Miss Atherley to me. "Think of something sensible now."

"Yes," said Mrs. Atherley. "What's the latest word from London?"

"Kikuyu."

"What?"

"I can't say it again," I protested.

"If you can't even say it twice, it's no good for Evangeline."

A thoughtful silence fell upon us.

"Have you fixed on a name for her yet?" Miss Atherley asked her mother.

"Evangeline, of course."

"No, I mean a name for her to call you. Because if she's going to call you 'Auntie' or 'Darling,' or whatever you decide on, you'd better start by teaching her that."

And then I had a brilliant idea.

"I've got the very word," I said. "It's 'hallo.' You see, it's a pleasant form of greeting to any stranger, and it will go perfectly with the next word that she's taught, whatever it may be."

"Supposing it's 'wardrobe,'" suggested Reggie, "or 'sardine'?"

"Why not? 'Hallo, Sardine' is the perfect title for a revue. Witty, subtle, neat—probably the great brain of the Revue King has already evolved it, and is planning the opening scene."

"Yes, 'hallo' isn't at all bad," said Mr. Atherley. "Anyway, it's better than 'Poor Polly,' which is simply morbid. Let's fix on 'hallo.'"

"Good," said Mrs. Atherley.

Evangeline said nothing, being asleep under her blanket.

I was down first next morning, having forgotten to wind up my watch overnight. Longing for company, I took the blanket off Evangeline's cage and introduced her to the world again. She stirred sleepily, opened her eyes and blinked at me.

"Hallo, Evangeline," I said.

She made no reply.

Suddenly a splendid scheme occurred to me. I would teach Evangeline her word now. How it would surprise the others when they came down and said "Hallo" to her, to find themselves promptly answered back!

"Evangeline," I said, "listen. Hallo, hallo, hallo, hallo." I stopped a moment and went on more slowly. "Hallo—hallo—hallo."

It was dull work.

"Hallo," I said, "hallo—hallo—hallo," and then very distinctly, "Hal-lo."

Evangeline looked at me with an utterly bored face.

"Hallo," I said, "hallo—hallo."

She picked up a monkey-nut and ate it languidly.

"Hallo," I went on, "hallo, hallo ... hallo, hallo, HALLO, HALLO ... hallo, hallo——"

She dropped her nut and roused herself for a moment.

"Number engaged," she snapped, and took another nut.

You needn't believe this. The others didn't when I told them.

THE SPREADING WALNUT TREE

We were having breakfast in the garden with the wasps, and Peter was enlarging on the beauties of the country round his new week-end cottage.

"Then there's Hilderton," he said; "that's a lovely little village, I'm told. We might explore it to-morrow."

Celia woke up suddenly.

"Is Hilderton near here?" she asked in surprise. "But I often stayed there when I was a child."

"This was years ago, when Edward the Seventh was on the throne," I explained to Mrs. Peter.

"My grandfather," went on Celia, "lived at Hilderton Hall."

There was an impressive silence.

"You see the sort of people you're entertaining," I said airily to Peter. "My wife's grandfather lived at Hilderton Hall. Celia, you should have spoken about this before. It would have done us a lot of good in Society." I pushed my plate away. "I can't go on eating bacon after this. Bring me peaches."

"I should love to see it again."

121

"If I'd had my rights," I said, "I should be living there now. I must put my solicitor on to this. There's been foul play somewhere."

Peter looked up from one of the maps which, being new to the country, he carries with him.

"I can't find Hilderton Hall here," he said. "It's six inches to the mile, so it ought to be marked."

"Celia, our grandfather's name is being aspersed. Let us look into this."

We crowded round the map and studied it anxiously. Hilderton was there, and Hilderton House, but no Hilderton Hall.

"But it's a great big place," protested Celia.

"I see what it is," I said regretfully. "Celia, you were young then."

"Ten."

"Ten. And naturally it seemed big to you, just as Yarrow seemed big to Wordsworth, and a shilling seems a lot to a baby. But really——"

"Really," said Peter, "it was semi-detached."

"And your side was called Hilderton Hall and the other side Hilderton Castle."

"I don't believe it was even called Hilderton Hall," said Peter. "It was Hilderton Villa."

"I don't believe she ever had a grandfather at all," said Mrs. Peter.

"She must have had a grandfather," I pointed out. "But I'm afraid he never lived at Hilderton Hall. This is a great blow to me, and I shall now resume my bacon."

I drew my plate back and Peter returned his map to his pocket.

"You're all very funny," said Celia, "but I know it was Hilderton Hall. I've a good mind to take you there this morning and show it to you."

"Do," said Peter and I eagerly.

"It's a great big place——"

"That's what we're coming to see," I reminded her.

"Of course they may have sold some of the land, or—I mean, I know when I used to stay there it was a—a great big place. I can't promise that it——"

"It's no good now, Celia," I said sternly. "You shouldn't have boasted."

Hilderton was four miles off, and we began to approach it— Celia palpably nervous—at about twelve o'clock that morning.

"Are you recognizing any of this?" asked Peter.

"N-no. You see I was only about eight——"

"You must recognise the church," I said, pointing to it. "If you don't, it proves either that you never lived at Hilderton or that you never sang in the choir. I don't know which thought is the more distressing. Now what about this place? Is this it?"

Celia peered up the drive.

"N-no; at least I don't remember it. I know there was a walnut tree in front of the house."

"Is that all you remember?"

"Well, I was only about six——"

Peter and I both had a slight cough at the same time.

"It's nothing," said Peter, finding Celia's indignant eye upon him. "Let's go on."

We found two more big houses, but Celia, a little doubtfully, rejected them both.

"My grandfather-in-law was very hard to please," I apologized to Peter. "He passed over place after place before he finally fixed on Hilderton Hall. Either the heronry wasn't ventilated properly, or the decoy ponds had the wrong kind of mud, or——"

There was a sudden cry from Celia.

"This is it," she said.

She stood at the entrance to a long drive. A few chimneys could be seen in the distance. On either side of the gates was a high wall.

"I don't see the walnut tree," I said.

"Of course not, because you can't see the front of the house. But I feel certain that this is the place."

"We want more proof than that," said Peter. "We must go in and find the walnut tree."

"We can't all wander into another man's grounds looking for walnut trees," I said, "with no better excuse than that Celia's great-grandmother was once asked down here for the week-end and stayed for a fortnight. We——"

"My grandfather," said Celia coldly, "lived here."

"Well, whatever it was," I said, "we must invent a proper reason. Peter, you might pretend you've come to inspect the gas-meter or the milk or something. Or perhaps Celia had better disguise herself as a Suffragette and say that she's come to borrow a box of matches. Anyhow, one of us must get to the front of the house to search for this walnut tree."

"It—it seems rather cheek," said Celia doubtfully.

"We'll toss up who goes."

We tossed, and of course I lost. I went up the drive nervously. At the first turn I decided to be an insurance inspector, at the next a scout-master, but, as I approached the front door, I thought of a very simple excuse. I rang the bell under the eyes of several people at lunch and looked about eagerly for the walnut tree.

There was none.

"Does Mr.—er—Erasmus—er—Percival live here?" I asked the footman.

"No, sir," he said—luckily.

"Ah! Was there ever a walnut—I mean was there ever a Mr. Percival who lived here? Ah! Thank you," and I sped down the drive again.

"Well?" said Celia eagerly.

"Mr. Percival doesn't live there."

"Whoever's Mr. Percival?"

"Oh, I forgot; you don't know him. Friends," I added solemnly, "I regret to tell you there is no walnut tree."

"I am not surprised," said Peter.

The walk home was a silent one. For the rest of the day Celia was thoughtful. But at the end of dinner she brightened up a little and joined in the conversation.

"At Hilderton Hall," she said suddenly, "we always——"

"H'r'm," I said, clearing my throat loudly. "Peter, pass Celia the walnuts."

I have had great fun in London this week with the walnut joke, though Celia says she is getting tired of it. But I had a letter from Peter to-day which ended like this:—

"By the way, I was an ass last week. I took you to Banfield in mistake for Hilderton. I went to Hilderton yesterday and found Hilderton Hall—a large place with a walnut tree. It's a little way out of the village, and is marked big on the next section of the map to the one we were looking at. You might tell Celia."

True, I might....

Perhaps in a week or two I shall.

DEFINITIONS

As soon as we had joined the ladies after dinner Gerald took up a position in front of the fire.

"Now that the long winter evenings are upon us," he began—

"Anyhow, it's always dark at half-past nine," said Norah.

"Not in the morning," said Dennis, who has to be excused for anything foolish he says since he became obsessed with golf.

"Please don't interrupt," I begged. "Gerald is making a speech."

"I was only going to say that we might have a little game of some sort. Norah, what's the latest parlour game from London?"

"Tell your uncle," I urged, "how you amuse yourselves at the Lyceum."

"Do you know 'Hunt the Pencil'?"

"No. What do you do?"

"You collect five pencils; when you've got them, I'll tell you another game."

"Bother these pencil games," said Dennis, taking an imaginary swing with a paper-knife. "I hope it isn't too brainy."

"You'll want to know how to spell," said Norah severely, and she went to the writing-desk for some paper.

In a little while—say, half an hour—we had each a sheet of paper and a pencil, and Norah was ready to explain.

"It's called Definitions. I expect you all know it."

We assured her we didn't.

"Well, you begin by writing down five or six letters, one underneath the other. We might each suggest one. 'E.'"

We weighed in with ours, and the result was E P A D U.

"Now you write them backwards."

There was a moment's consternation.

"Like 'bath-mat'?" said Dennis. "An 'e' backwards looks so silly."

"Stupid—like this," explained Norah. She showed us her paper.

E U

P D

A A

D P

U E

"This is thrilling," said Mrs. Gerald, pencilling hard.

"Then everybody has to fill in words all the way down, your first word beginning with 'e' and ending with 'u,' and so on. See?"

Gerald leant over Dennis and explained carefully to him, and in a little while we all saw.

"Then, when everybody's finished, we define our words in

turn, and the person who guesses a word first gets a mark. That's all."

"And a very good game too," I said, and I rubbed my head and began to think.

"Of course," said Norah, after a quarter of an hour's silence, "you want to make the words difficult and define them as subtly as possible."

"Of course," I said, wrestling with 'E—U.' I could only think of one word, and it was the one everybody else was certain to have.

"Are we all ready? Then somebody begin."

"You'd better begin, Norah, as you know the game," said Mrs. Gerald.

We prepared to begin.

"Mine," said Norah, "is a bird."

"Emu," we all shouted; but I swear I was first.

"Yes."

"I don't think that's a very subtle definition," said Dennis. "You promised to be as subtle as possible."

"Go on, dear," said Gerald to his wife.

"Well, this is rather awkward. Mine is——"

"Emu," I suggested.

"You must wait till she has defined it," said Norah sternly.

"Mine is a sort of feathered animal."

"Emu," I said again. In fact, we all said it.

Gerald coughed. "Mine," he said, "isn't exactly a—fish, because it——"

"Emu," said everybody.

"That was subtler," said Dennis, "but it didn't deceive us."

"Your turn," said Norah to me. And they all leant forward ready to say "Emu."

"Mine," I said, "is—all right, Dennis, you needn't look so excited—is a word I once heard a man say at the Zoo."

There was a shriek of "Emu!"

"Wrong," I said.

Everybody was silent.

"Where did he say it?" asked Norah at last. "What was he doing?"

"He was standing outside the Emu's cage."

"It must have been Emu."

"It wasn't."

"Perhaps there's another animal beginning with 'e' and ending with 'u,'" suggested Dennis. "He might have said,'Look here, I'm tired of this old Emu, let's go and see the E-doesn't-mu,' or whatever it's called."

126

"We shall have to give it up," said Norah at last. "What is it?"

"Ebu," I announced. "My man had a bad cold, and he said, 'Look, Baria, there's ad Ebu.' Er—what do I get for that?"

"Nothing," said Norah coldly. "It isn't fair. Now, Mr. Dennis."

"Mine is not Emu, and it couldn't be mistaken for Emu; not even if you had a sore throat and a sprained ankle. And it has nothing to do with the Zoo, and——"

"Well, what is it?"

"It's what you say at golf when you miss a short putt."

"I doubt it," I said.

"Not what Gerald says," said his wife.

"Well, it's what you might say. What Horace would have said."

"'Eheu'—good," said Gerald, while his wife was asking "Horace who?"

We moved on to the next word, P—D.

"Mine," said Norah, "is what you might do to a man whom you didn't like, but it's a delightful thing to have and at the same time you would hate to be in it."

"Are you sure you know what you are talking about, dear?" said Mrs. Gerald gently.

"Quite," said Norah with the confidence of extreme youth.

"Could you say it again very slowly," asked Dennis, "indicating by changes in the voice which character is speaking?"

She said it again.

"'Pound,'" said Gerald. "Good—one to me."

Mrs. Gerald had "pod," Gerald had "pond"; but they didn't define them very cleverly and they were soon guessed. Mine, unfortunately, was also guessed at once.

"It is what Dennis's golf is," I said.

"'Putrid,'" said Gerald correctly.

"Mine," said Dennis, "is what everybody has two of."

"Then it's not 'pound,'" I said, "because I've only got one and ninepence."

"At least, it's best to have two. Sometimes you lose one. They're very useful at golf. In fact, absolutely necessary."

"Have you got two?"

"Yes."

I looked at Dennis's enormous hands spread out on his knees.

"Is it 'pud'?" I asked. "It is? Are those the two? Good heavens!" and I gave myself a mark.

A—A was the next, and we had the old Emu trouble.

"Mine," said Norah—"mine is rather a meaningless word."

"'Abracadabra,'" shouted everybody.

"Mine," said Miss Gerald, "is a very strange word, which——"

"'Abracadabra,'" shouted everybody.

"Mine," said Gerald, "is a word which used to be——"

"'Abracadabra,'" shouted everybody.

"Mine," I said to save trouble, "is 'Abracadabra.'"

"Mine," said Dennis, "isn't. It's what you say at golf when——"

"Oh lor!" I groaned. "Not again."

"When you hole a long putt for a half."

"You generally say, 'What about that for a good putt, old thing? Thirty yards at least,'" suggested Gerald.

"No."

"Is it—is it 'Alleluia'?" suggested Mrs. Gerald timidly.

"Yes."

"Dennis," I said, "you're an ass."

"And now," said Norah at the end of the game, "who's won?"

They counted up their marks.

"Ten," said Norah.

"Fifteen," said Gerald.

"Three," said his wife.

"Fourteen," said Dennis.

They looked at me.

"I'm afraid I forgot to put all mine down," I said, "but I can easily work it out. There were five words, and five definitions of each word. Twenty-five marks to be gained altogether. You four have got—er—let's see—forty-two between you. That leaves me——"

"That leaves you minus seventeen," said Dennis. "I'm afraid you've lost, old man." He took up the shovel and practised a few approach shots. "It's rather a good game."

I think so too. It's a good game, but, like all paper games, its scoring wants watching.

A BILLIARD LESSON

I was showing Celia a few fancy strokes on the billiard-table. The other members of the house-party were in the library, learning their parts for some approaching theatricals—that is to say, they were sitting round the fire and saying to each other, "This is a rotten play." We had been offered the position of auditors to several of the company, but we were going to see Parsifal on the next day, and I was afraid that the constant excitement would be bad for Celia.

128

"Why don't you ask me to play with you?" she asked. "You never teach me anything."

"There's ingratitude. Why, I gave you your first lesson at golf only last Thursday."

"So you did. I know golf. Now show me billiards."

I looked at my watch.

"We've only twenty minutes. I'll play you thirty up."

"Right-o. What do you give me—a ball or a bisque or what?"

"I can't spare you a ball, I'm afraid. I shall want all three when I get going. You may have fifteen start, and I'll tell you what to do."

"Well, what do I do first?"

"Select a cue."

She went over to the rack and inspected them.

"This seems a nice brown one. Now then, you begin."

"Celia, you've got the half-butt. Put it back and take a younger one."

"I thought it seemed taller than the others." She took another. "How's this? Good. Then off you go."

"Will you be spot or plain?" I said, chalking my cue.

"Does it matter?"

"Not very much. They're both the same shape."

"Then what's the difference?"

"Well, one is more spotted than the other."

"Then I'll be less spotted."

I went to the table.

"I think," I said, "I'll try and screw in off the red." (I did this once by accident and I've always wanted to do it again.) "Or perhaps," I corrected myself, as soon as the ball had left me, "I had better give a safety miss."

I did. My ball avoided the red and came swiftly back into the left-hand bottom pocket.

"That's three to you," I said without enthusiasm.

Celia seemed surprised.

"But I haven't begun yet," she said. "Well, I suppose you know the rules, but it seems funny. What would you like me to do?"

"Well, there isn't much on. You'd better just try and hit the red ball."

"Right." She leant over the table and took long and careful aim. I held my breath.... Still she aimed.... Then, keeping her chin on the cue, she slowly turned her head and looked up at me with a thoughtful expression.

"Oughtn't there to be three balls on the table?" she said, wrinkling her forehead.

"No," I answered shortly.

129

"But why not?"

"Because I went down by mistake."

"But you said that when you got going, you wanted—— I can't argue bending down like this." She raised herself slowly. "You said—— Oh, all right, I expect you know. Anyhow, I have scored some already, haven't I?"

"Yes. You're eighteen to my nothing."

"Yes. Well, now I shall have to aim all over again." She bent slowly over her cue. "Does it matter where I hit the red?"

"Not much. As long as you hit it on the red part."

She hit it hard on the side, and both balls came into baulk.

"Too good," I said.

"Does either of us get anything for it?"

"No." The red and the white were close together, and I went up the table and down again on the off-chance of a cannon. I misjudged it, however.

"That's three to you," I said stiffly, as I took my ball out of the right-hand bottom pocket. "Twenty-one to nothing."

"Funny how I'm doing all the scoring," said Celia meditatively. "And I've practically never played before. I shall hit the red hard now and see what happens to it."

She hit, and the red coursed madly about the table, coming to rest near the top right-hand pocket and close to the cushion. With a forcing shot I could get in.

"This will want a lot of chalk," I said pleasantly to Celia, and gave it plenty. Then I let fly....

"Why did that want a lot of chalk?" said Celia with interest.

I went to the fire-place and picked my ball out of the fender.

"That's three to you," I said coldly. "Twenty-four to nothing."

"Am I winning?"

"You're leading," I explained. "Only, you see, I may make a twenty at any moment."

"Oh!" She thought this over. "Well, I may make my three at any moment."

She chalked her cue and went over to her ball.

"What shall I do?"

"Just touch the red on the right-hand side," I said, "and you'll go into the pocket."

"The right-hand side? Do you mean my right-hand side, or the ball's?"

"The right-hand side of the ball, of course; that is to say, the side opposite your right hand."

"But its right-hand side is opposite my left hand, if the ball is facing this way."

130

"Take it," I said wearily, "that the ball has its back to you."

"How rude of it," said Celia, and hit it on the left-hand side, and sank it. "Was that what you meant?"

"Well ... it's another way of doing it."

"I thought it was. What do I give you for that?"

"You get three."

"Oh, I thought the other person always got the marks. I know the last three times——"

"Go on," I said freezingly. "You have another turn."

"Oh, is it like rounders?"

"Something. Go on, there's a dear. It's getting late."

She went, and left the red over the middle pocket.

"A-ha!" I said. I found a nice place in the "D" for my ball. "Now then. This is the Gray stroke, you know."

I suppose I was nervous. Anyhow, I just nicked the red ball gently on the wrong side and left it hanging over the pocket. The white travelled slowly up the table.

"Why is that called the grey stroke?" asked Celia with great interest.

"Because once, when Sir Edward Grey was playing the German Ambassador—but it's rather a long story. I'll tell you another time."

"Oh! Well, anyhow, did the German Ambassador get anything for it?"

"No."

"Then I suppose I don't. Bother."

"But you've only got to knock the red in for game."

"Oh!... There, what's that?"

"That's a miss-cue. I get one."

"Oh!... Oh well," she added magnanimously, "I'm glad you've started scoring. It will make it more interesting for you."

There was just room to creep in off the red, leaving it still over the pocket. With Celia's ball nicely over the other pocket there was a chance of my twenty break. "Let's see," I said, "how many do I want?"

"Twenty-nine," replied Celia.

"Ah," I said ... and I crept in.

"That's three to you," I said icily. "Game."

BURLESQUES

THE SEASIDE NOVELETTE

[MAY BE READ ON THE PIER]

No. XCVIII—A SIMPLE ENGLISH GIRL

CHAPTER I

PRIMROSE FARM

Primrose Farm stood slumbering in the sunlight of an early summer morn. Save for the gentle breeze which played in the tops of the two tall elms all Nature seemed at rest. Chanticleer had ceased his song; the pigs were asleep; in the barn the cow lay thinking. A deep peace brooded over the rural scene, the peace of centuries. Terrible to think that in a few short hours ... but perhaps it won't. The truth is I have not quite decided whether to have the murder in this story or in No. XCIX.—The Severed Thumb. We shall see.

As her alarum clock (a birthday present) struck five, Gwendolen French sprang out of bed and plunged her face into the clump of nettles which grew outside her lattice window. For some minutes she stood there, breathing in the incense of the day; then dressing quickly she went down into the great oak-beamed kitchen to prepare breakfast for her father and the pigs. As she went about her simple duties she sang softly to herself, a song of love and knightly deeds. Little did she think that a lover, even at that moment, stood outside her door.

"Heigh-ho!" sighed Gwendolen, and she poured the bran-mash into a bowl and took it up to her father's room.

For eighteen years Gwendolen French had been the daughter of John French of Primrose Farm. Endowed by Nature with a beauty that is seldom seen outside this sort of story, she was yet as modest and as good a girl as was to be found in the county. Many a fine lady would have given all her Parisian diamonds for the peach-like complexion which bloomed on the fair face of Gwendolen. But the gifts of Nature are not to be bought and sold.

132

There was a sudden knock at the door.

"Come in," cried Gwendolen in surprise. Unless it was the cow, it was an entirely unexpected visitor.

A tall and handsome young man entered, striking his head violently against a beam as he stepped into the low-ceilinged kitchen.

"Good morning," he said, repressing the remark which came more readily to his lips. "Pray forgive this intrusion. The fact is I have lost my way, and I wondered whether you would be kind enough to inform me as to my whereabouts."

Recognizing from his conversation that she was being addressed by a gentleman, Gwendolen curtsied.

"This is Primrose Farm, sir," she said.

"I fear," he replied with a smile, "it has been my misfortune never to have heard so charming a name before. I am Lord Beltravers, of Beltravers Castle, Beltravers. Having returned last night from India I came out for an early stroll this morning, and I fear that I have wandered out of my direction."

"Why," cried Gwendolen, "your lordship is miles from Beltravers Castle. How tired and hungry you must be." She removed a lettuce from the kitchen chair, dusted it, and offered it to him. (That is to say, the chair, not the lettuce.) "Let me get you some milk," she added. Picking up a pail, she went out to inspect the cow.

"Gad," said Lord Beltravers as soon as he was alone. He paced rapidly up and down the tiled kitchen. "Deuce take it," he added recklessly, "she's a lovely girl." The Beltraverses were noted in two continents for their hard swearing.

"Here you are, sir," said Gwendolen, returning with the precious liquid.

Lord Beltravers seized the pail and drained it at a draught.

"Heavens, but that was good!" he said. "What was it?"

"Milk," said Gwendolen.

"Milk; I must remember. And now may I trespass on your hospitality still further by trespassing on your assistance so far as to solicit your help in putting me far enough on my path to discover my way back to Beltravers Castle?" (When he was alone he said that sentence again to himself, and wondered what had happened to it.)

"I will show you," she said simply.

They passed out into the sunlit orchard. In an apple tree a thrush was singing; the gooseberries were over-ripe; beetroots were flowering everywhere.

"You are very beautiful," he said.

"Yes," said Gwendolen.

"I must see you again. Listen! To-night my mother, Lady Beltravers, is giving a ball. Do you dance?"

"Alas, not the tango," she said sadly.

"The Beltraverses do not tang," he announced with simple dignity. "You valse? Good. Then will you come?"

"Thank you, my lord. Oh, I should love to!"

"That is excellent. And now I must bid you good-bye. But first, will you not tell me your name?"

"Gwendolen French, my lord."

"Ah! One 'f' or two?"

"Three," said Gwendolen simply.

CHAPTER II

BELTRAVERS CASTLE

Beltravers Castle was a blaze of lights. At the head of the old oak staircase (a magnificent example of the Selfridge period) the Lady Beltravers stood receiving her guests. Magnificently gowned in one of Sweeting's latest creations, and wearing round her neck the famous Beltravers seed-pearls, she looked the picture of stately magnificence. As each guest was announced by a bevy of footmen, she extended her perfectly gloved hand and spoke a few words of kindly welcome.

"Good evening, Duchess; so good of you to look in. Ah, Earl, charmed to meet you; you'll find some sandwiches in the billiard-room. Beltravers, show the Earl some sandwiches. How-do-you-do, Professor? Delighted you could come. Won't you take off your goloshes?"

All the county was there.

Lord Hobble was there wearing a magnificent stud; Erasmus Belt, the famous author, whose novel, Bitten: A Romance, went into two editions; Sir Septimus Root, the inventor of the fire-proof spat; Captain the Honourable Alfred Nibbs, the popular breeder of blood-tortoises—the whole world and his wife were present. And towering above them all stood Lord Beltravers, of Beltravers Castle, Beltravers.

Lord Beltravers stood aloof in a corner of the great ball-room. Above his head was the proud coat-of-arms of the Beltraverses—a

134

headless sardine on a field of tomato. As each new arrival entered Lord Beltravers scanned his or her countenance eagerly, and then turned away with a snarl of disappointment. Would his little country maid never come?

She came at last. Attired in a frock which had obviously been created in Little Popley, she looked the picture of girlish innocence as she stood for a moment hesitating in the doorway. Then her eyes brightened as Lord Beltravers came towards her with long swinging strides.

"You're here!" he exclaimed. "How good of you to come. I have thought about you ever since this morning. There is a valse beginning. Will you valse it with me?"

"Thank you," said Gwendolen shyly.

Lord Beltravers, who valsed divinely, put his arm round her waist and led her into the circle of dancers.

CHAPTER III

AFFIANCED

The ball was at its height. Gwendolen, who had been in to supper eight times, placed her hand timidly on the arm of Lord Beltravers, who had just begged a polka of her.

"Let us sit this out," she said. "Not here—in the garden."

"Yes," said Lord Beltravers gravely. "Let us go. I have something to say to you."

Offering her his arm, he led her down the great terrace which ran along the back of the house.

"How wonderful to have your ancestors always around you like this!" cooed Gwendolen, as she gazed with reverence at the two statues which fronted them.

"Venus," said Lord Beltravers shortly, "and Samson."

He led her down the steps and into the ornamental garden, and there they sat down.

"Miss French," said Lord Beltravers, "or, if I may call you by that sweet name, Gwendolen, I have brought you here for the purpose of making an offer to you. Perhaps it would have been more in accordance with etiquette had I approached your mother first."

"Mother is dead," said the girl simply.

"I am sorry," said Lord Beltravers, bending his head in courtly sympathy. "In that case I should have asked your father to hear my suit."

"Father is deaf," she replied. "He couldn't have heard it."

"Tut, tut," said Lord Beltravers impatiently. "I beg your pardon," he added at once, "I should have controlled myself. That being so," he went on, "I have the honour to make to you, Miss French, an offer of marriage. May I hope?"

Gwendolen put her hand suddenly to her heart. The shock was too much for her fresh young innocence. She was not really engaged to Giles Earwaker, though he, too, was hoping; and the only three times that Thomas Ritson had kissed her she had threatened to box his ears.

"Lord Beltravers," she began——

"Call me Beltravers," he begged.

"Beltravers, I love you. I give you a simple maiden's heart."

"My darling!" he cried, clasping her thumb impulsively. "Then we are affianced."

He slipped a ring off his finger and fitted it affectionately on two of hers.

"Wear this," he said gravely. "It was my mother's. She was a de Dindigul. See, this is their crest—a roe-less herring over the motto Dans l'huile." Observing that she looked puzzled he translated the noble French words to her. "And now let us go in. Another dance is beginning. May I beg for the honour?"

"Beltravers," she whispered lovingly.

CHAPTER IV

EXPOSURE

The next dance was at its height. In a dream of happiness Gwendolen revolved with closed eyes round Lord Beltravers, of Beltravers Castle, Beltravers.

Suddenly above the music rose a voice, commanding, threatening.

"Stop!" cried the Lady Beltravers.

As if by magic the band ceased and all the dancers were still.

"There is an intruder here," said Lady Beltravers in a cold

voice. "A milkmaid, a common farmer's daughter. Gwendolen French, leave my house this instant!"

Dazed, hardly knowing what she did, Gwendolen moved forward. In an instant Lord Beltravers was after her.

"No, mother," he said, with the utmost dignity. "Not a common milkmaid, but the future Lady Beltravers."

An indescribable thrill of emotion ran through the crowded ball-room. Lord Hobble's stud fell out; and Lady Susan Golightly hurried across the room and fainted in the arms of Sir James Batt.

"What!" cried the Lady Beltravers. "My son, the last of the Beltraverses, the Beltraverses who came over with Julius Wernher, I should say Cæsar, marry a milkmaid?"

"No, mother. He is marrying what any man would be proud to marry—a simple English girl."

There was a cheer, instantly suppressed, from a Socialist in the band.

For just a moment words failed the Lady Beltravers. Then she sank into a chair, and waved her guests away.

"The ball is over," she said slowly. "Leave me. My son and I must be alone."

One by one, with murmured thanks for a delightful evening, the guests trooped out. Soon mother and son were alone. Lord Beltravers, gazing out of the window, saw the 'cellist laboriously dragging his 'cello across the park.

CHAPTER V

THE END

[And now, dear readers, I am in a difficulty. How shall the story go on? The editor of The Seaside Library asks quite frankly for a murder. His idea was that the Lady Beltravers should be found dead in the park next morning and that Gwendolen should be arrested. This seems to me both crude and vulgar. Besides, I want a murder for No. XCIX. of the series—The Severed Thumb.

No, I think I know a better way out.]

Old John French sat beneath a spreading pear tree, and waited. Early that morning a mysterious note had been brought to him, asking for an interview on a matter of the utmost importance. This was the trysting-place.

"I have come," said a voice behind him, "to ask you to beg your daughter——"

"I HAVE COME," cried the Lady Beltravers, "TO ASK YOU—

"I HAVE COME," shouted her ladyship, "TO——"

John French wheeled round in amazement. With a cry the Lady Beltravers shrank back.

"Eustace," she gasped—"Eustace, Earl of Turbot!"

"Eliza!"

"What are you doing here? I came to see John French."

"What?" he asked, with his hand to his ear.

She repeated her remark loudly several times.

"I am John French," he said at last. "When you refused me and married Beltravers I suddenly felt tired of Society; and I changed my name and settled down here as a simple farmer. My daughter helps me on the farm."

"Then your daughter is——"

"Lady Gwendolen Hake."

A beautiful double wedding was solemnized at Beltravers in October, the Earl of Turbot leading Eliza, Lady Beltravers to the altar, while Lord Beltravers was joined in matrimony to the beautiful Lady Gwendolen Hake. There were many presents on both sides, which partook equally of the beautiful and the costly.

Lady Gwendolen Beltravers is now the most popular hostess in the county; but to her husband she always seems the simple English milkmaid that he first thought her. Ah!

THE SECRET OF THE ARMY AEROPLANE

[In the thrilling manner of Mr. William le Queux.]

"Yes," said my friend, Ray Raymond, as a grim smile crossed his typically English face, looking round the chambers which we shared together, though he never had occasion to practise, though I unfortunately had, "it is a very curious affair indeed."

"Tell us the whole facts, Ray," urged Vera Vallance, the pretty fair-haired daughter of Admiral Sir Charles Vallance, to whom he was engaged.

"Well, dear, they are briefly as follows," he replied, with an affectionate glance at her. "It is well known that the Germans are anxious to get hold of our new aeroplane, and that the secret of it is at present locked in the inventor's breast. Last Tuesday a man with his moustache brushed up the wrong way alighted at Basingstoke station and enquired for the refreshment-room. This leads me to believe that a dastardly attempt is about to be made to wrest the supremacy of the air from our grasp!" Immediately I swooned.

"And even in the face of this the Government denies the activity of German spies in England!" I exclaimed bitterly as soon as I had recovered consciousness.

"Jacox," said my old friend, "as a patriot it is none the less my duty to expose these miscreants. To-morrow we go to Basingstoke."

Next Thursday, then, saw us ensconced in our private sitting-room at the Bull Hotel, Basingstoke. On our way from the station I had noticed how ill-prepared the town was to resist invasion, and I had pointed this out bitterly to my dear old friend, Ray Raymond.

"Yes," he remarked, grimly; "and it is simply infested with spies. Jack, my surmises are proving correct. There will be dangerous work afoot to-night. Have you brought your electric torch with you?"

"Since that Rosyth affair, I never travel without it," I replied, as I stood with my back to the cheap mantel-shelf so common in English hotels.

The night was dark, therefore we proceeded with caution as we left the inn. The actions of Ray Raymond were curious. As we passed each telegraph pole he stopped and said grimly, "Ah, I thought so"; and drew his revolver. When we had covered fifteen miles we looked at our watches by the aid of our electric torches and discovered that it was time to get back to the hotel unless we wished our presence, or rather absence, to be made known to the German spies; therefore we returned hastily.

Next morning Ray was recalled to town by an urgent telegram, therefore I was left alone at Basingstoke to foil the dastardly spies. I stayed there for thirteen weeks, and then went with my old friend to Grimsby, he having received news that a German hairdresser, named Macdonald, was resident in that town.

"My dear Jack," said my friend Ray Raymond, his face assuming the sphinx-like expression by which I knew that he had formed some theory for the destruction of his country's dastardly enemies, "to-night we shall come to grips with the Teuton!"

"And yet," I cried, "the Government refuses to admit the activity of German spies in England!"

"Ha!" said my friend grimly.

He opened a small black bag and produced a dark lantern, a coil of strong silk rope, and a small but serviceable jemmy. All that burglarious outfit belonged to my friend!

At this moment the pretty fair girl to whom he was engaged, Vera Vallance, arrived, but returned to London by the next train.

At ten o'clock we proceeded cautiously to the house of Macdonald the hairdresser, whom Ray had discovered to be a German spy!

"Have you your electric torch with you?" inquired my dear old college friend.

"I have," I answered grimly.

"Good! Then let us enter!"

"You mean to break in?" I cried, amazed at the audacity of my friend.

"Bah!" he said. "Spies are always cowards!"

Therefore we knocked at the door. It was opened by two men, the elder of whom gave vent to a quick German imprecation. The younger had a short beard.

"You are a German spy?" enquired Ray Raymond.

"No," replied the bearded German in very good English, adding with marvellous coolness: "To what, pray, do we owe this unwarrantable intrusion?"

"To the fact that you are a spy who has been taking secret tracings of our Army aeroplane!" retorted my friend.

But the spy only laughed in open defiance.

"Well, there's no law against it," he replied.

"No," retorted Ray grimly, "thanks to the stupidity of a crass Government, there is no law against it."

"My God!" I said hoarsely, and my face went the colour of ashes.

"But my old friend Jacass—I mean Jacox—and I," continued Ray Raymond, fixing the miserable spy with his eye, "have decided to take the law into our own hands. I have my revolver and my friend has his electric torch. Give me the tracings."

"Gott—no!" cried the German spies in German. "Never, you English cur!"

But Ray had already extracted a letter from the elder man's pocket, and was making for the door! I followed him. When we got back to our hotel he drew the letter from his pocket and eagerly examined it. I give here an exact copy of it, and I may state that when we sent it to His Majesty's Minister for War he returned it without a word!

"Berkeley Chambers,
Cannon Street, E.C.

Dear Sir,—In reply to yours of the 29th ult. we beg to say that we can do you a good line in shaving brushes at the following wholesale prices:

Badger   70s. a gross.
Pure Badger 75s. a gross.
Real Badger 80s. a gross.

Awaiting your esteemed order, which we shall have pleasure in promptly executing,

We are, sir,
Yours obediently,
Wilkinson and Allbutt.

Mr. James Macdonald."

That letter, innocent enough upon the face of it, contained dastardly instructions from the Chief of Police to a German spy! Read by the alphabetical code supplied to every German secret agent in England, it ran as follows:

(*Phrase 1*). "Discover without delay secret of new aeroplane."
(*Phrase 2*). "Forward particulars of best plan for blowing up

(1) Portsmouth Dockyard.
(2) Woolwich Arsenal.
(3) Albert Memorial."

(*Phrase 3*). "Be careful of Jack Jacox. He carries a revolver and an electric torch."

"Ah!" said my friend grimly, "we were only just in time. Had we delayed longer, England might have knelt at the proud foot of a conqueror!"
"Ha!" I replied briefly.
Next morning we returned to the chambers which we shared together in London, and were joined by Vera Vallance, the pretty fair daughter of Admiral Sir Charles Vallance, to whom my old

141

friend was engaged. And, as he stroked her hair affectionately, I realised thankfully that he and I had indeed been the instruments of Providence in foiling the plots of the German spies!

BUT HOW WILL IT ALL END?
WHEN WILL GERMANY STRIKE?

THE HALO THEY GAVE THEMSELVES

[A collaboration by the Authors of "The Broken Halo" and "The Woman Thou Gavest Me."

CHAPTER I

SUNDAY MORNING

(Mrs. Barclay begins)

It was a beautiful Sunday morning. All nature browsed in solemn Sabbath stillness. The Little Grey Woman of the Night-Light was hurrying, somewhat late, to church.

Down the white ribbon of road the Virile Benedict of the Libraries came bicycling, treadling easily from the ankles. He rode boldly, with only one hand on the handle-bars, the other in the pocket of his white flannel cricketing trousers. His footballing tie, with his college arms embroidered upon it, flapped gently in the breeze. To look at him you would have said that he was probably a crack polo player on his way to defend the championship against all comers, or the captain of a county golf eleven. As he rode, his soul overflowing with the joy of life, he hummed the Collect for the Day.

It was exactly opposite the church that he ran into the Little Grey Woman of the Night-Light. He had just flashed past a labourer in the road—known to his cronies as the Flap-eared Denizen of the Turnip-patch—a labourer who in the dear dead days of Queen Victoria would have touched his hat humbly, but who now, in this horrible age of attempts to level all class distinctions, actually went on lighting his pipe! Alas, that the respectful deference of the poor toward the rich is now a thing of the past! So thought the Virile

Benedict of the Libraries, and in thinking this he had let his mind wander from the important business of guiding his bicycle! In another moment he had run into the Little Grey Woman of the Night-Light!

She had seen him coming and had given a warning cry, but it was too late. The next moment he shot over his handle-bars; but even as he revolved through the air he wondered how old she really was, and what, if any, was her income. For since the death of the Little White Lady he had formed a habit of marrying elderly women for their money, and his fifth or sixth wife had perished of old age only a few months ago.

[Hall Caine (waking up). Who, pray, is the Little White Lady?

Mrs. Barclay. His first wife. She comes in my book, "The Broken Halo," now in its two hundredth edition.

Hall Caine (annoyed). Tut!]

"Jove," he said cheerily, as he picked himself and her and his bicycle up, "that was a nasty spill. As my Aunt Louisa used to say to the curate when he upset the milk-jug into her lap, 'No milk, thank you.'" His brown eyes danced with amusement as he related this reminiscence of his boyhood. To the Little Grey Woman he seemed to exhale youth from every pore.

"What did your Aunt Louisa say when her ankle was sprained?" she asked with a rueful smile.

In an instant the merry banter faded from the Virile Benedict's brown eyes, and was replaced by the commanding look of one who has taken a brilliant degree in all his medical examinations.

"Allow me," he said brusquely; "I am a doctor." He bent down and listened to her ankle.

It did not take Dr. Dick Cameron's quick ear long to find out all there was to know. His manner became very gentle and his voice very low; and, though he continued to exhale youth, he did it less ostentatiously than before.

"I must carry you home," he said, picking her up in his strong young arms; "you cannot go to church to-day."

"But the curate is preaching!"

Dr. Dick murmured something profane under his breath about curates. He had, alas! these moments of irreverence; as, for instance, on one occasion when he had spoken of Mr. Louis N. Parker's noble picture-play, "Joseph and his Brethren," quite shortly as "Jos. Bros."

"I will carry you home," he said gently. "Tell me where you live, Little Grey Woman."

She smiled up at him bravely. "The Manor House," she said.

143

His voice became yet more gentle. "And now tell me your income," he whispered; and his whole being trembled with emotion as he waited for her reply.

[Mrs. Barclay. There! That's the end of the chapter. Now it's your turn.

Hall Caine (waking up). I don't know if I told you that in my last great work of the imagination, in which I collaborated with the Bishop of London, I wrote throughout in the first person. Nearly a million copies were sold, thus showing that the heart of the great public approved of my method of telling my story through the mouth of a young and innocent girl, exposed to great temptation. I should wish, therefore, to repeat that method in this story, if you could so arrange it.

Mrs. Barclay. But that's easy. The Little Grey Woman shall tell Dr. Dick the story of her first marriage. I did that in my last book, "The Broken Halo," now in its two hundredth edition.

Hall Caine (annoyed). Tut!]

CHAPTER II

UNDER THE CEDAR

(Mrs. Barclay continues)

They were having tea in the garden—the Little Grey Woman and Dr. Dick. More than six months had elapsed since the accident outside the church, and Dr. Dick still remained on at the Manor House in charge of his patient, wishing to be handy in case the old sprain came on again suddenly. She was eighty-two and had twelve thousand a year. On the lawn a thrush was singing.

"How fresh and green the world is to-day," sighed Dr. Dick, leaning back and exhaling youth. "As the curate used to say to my Aunt Louisa, 'A delightful shower after the rain.'" He laughed merrily, and threw a crumb at the thrush with the perfect aim of a good cricketer throwing the ball at the wickets.

"My dear boy," said the Little Grey Woman, "the world is always fresh and green to youth like yours. But to an old woman like me——"

"Not old," said Dick, with an ardent glance; "only eighty-two. Mrs. Beauchamp, will you marry me?"

She looked at him with a sad but tender smile.

"What would my friends say?" she asked.

"Bother your friends."

"My dear boy, you would be considerably surprised if you could glance through an approximate list of the friends I possess to-day. Do you know that if I marry you I shall be required to make an explanation to several royal ladies—that is, if they graciously grant me the opportunity so to do."

"But I want your mon—I mean I love you," he pleaded, the light of youth shining in his brown eyes.

The Little Grey Woman looked at him tenderly. Their eyes met.

"Listen," she said. "I will tell you the story of my first marriage, and then if you wish you shall ask me again."

Dr. Dick helped himself to another slice of cake and leant back to listen.

[Mrs. Barclay. There you are. Now you can do Chapter Three.

Hall Caine. Excellent. It is quite time that one got some emotion into this story. In "The Woman Thou Gavest Me," of which more than a million——

Mrs. Barclay. Emotion, indeed! My last book is already in its two hundredth edition.

Hall Caine (annoyed). Tut!]

CHAPTER III

MRS. BEAUCHAMP'S STORY

(Mr. Hall Caine takes up the tale)

I have always had a wonderful memory, and my earliest recollection is of hearing my father ask, on the day when I was born, whether it was a boy or a girl. When they told him "a girl," he let fall a rough expression which sent the blood coursing over my mother's pale cheeks like lobster-sauce coursing over a turbot. My father, John Boomster, was a great advertising agent, perhaps the greatest in the island, though he always said that there was one man who could beat him. He wanted a son to succeed him in the business, and in the years to come he never forgave me for being a girl. He would often glare at me in silence for three-quarters of an hour, and then, letting fall the same rough expression, throw a boot at me and stride from the room. A hard, cruel man, my father, and yet, in his fashion, he was fond of me.

It was not until I was eighteen that he first spoke to me. To my dying day I shall never forget that evening; nor his words, which bit themselves into my mind as a red-hot iron bites its way into cheese.

"Nell," he said, for that was my name, though he had never used it before, "I've arranged that you are to marry Lord Wurzel two months from to-day."

At these terrible words the blood ebbed slowly from my ears and my hands grew hot.

"I do not know him," I said in a stifled voice.

"You will to-morrow," he laughed brutally, and with another rough word he strode from the room.

Lord Wurzel! I ran upstairs to my room and flung myself face downwards on the bed. In my agony I bit a large piece out of my pillow. The blood flowed forward and backward over me in waves, and I burst every now and then into a passion of weeping.

By and by I began to feel more serene. I decided that it was my duty to obey my father. My heart leapt within me at the thought of doing my duty, and to calm myself I put on my hat and wandered into the glen. It was very silent in the glen. There was no sound but the rustling of the leaves overhead, the popping of the insects underfoot, the sneezing of the cattle, the whistling of the pigs, the coughing of the field-mice, the roaring of the rabbits, and the deep organ-song of the sea.

But suddenly, above all these noises, I heard a voice which sent the blood ebbing and flowing in my heart and caused the back of my neck to quiver with ecstasy.

"Nell!" it said.

It was the voice of my old comrade, Andrew Spinnaker, who had played with me in our childhood's days, and whom I had not seen now for eight years.

"Andrew!" I cried, as I turned round. "What are you doing here?"

"I am just off to discover the South Pole," he said. "My shipmates are waiting for me to command the expedition."

I noticed then for the first time that he was dressed in a seal-skin cap and a pair of sleeping-bags.

"Nell," he went on, "before I go, tell me you love me."

My heart fluttered like a captured bird; my knees trembled like a drunken spider's; my throat was stifled like a stifled throat. A huge wave of something or other surged over me and told me that the great mystery of the world had happened to me.

I was in love.

I was in love with Andrew Spinnaker.

"Andrew," I cried, falling on his startled chin, "I love you." All the back of my neck thrilled with joy.

But my joy was shortlived. No sooner had I become aware that I loved Andrew Spinnaker than my conscience told me I had no right to do so. I was going to marry Lord Wurzel, and to love another than my husband was sin. I shook Andrew off my lips.

"I love you," I said, "but I cannot marry you. I am marrying Lord Wurzel."

"That beast?" cried Andrew, in the impetuous sailor fashion which so endeared him to his shipmates. "When I come back I will thrash him as I would thrash a vicious ape."

"When will that be?"

"In about two months," said my darling boy. "This is going to be a very quick expedition."

"Alas, that will be my wedding day," I said with a low sob like that of a buffalo yearning for its mate. "It will be too late."

Andrew took me in his strong arms. I should not have let him, but I could not help it.

"Listen," he said, "I will start back from the Pole a day before my shipmates, and save you from that d-sh-d beast. And then I will marry you, Nell."

There was a roaring in my ears like the roaring of the bath when the tap is left on; many waters seemed to rush upon me; my hat fell off, and then deep oblivion came over me and I swooned.

To go through my emotions in detail during the next two months would be but to harrow you needlessly. Suffice it to say that seventeen times I flung myself face downwards on my bed and bit a piece out of the pillow, on twenty-nine occasions the blood ebbed slowly from my face, and my heart fluttered like a captured bird, while in a hundred and forty instances a wave of emotion surged slowly over my whole body, leaving me trembling like an aspen leaf. Otherwise my health remained good.

It was the night before the wedding. The bad Lord Wurzel had just left me with words of love upon his lying lips. To-morrow, unless Andrew Spinnaker saved me, I should be Lady Wurzel.

"A marconigram for you, miss," said our faithful old gardener, William, entering the drawing-room noiselessly by the chimney. "I brought it myself to be sure you got it."

147

With trembling fingers I tore it open. How my heart leapt and the hot colour flooded my neck and brow when I recognised the dear schoolboy writing of my beloved Andrew! I have the message still. It went like this:

"*Wireless—South Pole.*

Arrived safe. Found Pole. Weather charming. Blue sky. Not a breath of wind. Am wearing my thick socks. Sun never going down. Constellations revolving without dipping. Moon going sideways. Am starting for England to-morrow. Arrive Victoria twelve o'clock, Wednesday.—Andrew."

Back on Wednesday! And to-morrow was Tuesday—my wedding day! There was no hope. I felt like a shipwrecked voyager. For the thirty-fifth time since the beginning of the month deep oblivion came over me, and I swooned.

[Hall Caine. I think you might go on now. I have put a little life into the story. It is, perhaps, not quite so vivid as my last work, "The Woman Thou Gavest Me," of which more than a million copies——

Mrs. Barclay. In the two hundredth edition of "The Broken Halo"——

Hall Caine (annoyed). Tut!]

CHAPTER IV

THE END

(Mrs. Barclay resumes)

At this point in The Little Grey Woman's story handsome Dr. Dick put down his third piece of cake and got up. There was a baffled look on his virile face which none of his previous wives had ever seen there. For once Dr. Dick was nonplussed!

"Is there much more of your story?" he asked.

"Five hundred and nineteen pages," she said.

The Virile Benedict of the Libraries took up his hat. Never had he exhaled youth so violently, yet never had he looked such a man.

He had made up his mind. She was rich; but, after all, money was not everything.

"Good-bye," he said.

A DIDACTIC NOVEL

[In humble imitation of Mr. Eustace Miles's serial in Healthward Ho! (Help!), and in furtherance of the great principle of self-culture]

THE MYSTERY OF GORDON SQUARE

Synopsis of Previous Chapters

Roger Dangerfield, the famous barrister, is passing through Gordon Square one December night when he suddenly comes across the dead body of a man of about forty years. To his horror he recognises it to be that of his friend, Sir Eustace Butt, M.P., who has been stabbed in seven places. Much perturbed by the incident, Roger goes home and decides to lead a new life. Hitherto he had been notorious in the London clubs for his luxurious habits, but now he rises at 7.30 every morning and breathes evenly through the nose for five minutes before dressing.

After three weeks of the breathing exercise, Roger adds a few simple lunges to his morning drill. Detective-Inspector Frenchard tells him that he has a clue to the death of Sir Eustace, but that the murderer is still at large. Roger sells his London house and takes a cottage in the country, where he practises the simple life. He is now lunging ten times to the right, ten times to the left and ten times backwards every morning, besides breathing lightly through the nose during his bath.

One day he meets a Yogi, who tells him that if he desires to track the murderer down he must learn concentration. He suggests that Roger should start by concentrating on the word "wardrobe," and then leaves this story and goes back to India. Roger sells his house in the country and comes back to town, where he concentrates for half an hour daily on the word "wardrobe," besides, of course, persevering with his breathing and lunging exercises. After a heavy morning's drill he is passing through Gordon Square when he comes across the body of his old friend, Sir Joshua Tubbs, M.P., who has been stabbed nine times. Roger returns home quickly, and decides to practise breathing through the ears.

CHAPTER XCI

PREPARATION

The appalling death of Sir Joshua Tubbs, M.P., following so closely upon that of Sir Eustace Butt, M.P., meant the beginning of a new life for Roger. His morning drill now took the following form:—

On rising at 7.30 a.m. he sipped a glass of distilled water, at the same time concentrating on the word "wardrobe." This lasted for ten minutes, after which he stood before the open window for five minutes, breathing alternately through the right ear and the left. A vigorous series of lunges followed, together with the simple kicking exercises detailed in chapter LIV.

These over, there was a brief interval of rest, during which our hero, breathing heavily through the back of the head, concentrated on the word "dough-nut." Refreshed by the mental discipline, he rose and stood lightly on the ball of his left foot, at the same time massaging himself vigorously between the shoulders with his right. After five minutes of this he would rest again, lying motionless except for a circular movement of the ears. A cold bath, a brisk rub down and another glass of distilled water completed the morning training.

But it is time we got on with the story. The murder of Sir Joshua Tubbs, M.P. had sent a thrill of horror through England, and hundreds of people wrote indignant letters to the Press, blaming the police for their neglect to discover the assassin. Detective-Inspector Frenchard, however, was hard at work, and he was inspired by the knowledge that he could always rely upon the assistance of Roger Dangerfield, the famous barrister, who had sworn to track the murderer down.

To prepare himself for the forthcoming struggle Roger decided, one sunny day in June, to give up the meat diet upon which he had relied so long, and to devote himself entirely to a vegetable régime. With that thoroughness which was now becoming a characteristic of him, he left London and returned to the country, with the intention of making a study of food values.

CHAPTER XCII

LOVE COMES IN

It was a beautiful day in July and the country was looking its best. Roger rose at 7.30 a.m. and performed those gentle, health-giving exercises which have already been described in previous chapters. On this glorious morning, however, he added a simple exercise for the elbows to his customary ones, and went down to his breakfast as hungry as the proverbial hunter. A substantial meal of five dried beans and a stewed nut awaited him in the fine oak-panelled library; and as he did ample justice to the banquet his thoughts went back to the terrible days when he lived the luxurious meat-eating life of the ordinary man-about-town; to the evening when he discovered the body of Sir Eustace Butt, M.P., and swore to bring the assassin to vengeance; to the day when——

Suddenly he realised that his thoughts were wandering. With iron will he controlled them and concentrated fixedly on the word "dough-nut" for twelve minutes. Greatly refreshed, he rose and strode out into the sun.

At the door of his cottage a girl was standing. She was extremely beautiful, and Roger's heart would have jumped if he had not had that organ (thanks to Twisting Exercise 23) under perfect control.

"Is this the way to Denfield?" she asked.

"Straight on," said Roger.

He returned to his cottage, breathing heavily through his ears.

151

CHAPTER XCIII

ANOTHER SURPRISE

Six months went by, and the murderer of Sir Joshua Tubbs, M.P. and Sir Eustace Butt, M.P. still remained at large. Roger had sold his cottage in the country and was now in London, performing his exercises with regularity, concentrating daily upon the words "wardrobe," "dough-nut," and "wasp," and living entirely upon proteids.

One day he had the idea that he would start a restaurant in the East-End for the sale of meatless foods. This would bring him in touch with the lower classes, among whom he expected to find the assassin of his two oldest friends.

In less than three or four years the shop was a tremendous success. In spite of this, however, Roger did not neglect his exercises; taking particular care to keep the toes well turned in when lunging ten times backwards. (Exercise 17.) Once, to his joy, the girl whom he had first met outside his country cottage came in and had her simple lunch of Smilopat (ninepence the dab) at his shop. That evening he lunged twelve times to the right instead of ten.

One day business had taken Roger to the West-End. As he was returning home at midnight through Gordon Square, he suddenly stopped and staggered back.

A body lay on the ground before him!

Hastily turning it over upon its face, Roger gave a cry of horror.

It was Detective-Inspector Frenchard! Stabbed in eleven places!

Roger hurried madly home, and devised an entirely new set of exercises for his morning drill. A full description of these, however, must be reserved for another chapter.

(And so on for ever.)

MERELY PLAYERS

ON THE BAT'S BACK

With the idea of brightening cricket, my friend Twyford has given me a new bat. I have always felt that, in my own case, it was the inadequacy of the weapon rather than of the man behind it which accounted for a certain monotony of low-scoring; with this new bat I hope to prove the correctness of my theory.

My old bat has always been a trier, but of late it has been manifestly past its work. Again and again its drive over long-off's head has failed to carry the bunker at mid-off. More than once it has proved itself an inch too narrow to ensure that cut-past-third-man-to-the-boundary which is considered one of the most graceful strokes in my repertoire. Worst of all, I have found it at moments of crisis (such as the beginning of the first over) utterly inadequate to deal with the ball which keeps low. When bowled by such a ball—and I may say that I am never bowled by any other—I look reproachfully at the bottom of my bat as I walk back to the pavilion. "Surely," I say to it, "you were much longer than this when we started out?"

Perhaps it was not magnanimous always to put the blame on my partner for our accidents together. It would have been more chivalrous to have shielded him. "No, no," I should have said to my companions as they received me with sympathetic murmurs of "Bad luck,"—"no, no, you mustn't think that. It was my own fault. Don't reproach the bat." It would have been well to have spoken thus; and indeed, when I had had time to collect myself, I did so speak. But out on the field, in the first shame of defeat, I had to let the truth come out. That one reproachful glance at my bat I could not hide.

But there was one habit of my bat's—a weakness of old age, I admit, but not the less annoying—about which it was my duty to let all the world know. One's grandfather may have a passion for the gum on the back of postage-stamps, and one hushes it up; but if he be deaf the visitor must be warned. My bat had a certain looseness in the shoulder, so that, at any quick movement of it, it clicked. If I struck the ball well and truly in the direction of point this defect did not matter; but if the ball went past me into the hands of the wicket-keeper, an unobservant bowler would frequently say, "How's that?" And an ill-informed umpire would reply, "Out." It was my duty before the game began to take the visiting umpire on one side and give him a practical demonstration of the click ...

But these are troubles of the past. I have my new bat now, and I can see that cricket will become a different game for me. My practice of this morning has convinced me of this. It was not one of your stupid practices at the net, with two burly professionals bumping down balls at your body and telling you to "Come out to them, Sir." It was a quiet practice in my rooms after breakfast, with no moving object to distract my attention and spoil my stroke. The bat comes up well. It is light, and yet there is plenty of wood in it. Its drives along the carpet were excellent; its cuts and leg glides all that could be wished. I was a little disappointed with its half-arm hook, which dislodged a teacup and gave what would have been an easy catch to mid-on standing close in by the sofa; but I am convinced that a little oil will soon put that right.

And yet there seemed to be something lacking in it. After trying every stroke with it; after tucking it under my arm and walking back to the bathroom, touching my cap at the pianola on the way; after experiments with it in all positions, I still felt that there was something wanting to make it the perfect bat. So I put it in a cab and went round with it to Henry. Henry has brightened first-class cricket for some years now.

"Tell me, Henry," I said, "what's wrong with this bat?"

"It seems all right," he said, after waving it about. "Rather a good one."

I laid it down on the floor and looked at it. Then I turned it on its face and looked at it. And then I knew.

"It wants a little silver shield on the back," I said. "That's it."

"Why, is it a presentation bat?" asked Henry.

"In a sense, yes. It was presented to me by Twyford."

"What for?"

"Really," I said modestly, "I hardly like—— Why do people give one things? Affection, Henry; pity, generosity—er——"

"Are you going to put that on the shield? 'Presented out of sheer pity to——'"

"Don't be silly; of course not. I shall put 'Presented in commemoration of his masterly double century against the Authentics,' or something like that. You've no idea how it impresses the wicket-keeper. He really sees quite a lot of the back of one's bat."

"Your inscription," said Henry, as he filled his pipe slowly, "will be either a lie or extremely unimpressive."

"It will be neither, Henry. If I put my own name on it, and talked about my double century, of course it would be a lie; but the inscription will be to Stanley Bolland."

154

"Who's he?"

"I don't know. I've just made him up. But now, supposing my little shield says, 'Stanley Bolland. H.P.C.C.—Season 1912. Batting average 116.34.'—how is that a lie?"

"What does H.P.C.C. stand for?"

"I don't know. It doesn't mean anything really. I'll leave out 'Batting average' if it makes it more truthful. 'Stanley Bolland. H.P.C.C., 1912. 116.34.' It's really just a little note I make on the back of my bat to remind me of something or other I've forgotten. 116.34 is probably Bolland's telephone number or the size of something I want at his shop. But by a pure accident the wicket-keeper thinks it means something else; and he tells the bowler at the end of the over that it's that chap Bolland who had an average of over a century for the Hampstead Polytechnic last year. Of course that makes the bowler nervous and he starts sending down long-hops."

"I see," said Henry; and he began to read his paper again.

So to-morrow I take my bat to the silversmith's and have a little engraved shield fastened on. Of course, with a really trustworthy weapon I am certain to collect pots of runs this season. But there is no harm in making things as easy as possible for oneself.

And yet there is this to be thought of. Even the very best bat in the world may fail to score, and it might so happen that I was dismissed (owing to some defect in the pitch) before my silver shield had time to impress the opposition. Or again, I might (through ill-health) perform so badly that quite a wrong impression of the standard of the Hampstead Polytechnic would be created, an impression which I should hate to be the innocent means of circulating.

So on second thoughts I lean to a different inscription. On the back of my bat a plain silver shield will say quite simply this:—

TO
STANLEY BOLLAND,
FOR SAVING LIFE AT SEA.
FROM A FEW ADMIRERS.

Thus I shall have two strings to my bow. And if, by any unhappy chance, I fail as a cricketer, the wicket-keeper will say to his comrades as I walk sadly to the pavilion, "A poor bat perhaps, but a brave—a very brave fellow."

It becomes us all to make at least one effort to brighten cricket.

155

UNCLE EDWARD

Celia has more relations than would seem possible. I am gradually getting to know some them by sight and a few more by name, but I still make mistakes. The other day, for instance, she happened to say she was going to a concert with Uncle Godfrey.

"Godfrey," I said, "Godfrey. No, don't tell me—I shall get it in a moment. Godfrey ... Yes, that's it; he's the architect. He lives at Liverpool, has five children, and sent us the asparagus-cooler as a wedding present."

"No marks," said Celia.

"Then he's the unmarried one in Scotland who breeds terriers. I knew I should get it."

"As a matter of fact he lives in London and breeds oratorios."

"It's the same idea. That was the one I meant. The great point is that I placed him. Now give me another one." I leant forward eagerly.

"Well, I was just going to ask you—have you arranged anything about Monday?"

"Monday," I said, "Monday. No, don't tell me—I shall get it in a moment. Monday ... He's the one who—— Oh, you mean the day of the week?"

"Who's a funny?" asked Celia of the teapot.

"Sorry; I really thought you meant another relation. What am I doing? I'm playing golf if I can find somebody to play with."

"Well, ask Edward."

I could place Edward at once. Edward, I need hardly say, is Celia's uncle; one of the ones I have not yet met. He married a very young aunt of hers, not much older than Celia.

"But I don't know him," I said.

"It doesn't matter. Write and ask him to meet you at the golf club. I'm sure he'd love to."

"Wouldn't he think it rather cool, this sudden attack from a perfectly unknown nephew? I fancy the first step ought to come from uncle."

"But you're older than he is."

"True. It's rather a tricky point in etiquette. Well, I'll risk it." This was the letter I sent to him:—

"MY DEAR UNCLE EDWARD,—Why haven't you written to me this term? I have spent the five shillings you gave me when I came back; it was awfully ripping of you to give it to me, but I have spent it now. Are you coming down

156

to see me this term? If you aren't you might write to me; there is a post-office here where you can change postal orders.

"What I really meant to say was, can you play golf with me on Monday at Mudbury Hill? I am your new and favourite nephew, and it is quite time we met. Be at the club-house at 2.30, if you can. I don't quite know how we shall recognize each other, but the well-dressed man in the nut-brown suit will probably be me. My features are plain but good, except where I fell against the bath-taps yesterday. If you have fallen against anything which would give me a clue to your face you might let me know. Also you might let me know if you are a professor at golf; if you are, I will read some more books on the subject between now and Monday. Just at the moment my game is putrid.

"Your niece and my wife sends her love. Good-bye. I was top of my class in Latin last week. I must now stop, as it is my bath-night.
"I am,
"Your loving
"Nephew."

The next day I had a letter from my uncle:—

"My dear Nephew,—I was so glad to get your nice little letter and to hear that you were working hard. Let me know when it is your bath-night again; these things always interest me. I shall be delighted to play golf with you on Monday. You will have no difficulty in recognizing me. I should describe myself roughly as something like Apollo and something like Little Tich, if you know what I mean. It depends how you come up to me. I am an excellent golfer and never take more than two putts in a bunker.

"Till 2.30 then. I enclose a postal-order for sixpence, to see you through the rest of the term.
"Your favourite uncle,
"Edward."

I showed it to Celia.

"Perhaps you could describe him more minutely," I said. "I hate wandering about vaguely and asking everybody I see if he's my uncle. It seems so odd."

"You're sure to meet all right," said Celia confidently. "He's—well, he's nice-looking and—and clean-shaven—and, oh, you'll recognize him."

At 2.30 on Monday I arrived at the club-house and waited for my uncle. Various people appeared, but none seemed in want of a nephew. When 2.45 came there was still no available uncle. True, there was one unattached man reading in a corner of the smoke-room, but he had a moustache—the sort of heavy moustache one associates with a major.

At three o'clock I became desperate. After all, Celia had not seen Edward for some time. Perhaps he had grown a moustache lately; perhaps he had grown one specially for to-day. At any rate there would be no harm in asking this major man if he was my uncle. Even if he wasn't he might give me a game of golf.

"Excuse me," I said politely, "but are you by any chance my Uncle Edward?"

"Your what?"

"I was almost certain you weren't, but I thought I'd just ask. I'm sorry."

"Not at all. Naturally one wants to find one's uncle. Have you—er—lost him long?"

"Years," I said sadly. "Er—I wonder if you would care to adopt me—I mean, give me a game this afternoon. My man hasn't turned up."

"By all means. I'm not very great."

"Neither am I. Shall we start now? Good."

I was sorry to miss Edward, but I wasn't going to miss a game of golf on such a lovely day. My spirits rose. Not even the fact that there were no caddies left and I had to carry my own clubs could depress me.

The Major drove. I am not going to describe the whole game; though my cleek shot at the fifth hole, from a hanging lie to within two feet of the—— However, I mustn't go into that now. But it surprised the Major a good deal. And when at the next hole I laid my brassie absolutely dead, he—— But I can tell you about that some other time. It is sufficient to say now that, when we reached the seventeenth tee, I was one up.

We both played the seventeenth well. He was a foot from the hole in four. I played my third from the edge of the green, and was ridiculously short, giving myself a twenty-foot putt for the hole. Leaving my clubs I went forward with the putter, and by the absurdest luck pushed the ball in.

"Good," said the Major. "Your game."

I went back for my clubs. When I turned round the Major was walking carelessly off to the next tee, leaving the flag lying on the green and my ball still in the tin.

"Slacker," I said to myself, and walked up to the hole.

And then I had a terrible shock. I saw in the tin, not my ball, but a moustache!

"Am I going mad?" I said. "I could have sworn that I drove off with a 'Colonel,' and yet I seem to have holed out with a Major's moustache!" I picked it up and hurried after him.

"Major," I said, "excuse me, you've dropped your moustache. It fell off at the critical stage of the match; the shock of losing was too much for you; the strain of——"

He turned his clean-shaven face round and grinned at me.

"On second thoughts," he said, "I am your long-lost uncle."

THE RENASCENCE OF BRITAIN

Peter Riley was one of those lucky people who take naturally to games. Actually he got his blue for cricket, rugger, and boxing, but his perfect eye and wrist made him a beautiful player of any game with a ball. Also he rode and shot well, and knew all about the inside of a car. But, although he was always enthusiastic about anything he was doing, he was not really keen on games. He preferred wandering about the country looking for birds' nests or discovering the haunts of rare butterflies; he liked managing a small boat single-handed in a stiff breeze; he would have enjoyed being upset and having to swim a long way to shore. Most of all, perhaps, he loved to lie on the top of the cliffs and think of the wonderful things that he would do for England when he was a Cabinet Minister. For politics was to be his profession, and he had just taken a first in History by way of preparation for it.

There were a lot of silly people who envied Peter's mother. They thought, poor dears, that she must be very, very proud of him, for they regarded Peter as the ideal of the modern young Englishman. "If only my boy grows up to be like Peter Riley!" they used to say to themselves; and then add quickly, "But of course he'll be much nicer." In their ignorance they didn't see that it was the Peters of England who were making our country the laughing-stock of the world.

If you had been in Berlin in 1916, you would have seen Peter; for he had been persuaded, much against his will, to uphold the honour of Great Britain in the middle-weights at the Olympic Games. He got a position in the papers as "P. Riley, disqualified"—

the result, he could only suppose, of his folly in allowing his opponent to butt him in the stomach. He was both annoyed and amused about it; offered to fight his vanquisher any time in England; and privately thanked Heaven that he could now get back to London in time for his favourite sister's wedding.

But he didn't. The English trainer, who had been sent, at the public expense, to America for a year, to study the proper methods, got hold of him.

"I've been watching you, young man," he said. "You'll have to give yourself up to me now. You're the coming champion."

"I'm sorry," said Peter politely, "but I shan't be fighting again."

"Fighting!" said the trainer scornfully. "Don't you worry; I'll take good care that you don't fight any more. The event you're going to win is 'Pushing the Chisel.' I've been watching you, and you've got the most perfect neck and calf-muscles for it I've ever seen. No more fighting for you, my boy; nor cricket, nor anything else. I'm not going to let you spoil those muscles."

"I don't think I've ever pushed the Chisel," said Peter. "Besides, it's over, isn't it?"

"Over? Of course it's over, and that confounded American won. 'Poor old England,' as all the papers said."

"Then it's too late to begin to practise," said Peter thankfully.

"Well, it's too late for the 1920 games. But we can do a lot in eight years, and I think I can get you fit for the 1924 games at Pekin."

Peter stared at him in amazement.

"My good man," he said at last, "in 1924 I shall be in London; and I hope in the House of Commons."

"And what about the honour of your country? Do you want to read the jeers in the American papers when we lose 'Pushing the Chisel' in 1924?"

"I don't care a curse what the American papers say," said Peter angrily.

"Then you're very different from other Englishmen," said the trainer sternly.

Of course, Peter was persuaded; he couldn't let England be the laughing-stock of the world. So for eight years he lived under the eye of the trainer, rising at five and retiring to bed at seven-thirty. This prevented him from taking much part in the ordinary social activities of the evening; and even his luncheon and garden-party invitations had to be declined in some such words as "Mr. Peter Riley regrets that he is unable to accept Lady Vavasour's kind invitation for Monday the 13th, as he will be hopping round the

160

garden on one leg then." His career, too, had to be abandoned; for it was plain that, even if he had the leisure to get into Parliament, the early hours he kept would not allow him to take part in any important divisions.

But there were compensations. As he watched his calves swell; as he looked in the glass and noticed each morning that his head was a little more on one side—sure sign of the expert Chisel-pusher; as, still surer sign, his hands became more knuckly and his mouth remained more permanently open, he knew that his devotion to duty would not be without its reward. He saw already his country triumphing, and heard the chorus of congratulation in the newspapers that England was still a nation of sportsmen....

In 1924 Pekin was crowded. There were, of course, the ordinary million inhabitants; and, in addition, people had thronged from all parts to see the great Chisel-pusher of whom so much had been heard. That they did not come in vain, we in London knew one July morning as we opened our papers.

"Pushing the Chisel *(Free Style)*.

"1. P. Riley (Great Britain), 5-3/4 in. (World's Record). 2. H. Biffpoffer (America), 5-1/2 in. A. Wafer (America) was disqualified for going outside the wood."

And so England was herself again. There was only one discordant note in her triumph. Mr. P. A. Vaile pointed out in all the papers that Peter Riley, in the usual pig-headed English way, had been employing entirely the wrong grip. Mr. Vaile's book, How to Push the Chisel, illustrated with 50 full plates of Mr. Vaile in knickerbockers pushing the Chisel, explained the correct method.

THE BIRTHDAY PRESENT

"It's my birthday to-morrow," said Mrs. Jeremy as she turned the pages of her engagement book.

"Bless us, so it is," said Jeremy. "You're thirty-nine or twenty-seven or something. I must go and examine the wine-cellar. I believe there's one bottle left in the Apollinaris bin. It's the only stuff in the house that fizzes."

161

"Jeremy! I'm only twenty-six."

"You don't look it, darling; I mean you do look it, dear. What I mean—well, never mind that. Let's talk about birthday presents. Think of something absolutely tremendous for me to give you."

"A rope of pearls."

"I didn't mean that sort of tremendousness," said Jeremy quickly. "Anyone could give you a rope of pearls; it's simply a question of overdrawing enough from the bank. I meant something difficult that would really prove my love for you—like Lloyd George's ear or the Kaiser's cigar-holder. Something where I could kill somebody for you first. I am in a very devoted mood this morning."

"Are you really?" smiled Mrs. Jeremy. "Because——"

"I am. So is Baby, unfortunately. She will probably want to give you something horribly expensive. Between ourselves, dear, I shall be glad when Baby is old enough to buy her own presents for her mamma. Last Christmas her idea of a complete edition of Meredith and a pair of silver-backed brushes nearly ruined me."

"You won't be ruined this time, Jeremy. I don't want you to give me anything; I want you to show that devotion of yours by doing something for me."

"Anything," said Jeremy grandly. "Shall I swim the Channel? I was practising my new trudgeon stroke in the bath this morning." He got up from his chair and prepared to give an exhibition of it.

"No, nothing like that." Mrs. Jeremy hesitated, looked anxiously at him, and then went boldly at it. "I want you to go in for that physical culture that everyone's talking about."

"Who's everyone? Cook hasn't said a word to me on the subject; neither has Baby; neither has——"

"Mrs. Hodgkin was talking to me about it yesterday. She was saying how thin you were looking."

"The scandal that goes on in these villages," sighed Jeremy. "And the Vicar's wife too. Dear, all this is weeks and weeks old; I suppose it has only just reached the Vicarage. Do let us be up-to-date. Physical culture has been quite démodé since last Thursday."

"Well, I never saw anything in the paper"——

"Knowing what wives are, I hid it from you. Let us now, my dear wife, talk of something else."

"Jeremy! Not for my birthday present?" said his wife in a reproachful voice. "The Vicar does them every morning," she added casually.

"Poor beggar! But it's what Vicars are for." Jeremy chuckled to himself. "I should love to see him," he said. "I suppose it's private, though. Perhaps if I said 'Press'——"

"You are thin, you know."

"My dear, the proper way to get fat is not to take violent exercise, but to lie in a hammock all day and drink milk. Besides, do you want a fat husband? Does Baby want a fat father? You wouldn't like, at your next garden party, to have everybody asking you in a whisper, 'Who is the enormously stout gentleman?' If Nature made me thin—or, to be more accurate, slender and of a pleasing litheness—let us believe that she knew best."

"It isn't only thinness; these exercises keep you young and well and active in mind."

"Like the Vicar?"

"He's only just begun," said his wife hastily.

"Let's wait a bit and watch him," suggested Jeremy. "If his sermons really get better, then I'll think about it seriously. I make you a present of his baldness; I shan't ask for any improvement there."

Mrs. Jeremy went over to her husband and patted the top of his head.

"'In a very devoted mood this morning,'" she quoted.

Jeremy looked unhappy.

"What pains me most about this," he said, "is the revelation of your shortcomings as a wife. You ought to think me the picture of manly beauty. Baby does. She thinks that, next to the postman, I am one of the——"

"So you are, dear."

"Well, why not leave it? Really, I can't waste my time fattening refined gold and stoutening the lily. I am a busy man. I walk up and down the pergola, I keep a dog, I paint little water-colours, I am treasurer of the cricket club; my life is full of activities."

"This only takes a quarter of an hour before your bath, Jeremy."

"I am shaving then; I should cut myself and get all the soap in my eyes. It would be most dangerous. When you were a widow, and Baby and the pony were orphans, you and Mrs. Hodgkin would be sorry. But it would be too late. The Vicar, tearing himself away from Position 5 to conduct the funeral service——"

"Jeremy, don't!"

"Ah, woman, now I move you. You are beginning to see what you were in danger of doing. Death I laugh at; but a fat death—the death of a stout man who has swallowed the shaving-brush through taking too deep a breath before beginning Exercise 3, that is more than I can bear."

"Jeremy!"

"When I said I wanted to kill someone for you, I didn't think

163

you would suggest myself, least of all that you wanted me fattened up like a Christmas turkey first. To go down to posterity as the large-bodied gentleman who inhaled the badger's hair; to be billed in the London press in the words, 'Curious Fatal Accident to Adipose Treasurer'—to do this simply by way of celebrating your twenty-sixth birthday, when we actually have a bottle of Apollinaris left in the Apollinaris bin—darling, you cannot have been thinking-"

His wife patted his head again gently. "Oh, Jeremy, you hopeless person," she sighed. "Give me a new sunshade. I want one badly."

"No," said Jeremy, "Baby shall give you that. For myself I am still feeling that I should like to kill somebody for you. Lloyd George? No. F. E. Smith? N-no...." He rubbed his head thoughtfully. "Who invented those exercises?" he asked suddenly.

"A German, I think."

"Then," said Jeremy, buttoning up his coat, "I shall go and kill him."

ONE OF OUR SUFFERERS

There is no question before the country of more importance than that of National Health. In my own small way I have made something of a study of it, and when a Royal Commission begins its enquiries, I shall put before it the evidence which I have accumulated. I shall lay particular stress upon the health of Thomson.

"You'll beat me to-day," he said, as he swung his club stiffly on the first tee; "I shan't be able to hit a ball."

"You should have some lessons," I suggested.

Thomson gave a snort of indignation.

"It's not that," he said. "But I've been very seedy lately, and—"

"That's all right; I shan't mind. I haven't played a thoroughly well man for a month, now."

"You know, I think my liver——"

I held up my hand.

"Not before my caddie, please," I said severely; "he is quite a child."

Thomson said no more for the moment, but hit his ball hard and straight along the ground.

"It's perfectly absurd," he said with a shrug; "I shan't be able to give you a game at all. Well, if you don't mind playing a sick man——"

"Not if you don't mind being one," I replied, and drove a ball which also went along the ground, but not so far as my opponent's. "There! I'm about the only man in England who can do that when he's quite well."

The ball was sitting up nicely for my second shot, and I managed to put it on the green. Thomson's, fifty yards farther on, was reclining in the worst part of a bunker which he had forgotten about.

"Well, really," he said, "there's an example of luck for you. Your ball——"

"I didn't do it on purpose," I pleaded. "Don't be angry with me."

He made two attempts to get out, and then picked his ball up. We walked in silence to the second tee.

"This time," I said, "I shall hit the sphere properly," and with a terrific swing I stroked it gently into a gorse bush. I looked at the thing in disgust and then felt my pulse. Apparently I was still quite well. Thomson, forgetting about his liver, drove a beauty. We met on the green.

"Five," I said.

"Only five?" asked Thomson suspiciously.

"Six," I said, holing a very long putt.

Thomson's health had a relapse. He took four short putts and was down in seven.

"It's really rather absurd," he said, in a conversational way, as we went to the next tee, "that putting should be so ridiculously important. Take that hole, for instance. I get on the green in a perfect three; you fluff your drive completely and get on in—what was it?"

"Five," I said again.

"Er—five. And yet you win the hole. It is rather absurd, isn't it?"

"I've often thought so," I admitted readily. "That is to say, when I've taken four putts. I'm two up."

On the third tee Thomson's health became positively alarming. He missed the ball altogether.

"It's ridiculous to try to play," he said, with a forced laugh. "I can't see the ball at all."

"It's still there," I assured him.

He struck at it again and it hurried off into a ditch.

"Look here," he said, "wouldn't you rather play the pro.? This is not much of a match for you."

I considered. Of course, a game with the pro. would be much pleasanter than a game with Thomson, but ought I to leave him in his present serious condition of health? His illness was approaching its critical stage, and it was my duty to pull him through if I could.

"No, no," I said. "Let's go on. The fresh air will do you good."

"Perhaps it will," he said hopefully. "I'm sorry I'm like this, but I've had a cold hanging about for some days, and that on the top of my liver——"

"Quite so," I said.

The climax was reached, at the next hole, when, with several strokes in hand, he topped his approach shot into a bunker. For my sake he tried to look as though he had meant to run it up along the ground, having forgotten about the intervening hazard. It was a brave effort to hide from me the real state of his health, but he soon saw that it was hopeless. He sighed and pressed his hand to his eyes. Then he held his fingers a foot away from him, and looked at them as if he were trying to count them correctly. His state was pitiable, and I felt that at any cost I must save him.

I did. The corner was turned at the fifth, where I took four putts.

"You aren't going to win all the holes," he said grudgingly, as he ran down his putt.

Convalescence set in at the sixth, when I got into an impossible place and picked up.

"Oh, well, I shall give you a game yet," he said. "Two down."

The need for further bulletins ceased at the seventh hole, which he played really well and won easily.

"A-ha, you won't beat me by much," he said, "in spite of my liver."

"By the way, how is the liver?" I asked.

"Your fresh-air cure is doing it good. Of course, it may come on again, but——" He drove a screamer. "I think I shall be all right," he announced.

"All square," he said cheerily at the ninth. "I fancy I'm going to beat you now. Not bad, you know, considering you were four up. Practically speaking, I gave you a start of four holes."

I decided that it was time to make an effort again, seeing that Thomson's health was now thoroughly re-established. Of the next seven holes I managed to win three and halve two. It is only fair to say, though (as Thomson did several times), that I had an extraordinary amount of good luck, and that he was dogged by ill-fortune throughout. But this, after all, is as nothing so long as one's

166

health is above suspicion. The great thing was that Thomson's liver suffered no relapse; even though, at the seventeenth tee, he was one down and two to play.

And it was on the seventeenth tee that I had to think seriously how I wanted the match to end. Thomson at lunch when he has won is a very different man from Thomson at lunch when he has lost. The more I thought about it, the more I realized that I was in rather a happy position. If I won, I won—which was jolly; if I lost, Thomson won—and we should have a pleasant lunch.

However, as it happened, the match was halved.

"Yes, I was afraid so," said Thomson; "I let you get too long a start. It's absurd to suppose that I can give you four holes up and beat you. It practically amounts to giving you four bisques. Four bisques is about six strokes—I'm not really six strokes better than you."

"What about lunch?" I suggested.

"Good; and you can have your revenge afterwards." He led the way into the pavilion. "Now I wonder," he said, "what I can safely eat. I want to be able to give you some sort of a game this afternoon."

Well, if there is ever a Royal Commission upon the national physique I shall insist on giving evidence. For it seems to me that golf, far from improving the health of the country, is actually undermining it. Thomson, at any rate, since he has taken to the game, has never been quite fit.

IN THE SWIM

"Do you tango?" asked Miss Hopkins, as soon as we were comfortably seated. I know her name was Hopkins, because I had her down on my programme as Popkins, which seemed too good to be true; and, in order to give her a chance of reconsidering it, I had asked her if she was one of the Popkinses of Hampshire. It had then turned out that she was really one of the Hopkinses of Maida Vale.

"No," I said, "I don't." She was only the fifth person who had asked me, but then she was only my fifth partner.

"Oh, you ought to. You must be up-to-date, you know."

"I'm always a bit late with these things," I explained. "The waltz came to England in 1812, but I didn't really master it till 1904."

"I'm afraid if you wait as long as that before you master the tango it will be out."

"That's what I thought. By the time I learnt the tango, the bingo would be in. My idea was to learn the bingo in advance, so as to be ready for it. Think how you'll all envy me in 1917. Think how Society will flock to my Bingo Quick Lunches. I shall be the only man in London who bingoes properly. Of course, by 1918 you'll all be at it."

"Then we must have one together in 1918," smiled Miss Hopkins.

"In 1918," I pointed out coldly, "I shall be learning the pongo."

My next partner had no name that I could discover, but a fund of conversation.

"Do you tango?" she asked me as soon as we were comfortably seated.

"No," I said, "I don't. But," I added, "I once learned the minuet."

"Oh, they're not very much alike, are they?"

"Not a bit. However, luckily that doesn't matter, because I've forgotten all the steps now."

She seemed a little puzzled and decided to change the subject.

"Are you going to learn the tango?" she asked.

"I don't think so. It took me four months to learn the minuet."

"But they're quite different, aren't they?"

"Quite," I agreed.

As she seemed to have exhausted herself for the moment, it was obviously my business to say something. There was only one thing to say.

"Do you tango?" I asked.

"No," she said, "I don't."

"Are you going to learn?"

"Oh, yes!"

"Ah!" I said; and five minutes later we parted for ever.

The next dance really was a tango, and I saw to my horror that I had a name down for it. With some difficulty I found the owner of it, and prepared to explain to her that unfortunately I couldn't dance the tango, but that for profound conversation about it I was undoubtedly the man. Luckily she explained first.

"I'm afraid I can't do this," she apologised. "I'm so sorry."

"Not at all," I said magnanimously. "We'll sit it out."

We found a comfortable seat.

"Do you tango?" she asked.

I was tired of saying "No."

"Yes," I said.

"Are you sure you wouldn't like to find somebody else to do it with?"

"Quite, thanks. The fact is I do it rather differently from the way they're doing it here to-night. You see, I actually learnt it in the Argentine."

She was very much interested to hear this.

"Really? Are you out there much? I've got an uncle living there now. I wonder if——"

"When I say I learnt it in the Argentine," I explained, "I mean that I was actually taught it in St. John's Wood, but that my dancing mistress came from——"

"In St. John's Wood?" she said eagerly. "But how funny! My sister is learning there. I wonder if——"

She was a very difficult person to talk to. Her relations seemed to spread themselves all over the place.

"Perhaps that is hardly doing justice to the situation," I explained again. "It would be more accurate to put it like this. When I decided—by the way, does your family frequent Paris? No? Good. Well, when I decided to learn the tango, the fact that my friends the Hopkinses of St. John's Wood, or rather Maida Vale, had already learnt it in Paris naturally led me to—— I say, what about an ice? It's getting awfully hot in here."

"Oh, I don't think——"

"I'll go and get them," I said hastily; and I went and took a long time getting them, and, as it turned out that she didn't want hers after all, a longer time eating them. When I was ready for conversation again the next dance was beginning. With a bow I relinquished her to another.

"Come along," said a bright voice behind me; "this is ours."

"Hallo, Norah, is that you? Come on."

We hurried in, danced in silence, and then found ourselves a comfortable seat. For a moment neither of us spoke....

"Have you learnt the tango yet?" asked Norah.

"Fourteen," I said aloud.

"Help! Does that mean that I'm the fourteenth person who has asked you?"

"The night is yet young, Norah. You are only the eighth. But I was betting that you'd ask me before I counted twenty. You lost, and you owe me a pair of ivory-backed hair-brushes and a cigar-cutter."

"Bother! Anyhow, I'm not going to be stopped talking about the tango if I want to. Did you know I was learning? I can do the scissors."

"Good. We'll do the new Fleet Street movement together, the scissors-and-paste. You go into the ball-room and do the scissors, and I'll—er—stick here and do the paste."

"Can't you really do any of it at all, and aren't you going to learn?"

"I can't do any of it at all, Norah. I am not going to learn, Norah."

"It isn't so very difficult, you know. I'd teach you myself for tuppence."

"Will you stop talking about it for threepence?" I asked, and I took out three coppers.

"No."

I sighed and put them back again.

It was the last dance of the evening. My hostess, finding me lonely, had dragged me up to somebody, and I and whatever her name was were in the supper-room drinking our farewell soup. So far we had said nothing to each other. I waited anxiously for her to begin. Suddenly she began.

"Have you thought about Christmas presents yet?" she asked.

I nearly swooned. With difficulty I remained in an upright position. She was the first person who had not begun by asking me if I danced the tango!

"Excuse me," I said. "I'm afraid I didn't—would you tell me your name again?"

I felt that it ought to be celebrated in some way. I had some notion of writing a sonnet to her.

"Hopkins," she said; "I knew you'd forgotten me."

"Of course I haven't," I said, suddenly remembering her. The sonnet would never be written now. "We had a dance together before."

"Yes," she said. "Let me see," she added, "I did ask you if you danced the tango, didn't I?"

THE MEN WHO SUCCEED

THE HEIR

Mr. Trevor Pilkington, of the well-known firm of Trevor Pilkington, fixed his horn spectacles carefully upon his nose, took a pinch of snuff, sneezed twice, gave his papers a preliminary rustle, looked slowly round the crowded room, and began to read the will. Through forty years of will-reading his method of procedure had always been the same. But Jack Summers, who was sharing an ottoman with two of the outdoor servants, thought that Mr. Pilkington's mannerisms were designed specially to annoy him, and he could scarcely control his impatience.

Yet no one ever had less to hope from the reading of a will than Jack. For the first twenty years of his life his parents had brought him up to believe that his cousin Cecil was heir to his Uncle Alfred's enormous fortune, and for the subsequent ten years his cousin Cecil had brought his Uncle Alfred up in the same belief. Indeed, Cecil had even roughed out one or two wills for signature, and had offered to help his uncle—who, however, preferred to do these things by himself—to hold the pen. Jack could not help feeling glad that his cousin was not there to parade his approaching triumph; a nasty cold, caught a week previously in attending his uncle to the Lord Mayor's Show, having kept Cecil in bed.

"To the Society for the Prevention of Cruelty to Children, ten shillings and sixpence"—the words came to him in a meaningless drone—"to the Fresh Air Fund, ten shillings and sixpence; to the King Edward Hospital Fund, ten shillings and sixpence"—was all the money going in charities?—"to my nephew Cecil Linley, who has taken such care of me"—Mr. Pilkington hesitated—"four shillings and ninepence; to my nephew, John Summers, whom, thank Heaven, I have never seen, five million pounds——"

A long whistle of astonishment came from the ottoman. The solicitor looked up with a frown.

"It's the surprise," apologised Jack. "I hardly expected so much. I thought that that brute—I mean I thought my cousin Cecil had nobbled—that is to say, was getting it all."

"The late Mr. Alfred made three wills," said the lawyer in a moment of expansion. "In the first he left his nephew Cecil a legacy of one shilling and tenpence, in the second he bequeathed him a sum of three shillings and twopence, and in the last he set aside the amount of four shillings and ninepence. The evidence seems to show that your cousin was rapidly rising in his uncle's estimation. You, on the other hand, have always been a legatee to the amount of five million pounds; but in the last will there is a trifling condition attached." He resumed his papers. "To my nephew, John Summers, five million pounds, on condition that, within one year from the date of my death, he marries Mary Huggins, the daughter of my old friend, now deceased, William Huggins."

Jack Summers rose proudly from his end of the ottoman.

"Thanks," he said curtly. "That tears it. It's very kind of the old gentleman, but I prefer to choose a wife for myself." He bowed to the company and strode from the room.

It was a cloudless August day. In the shadow of the great elms that fringed the Sussex lane a girl sat musing; on its side in the grass at her feet a bicycle, its back wheel deflated. She sat on the grassy bank with her hat in her lap, quite content to wait until the first passer-by with a repairing outfit in his pocket should offer to help her.

"Can I be of any assistance?" said a manly voice, suddenly waking her from her reverie.

She turned with a start. The owner of the voice was dressed in a stylish knickerbocker suit; his eyes were blue, his face was tanned, his hair was curly, and he was at least six foot tall. So much she noticed at a glance.

"My bicycle," she said; "punctured."

In a minute he was on his knees beside the machine. A rapid examination convinced him that she had not over-stated the truth, and he whipped from his pocket the repairing outfit without which he never travelled.

"I can do it in a moment," he said. "At least, if you can just help me a little."

As she knelt beside him he could not fail to be aware of her wonderful beauty. The repairs, somehow, took longer than he thought. Their heads were very close together all the time, and indeed on one occasion came violently into contact.

"There," he said at last, getting up and barking his shin against the pedal. "Conf—— That will be all right."

"Thank you," she said tenderly.

He looked at her without disguising his admiration; a tall, straight figure in the sunlight, its right shin rubbing itself vigorously against its left calf.

"It's absurd," he said at last; "I feel as if I've known you for years. And, anyway, I'm certain I've seen you before somewhere."

"Did you ever go to The Seaside Girl?" she asked eagerly.

"Often."

"Do you remember the Spanish princess who came on at the beginning of the Second Act and said, 'Wow-wow!' to the Mayor?"

"Why, of course! And you had your photograph in The Sketch, The Tatler, The Bystander, and The Sporting and Dramatic all in the same week?"

The girl nodded happily. "Yes, I'm Marie Huguenot!" she said.

"And I'm Jack Summers; so now we know each other." He took her hand. "Marie," he said, "ever since I have mended your bicycle—I mean, ever since I have known you, I have loved you. Will you marry me?"

"Jack!" she cooed. "You did say 'Jack,' didn't you?"

"Bless you, Marie. We shall be very poor, dear. Will you mind?"

"Not with you, Jack. At least, not if you mean what I mean by 'very poor.'"

"Two thousand a year."

"Yes, that's about what I meant."

Jack took her in his arms.

"And Mary Huggins can go and marry the Pope," he said, with a smile.

With a look of alarm in her eyes she pushed him suddenly away from her. There was a crash as his foot went through the front wheel of the bicycle.

"Mary Huggins?" she cried.

"Yes, I was left a fortune on condition that I married a person called Mary Huggins. Absurd! As though——"

"How much?"

"Oh, quite a lot if it wasn't for these confounded death duties. Five million pounds. You see——"

"Jack, Jack!" cried the girl. "Don't you understand? I am Mary Huggins."

He looked at her in amazement.

"You said your name was Marie Huguenot," he said slowly.

"My stage name, dear. Naturally I couldn't—I mean, one must—you know how particular managers are. When father died and I had to go on the stage for a living——"

"Marie, my darling!"

Mary rose and picked up her bicycle. The air had gone out of the back wheel again, and there were four spokes broken, but she did not heed it.

173

"You must write to your lawyer to-night," she said. "Won't he be surprised?"

But, being a great reader of the magazines, he wasn't.

THE STATESMAN

On a certain night in the middle of the season all London was gathered in Lady Marchpane's drawing-room; all London, that is, which was worth knowing—a qualification which accounted for the absence of several million people who had never heard of Lady Marchpane. In one corner of the room an Ambassador, with a few ribbons across his chest, could have been seen chatting to the latest American Duchess; in another corner one of our largest Advertisers was exchanging epigrams with a titled Newspaper Proprietor. Famous Generals rubbed shoulders with Post-Impressionist Artists; Financiers whispered sweet nothings to Breeders of prize Poms; even an Actor-Manager might have been seen accepting an apology from a Royalty who had jostled him.

"Hallo," said Algy Lascelles, catching sight of the dignified figure of Rupert Meryton in the crowd; "how's William?"

A rare smile lit up Rupert's distinguished features. He was Under Secretary for Invasion Affairs, and "William" was Algy's pleasant way of referring to the Bill which he was now piloting through the House of Commons. It was a measure for doing something or other by means of a what-d'you-call-it—I cannot be more precise without precipitating a European Conflict.

"I think we shall get it through," said Rupert calmly.

"Lady Marchpane was talking about it just now. She's rather interested, you know."

Rupert's lips closed about his mouth in a firm line. He looked over Algy's head into the crowd. "Oh!" he said coldly.

It was barely ten years ago that young Meryton, just down from Oxford, had startled the political world by capturing the important seat of Cricklewood (E.) for the Tariffadicals—as, to avoid plunging the country into Civil War, I must call them. This was at a by-election, and the Liberatives had immediately dissolved, only to come into power after the General Election with an increased majority. Through the years that followed, Rupert Meryton, by his

174

pertinacity in asking the Invasion Secretary questions which had been answered by him on the previous day, and by his regard for the dignity of the House, as shown in his invariable comment, "Come, come—not quite the gentleman," upon any display of bad manners opposite, established a clear right to a post in the subsequent Tariffadical Government. He had now been Under Secretary for two years, and in this Bill his first real chance had come.

"Oh, there you are, Mr. Meryton," said a voice. "Come and talk to me a moment." With a nod to a couple of Archbishops Lady Marchpane led the way to a little gallery whither the crowd had not penetrated. Priceless Correggios, Tintorettos, and G. K. Chestertons hung upon the walls, but it was not to show him these that she had come. Dropping into a wonderful old Chippendale chair, she motioned him to a Blundell-Maple opposite her, and looked at him with a curious smile.

"Well," she said, "about the Bill?"

Rupert's lips closed about his mouth in a firm line. (He was rather good at this.) Folding his arms, he gazed steadily into Lady Marchpane's still beautiful eyes.

"It will go through," he said. "Through all its stages," he added professionally.

"It must not go through," said Lady Marchpane gently.

Rupert could not repress a start, but he was master of himself again in a moment.

"I cannot add anything to my previous statement," he said.

"If it goes through," began Lady Marchpane——

"I must refer you," said Rupert, "to my answer of yesterday."

"Come, come, Mr. Meryton, what is the good of fencing with me? You know the position. Or shall I state it for you again?"

"I cannot believe you are serious."

"I am perfectly serious. There are reasons, financial reasons—and others—why I do not want this Bill to pass. In return for my silence upon a certain matter, you are going to prevent it passing. You know to what I refer. On the 4th of May last——"

"Stop!" cried Rupert hoarsely.

"On the 4th of May last," Lady Marchpane went on relentlessly, "you and I—in the absence of my husband abroad—had tea together at an A.B.C." (Rupert covered his face with his hands.) "I am no fonder of scandal than you are, but if you do not meet my wishes I shall certainly confess the truth to Marchpane."

"You will be ruined too!" said Rupert.

"My husband will forgive me and take me back." She paused significantly. "Will Marjorie Hale——" (Rupert covered his hands with his face)—"will the good Miss Hale forgive you? She is very strict, is she not? And rich? And rising young politicians want money more than scandal." She raised her head suddenly at the sound of footsteps. "Ah, Archbishop, I was just calling Mr. Meryton's attention to this wonderful Botticell——" (she looked at it more closely)——"this wonderful Dana Gibson. A beautiful piece of work, is it not?" The intruders passed on to the supper-room, and they were alone again.

"What am I to do?" said Rupert sullenly.

"The fate of the Bill is settled to-day week, when you make your big speech. You must speak against it. Confess frankly you were mistaken. It will be a close thing, anyhow. Your influence will turn the scale."

"It will ruin me politically."

"You will marry Marjorie Hale and be rich. No rich man is ever ruined politically. Or socially." She patted his hand gently. "You'll do it?"

He got up slowly. "You'll see next week," he said.

It is not meet that we should watch the unhappy Rupert through the long-drawn hours of the night, as he wrestled with the terrible problem. A moment's sudden madness on that May afternoon had brought him to the cross-roads. On the one hand, reputation, wealth, the girl that he loved; on the other, his own honour and—so, at least, he had said several times on the platform—the safety of England. He rose in the morning weary, but with his mind made up.

The Bill should go through!

Rupert Meryton was a speaker of a not unusual type. Although he provided the opinions himself, he always depended upon his secretary for the arguments with which to support them and the actual words in which to give them being. But on this occasion he felt that a special effort was required of him. He would show Lady Marchpane that the blackmail of yesterday had only roused him to a still greater effort on behalf of his country. He would write his own speech.

On the fateful night the House was crowded. It seemed that all the guests at Lady Marchpane's a week before were in the Distinguished Strangers' Gallery or behind the Ladies' Grille. From the Press Gallery "Our Special Word-painter" looked down upon the statesmen beneath him, his eagle eye ready to detect on the moment the Angry Flush, the Wince, or the Sudden Paling of enemy, the Grim Smile or the Lofty Calm of friend.

The Rt. Hon. Rupert Meryton, Tariffadical Member for Cricklewood (E.) rose to his feet amidst cheers.

"Mr. Speaker," he said, "I rise—er—to-night, sir—h'r'm, to—

176

er——" So much of his speech I may give, but urgent State reasons compel me to withhold the rest. Were it ever known with which Bill the secret history that I have disclosed concerns itself, the Great Powers in an instant would be at each other's throats. But though I may not disclose the speech I can tell of its effect on the House. And its effect was curious. It was, in fact, the exact opposite of what Rupert Meryton, that promising Under Secretary, had intended.

It was the first speech that he had ever prepared himself. Than Rupert there was no more dignified figure in the House of Commons; his honour was proof, as we have seen, against the most insidious temptations; yet, since one man cannot have all the virtues, he was distinctly stupid. It would have been a hopeless speech anyhow; but, to make matters worse, he had, in the most important part of it, attempted irony. And at the beginning of the ironical passage even the Tariffadical word-painters had to confess that it was their own stalwarts who "suddenly paled."

As Lady Marchpane had said, it was bound to be a close thing. The Liberatives and the Unialists, of course, were solid against the Bill, but there was also something of a cave in the Tariffadical Party. It was bound to be a close thing, and Rupert's speech just made the difference. When he sat down the waverers and doubters had made up their minds.

The Bill was defeated.

That the Tariffadicals should resign was natural; perhaps it was equally natural that Rupert's secretary should resign too. He said that his reputation would be gone if Rupert made any more speeches on his own, and that he wasn't going to risk it. Without his secretary Rupert was lost at the General Election which followed. Fortunately he had a grateful friend in Lady Marchpane. She exerted her influence with the Liberatives, and got him an appointment as Governor of the Stickjaw Islands. Here, with his beautiful and rich wife, Sir Rupert Meryton maintains a regal state, and upon his name no breath of scandal rests. Indeed, his only trouble so far has been with the Stickjaw language—a difficult language, but one which, perhaps fortunately, does not lend itself to irony.

THE MAGNATE

It was in October, 19— that the word "Zinc" first began to be heard in financial circles. City men, pushing their dominoes regretfully away, and murmuring "Zinc" in apologetic tones, were back in their offices by three o'clock, forgetting in their haste to leave the usual twopence under the cup for the waitress. Clubmen, glancing at the tape on their way to the smoking-room, said to their neighbours, "Zinc's moved a point, I see," before covering themselves up with The Times. In the trains, returning husbands asked each other loudly, "What's all this about zinc?"—all save the very innocent ones, who whispered, "I say, what is zinc exactly?" The music-halls took it up. No sooner had the word "Zinc" left the lips of an acknowledged comedian than the house was in roars of laughter. The furore at the Collodium when Octavius Octo, in his world-famous part of the landlady of a boarding-house, remarked, "I know why my ole man's so late. 'E's buying zinc," is still remembered in the bars round Piccadilly.

To explain it properly it will be necessary (my readers will be alarmed to hear) to go back some thirty years. This, as a simple calculation shows, takes us to June, 18—. It was in June, 18— that Felix Moses, a stout young man of attractive appearance (if you care for that style), took his courage in both hands, and told Phyllida Sloan that he was worth ten thousand a year and was changing his name to Mountenay. Miss Sloan, seeing that it was the beginning of a proposal, said hastily that she was changing hers to Abraham.

"You're marrying Leo Abraham?" asked Felix in amazement. "Ah!" A gust of jealousy swept over him. He licked his lips. There was a dangerous look in his eyes—a look that was destined in after days to make Emperors and rival financiers quail. "Ah!" he said softly. "Leo Abraham! I shall not forget!"

And now it will be necessary (my readers will be relieved to learn) to jump forward some thirty years. This obviously takes us to September 19—. Let us on this fine September morning take a peep into "No. — Throgneedle Street, E.C.," and see how the business of the mother city is carried on.

On the fourth floor we come to the sanctum of the great man himself. "Mr. Felix Mountenay—No admittance," is painted upon the outer door. It is a name which is known and feared all over Europe. Mr. Mountenay's private detective stands on one side of the door; on the other side is Mr. Mountenay's private wolf-hound. Murmuring the word "Press," however, we pass hastily through, and find ourselves before Mr. Mountenay himself. Mr. Mountenay is at work; let us watch him through a typical five minutes.

For a moment he stands meditating in the middle of the room. Kings are tottering on their thrones. Empires hang upon his nod. What will he decide? Suddenly he blows a cloud of smoke from his cigar, and rushes to the telephone.

"Hallo! Is that you, Jones?... What are Margarine Prefs. at?... What?... No, Margarine Prefs., idiot.... Ah! Then sell. Keep on selling till I tell you to stop.... Yes."

He hangs up the receiver. For two minutes he paces the room, smoking rapidly. He stops a moment ... but it is only to remove his cigar-band, which is in danger of burning. Then he resumes his pacings. Another minute goes rapidly by. He rushes to the telephone again.

"Hallo! Is that you, Jones?... What are Margarine Prefs. down to now?... Ah! Then buy. Keep on buying.... Yes."

He hangs up the receiver. By this master-stroke he has made a quarter of a million. It may seem to you or me an easy way of doing it. Ah, but what, we must ask ourselves, of the great brain that conceived the idea, the foresight which told the exact moment when to put it into action, the cool courage which seized the moment— what of the grasp of affairs, the knowledge of men? Ah! Can we grudge it him that he earns a quarter of a million more quickly than we do?

Yet Mr. Felix Mountenay is not happy. When we have brought off a coup for a hundred thousand even, we smile gaily. Mr. Mountenay did not smile. Fiercely he bit another inch off his cigar, and muttered to himself.

The words were "Leo Abraham! Wait!"

This is positively the last row of dots. Let us take advantage of them to jump forward another month. It was October 1st, 19—. (If that was a Sunday, then it was October 2nd. Anyhow, it was October.)

Mr. Felix Mountenay was sleeping in his office. For once that iron brain relaxed. He had made a little over three million in the last month, and the strain was too much for him. But a knock at the door restored him instantly to his own cool self.

"I beg your pardon, sir," said his secretary, "but somebody is selling zinc."

The word "zinc" touched a chord in Mr. Mountenay's brain which had lain dormant for years. Zinc! Why did zinc remind him of Leo Abraham?

"Fetch the Encyclopedia Britannica, quick!" he cried.

The secretary, a man of herculean build, returned with some

of it. With the luck which proverbially attends rich men, Mr. Mountenay picked up the "Z" volume at once. As he read the Zinc article it all came back to him. Leo Abraham had owned an empty zinc-mine! Was his enemy in his clutches at last?

"Buy!" he said briefly.

In a fortnight the secretary had returned.

"Well," said Mr. Mountenay, "have you bought all the zinc there is?"

"Yes, sir," said the secretary. "And a lot that there isn't," he added.

"Good!" He paused a moment. "When Mr. Leo Abraham calls," he added grimly, "show him up at once."

It was a month later that a haggard man climbed the stairs of No. — Throgneedle Street, and was shown into Mr. Mountenay's room.

"Well," said the financier softly, "what can I do for you?"

"I want some zinc," said Leo Abergavenny.

"Zinc," said Mr. Mountenay, with a smile, "is a million pounds a ton. Or an acre, or a gallon, or however you prefer to buy it," he added humorously.

Leo went white.

"You wish to ruin me?"

"I do. A promise I made to your wife some years ago."

"My wife?" cried Leo. "What do you mean? I'm not married."

It was Mr. Mountenay's turn to go white. He went it.

"Not married? But Miss Sloan——"

Mr. Leo Abergavenny sat down and mopped his face.

"I don't know what you mean," he said. "I asked Miss Sloan to marry me, and told her I was changing my name to Abergavenny. And she said that she was changing hers to Moses. Naturally, I thought——"

"Stop!" cried Mr. Mountenay. He sat down heavily. Something seemed to have gone out of his life; in a moment the world was empty. He looked up at his old rival, and forced a laugh.

"Well, well," he said; "she deceived us both. Let us drink to our lucky escape." He rang the bell.

"And then," he said in a purring voice, "we can have a little talk about zinc. After all, business is still business."

THE DOCTOR

His slippered feet stretched out luxuriously to the fire, Dr. Venables, of Mudford, lay back in his arm-chair and gave himself up to the delights of his Flor di Cabajo, No. 2, a box of which had been presented to him by an apparently grateful patient. It had been a busy day. He had prescribed more than half a dozen hot milk-puddings and a dozen changes of air; he had promised a score of times to look in again to-morrow; and the Widow Nixey had told him yet again, but at greater length than before, her private opinion of doctors.

Sometimes Gordon Venables wondered whether it was only for this that he had been the most notable student of his year at St. Bartholomew's. His brilliance, indeed, had caused something of a sensation in medical circles, and a remarkable career had been prophesied for him. It was Venables who had broken up one Suffrage meeting after another by throwing white mice at the women on the platform; who day after day had paraded London dressed in the costume of a brown dog, until arrested for biting an anti-vivisector in the leg. No wonder that all the prizes of the profession were announced to be within his grasp, and that when he buried himself in the little country town of Mudford he was thought to have thrown away recklessly opportunities such as were granted to few.

He had been in Mudford for five years now. An occasional paper in The Lancet on "The Recurrence of Anthro-philomelitis in Earth-worms" kept him in touch with modern medical thought, but he could not help feeling that to some extent his powers were rusting in Mudford. As the years went on his chance of Harley Street dwindled.

"Come in," he said in answer to a knock at the door.

The housekeeper's head appeared.

"There's been an accident, sir," she gasped. "Gentleman run over!"

He snatched up his stethoscope and, without even waiting to inquire where the accident was, hurried into the night. Something whispered to him that his chance had come.

After a quarter of an hour he stopped a small boy.

"Hallo, Johnny," he said breathlessly, "where's the accident?"

The boy looked at him with open mouth for some moments. Then he had an idea.

"Why, it's Doctor!" he said.

Dr. Venables pushed him over and ran on....

It was in the High Street that the accident had happened. Lord Lair, an eccentric old gentleman who sometimes walked when he might have driven, had, while dodging a motor-car, been run into by a child's hoop. He lay now on the pavement surrounded by a large and interested crowd.

"Look out," shouted somebody from the outskirts; "here comes Doctor."

Dr. Venables pushed his way through to his patient. His long search for the scene of the accident had exhausted him bodily, but his mind was as clear as ever.

"Stand back there," he said in an authoritative voice. Then, taking out his stethoscope, he made a rapid examination of his patient.

"Incised wound in the tibia," he murmured to himself. "Slight abrasion of the patella and contusion of the left ankle. The injuries are serious but not necessarily mortal. Who is he?"

The butcher, who had been sitting on the head of the fallen man, got up and disclosed the features of Lord Lair. Dr. Venables staggered back.

"His lordship!" he cried. "He is a patient of Dr. Scott's! I have attended the client of another practitioner! Professionally I am ruined!"

Lord Lair, who was now breathing more easily, opened his eyes.

"Take me home," he groaned.

Dr. Venables' situation was a terrible one. Medical etiquette demanded his immediate retirement from the case, but the promptings of humanity and the thought of his client's important position in the world were too strong for him. Throwing his scruples to the winds, he assisted the aged peer on to a hastily improvised stretcher and accompanied him to the Hall.

His lordship once in bed, the doctor examined him again. It was obvious immediately that there was only one hope of saving the patient's life. An injection of anthro-philomelitis must be given without loss of time.

Dr. Venables took off his coat and rolled up his sleeves. He never travelled without a small bottle of this serum in his waistcoat pocket—a serum which, as my readers know, is prepared from the earth-worm, in whose body (fortunately) large deposits of anthro-philomelitis are continually found. With help from a footman in holding down the patient, the injection was made. In less than a year Lord Lair was restored to health.

Dr. Gordon Venables' case came before the British Medical Council early in October. The counts in the indictment were two.

The first was that, "on the 17th of June last, Dr. Gordon Venables did feloniously and with malice aforethought commit the disgusting and infamous crime of attending professionally the client of another practitioner."

The second was that "in the course of rendering professional services to the said client, Dr. Venables did knowingly and wittingly employ the assistance of one who was not a properly registered medical man, to wit, Thomas Boiling, footman, thereby showing himself to be a scurvy fellow of infamous morals."

Dr. Venables decided to apologise. He also decided to send in an account to Lord Lair for two hundred and fifty guineas. He justified this to himself mainly on the ground that, according to a letter in that week's Lancet, the supply of anthro-philomelitis in earth-worms was suddenly giving out, and that it was necessary to recoup himself for the generous quantity he had injected into Lord Lair. Naturally, also, he felt that his lordship, as the author of the whole trouble, owed him something.

The Council, in consideration of his apology, dismissed the first count. On the second count, however, they struck him off the register.

It was a terrible position for a young doctor to be in, but Gordon Venables faced it like a man. With Lord Lair's fee in his pocket he came to town and took a house in Harley Street. When he had paid the first quarter's rent and the first instalment on the hired furniture, he had fifty pounds left.

Ten pounds he spent on embossed stationery.

Forty pounds he spent on postage-stamps.

For the next three months no journal was complete without a letter from 999 Harley Street, signed "Gordon Venables," in which the iniquity of his treatment by the British Medical Council was dwelt upon with the fervour of a man who knew his subject thoroughly; no such letter was complete without a side-reference to anthro-philomelitis (as found, happily, in earth-worms) and the anthro-philomelitis treatment (as recommended by peers). Six months previously the name of Venables had been utterly unknown to the man in the street. In three months' time it was better known even than ——'s, the well-known ——.

One-half of London said he was an infamous quack.

The other half of London said he was a martyred genius.

Both halves agreed that, after all, one might as well try this new what-you-may-call-it treatment, just to see if there was anything in it, don't you know.

It was only last week that Mr. Venables made an excellent speech against the super-tax.

THE NEWSPAPER PROPRIETOR

The great Hector Strong, lord of journalism and swayer of empires, paced the floor of his luxurious apartment with bowed head, his corrugated countenance furrowed with lines of anxiety. He had just returned from a lunch with all his favourite advertisers ... but it was not this which troubled him. He was thinking out a new policy for The Daily Vane.

Suddenly he remembered something. Coming up to town in his third motor, he had glanced through the nineteen periodicals which his house had published that morning, and in one case had noted matter for serious criticism. This was obviously the first business he must deal with.

He seated himself at his desk and pushed the bell marked "38." Instantly a footman presented himself with a tray of sandwiches.

"What do you want?" said Strong coldly.

"You rang for me, sir," replied the trembling menial.

"Go away," said Strong. Recognizing magnanimously, however, that the mistake was his own, he pressed bell "28." In another moment the editor of Sloppy Chunks was before him.

"In to-day's number," said Strong, as he toyed with a blue pencil, "you apologize for a mistake in last week's number." He waited sternly.

"It was a very bad mistake, sir, I'm afraid. We did a great injustice to——"

"You know my rule," said Strong. "The mistake of last week I could have overlooked. The apology of this week is a more serious matter. You will ask for a month's salary on your way out." He pressed a button and the editor disappeared through the trap-door.

Alone again, Hector Strong thought keenly for a moment. Then he pressed bell "38." Instantly a footman presented himself with a tray of sandwiches.

"What do you mean by this?" roared Strong, his iron self-control for a moment giving way.

"I b-beg your pardon, sir," stammered the man. "I th-thought——"

"Get out!" As the footman retired, Strong passed his hand across his forehead. "My memory is bad to-day," he murmured, and pushed bell "48."

A tall thin man entered.

"Ah, good afternoon, Mr. Brownlow," said the Proprietor. He

toyed with his blue pencil. "Let me see, which of our papers are under your charge at the moment?"

Mr. Brownlow reflected.

"Just now," he said, "I am editing Snippety Snips, The Whoop, The Girls' Own Aunt, Parings, Slosh, The Sunday Sermon, and Back Chat."

"Ah! Well, I want you to take on Sloppy Chunks too for a little while. Mr. Symes has had to leave us."

"Yes, sir." Mr. Brownlow bowed and moved to the door.

"By the way," Strong said, "your last number of Slosh was very good. Very good indeed. I congratulate you. Good day."

Left alone, Hector Strong, lord of journalism and swayer of empires, resumed his pacings. His two mistakes with the bell told him that he was distinctly not himself this afternoon. Was it only the need of a new policy for The Vane which troubled him? Or was it——

Could it be Lady Dorothy?

Lady Dorothy Neal was something of an enigma to Hector Strong. He was making more than a million pounds a year, and yet she did not want to marry him. Sometimes he wondered if the woman were quite sane. Yet, mad or sane, he loved her.

A secretary knocked and entered. He waited submissively for half an hour until the Proprietor looked up.

"Well?"

"Lady Dorothy Neal would like to see you for a moment, sir."

"Show her in."

Lady Dorothy came in brightly.

"What nice-looking men you have here," she said. "Who is the one in the blue waistcoat? He has curly hair."

"You didn't come to talk about him?" said Hector reproachfully.

"I didn't come to talk to him really, but if you keep me waiting half an hour—— Why, what are you doing?"

Strong looked up from the note he was writing. The tender lines had gone from his face, and he had become the stern man of action again.

"I am giving instructions that the services of my commissionaire, hall-boy, and fifth secretary will no longer be required."

"Don't do that," pleaded Dorothy.

Strong tore up the note and turned to her. "What do you want of me?" he asked.

She blushed and looked down. "I—I have written a—a play," she faltered.

185

He smiled indulgently. He did not write plays himself, but he knew that other people did.

"When does it come off?" he asked.

"The manager says it will have to at the end of the week. It came on a week ago."

"Well," he smiled, "if people don't want to go, I can't make them."

"Yes, you can," she said boldly.

He gave a start. His brain working at lightning speed saw the possibilities in an instant. At one stroke he could win Lady Dorothy's gratitude, provide The Daily Vane with a temporary policy, and give a convincing exhibition of the power of his press.

"Oh, Mr. Strong——"

"Hector," he whispered. As he rose from his desk to go to her, he accidentally pressed the button of the trap-door. The next moment he was alone.

"That the British public is always ready to welcome the advent of a clean and wholesome home-grown play is shown by the startling success of Christina's Mistake, which is attracting such crowds to The King's every night." So wrote The Daily Vane, and continued in the same strain for a column.

"Clubland is keenly exercised," wrote The Evening Vane, "over a problem of etiquette which arises in the Second Act of Christina's Mistake, the great autumn success at The King's Theatre. The point is shortly this. Should a woman ..." And so on.

"A pretty little story is going the rounds," said Slosh, "anent that charming little lady, Estelle Rito, who plays the part of a governess in Christina's Mistake, for which ('Manager' Barodo informs me) advance booking up to Christmas has already been taken. It seems that Miss Rito, when shopping in the purlieus of Bond Street ..."

Sloppy Chunks had a joke which set all the world laughing. It was called——

"Between the Acts

Flossie. 'Who's the lady in the box with Mr. Johnson?'

Gussie. 'Hush! It's his wife!'

And Flossie giggled so much that she could hardly listen to the last Act of Christina's Mistake, which she had been looking forward to for weeks!"

The Sunday Sermon offered free tickets to a hundred unmarried suburban girls, to which class Christina's Mistake might be supposed to make a special religious appeal. But they had to collect coupons first for The Sunday Sermon.

And, finally, The Times, of two months later, said:

"A marriage has been arranged between Lady Dorothy Neal, daughter of the Earl of Skye, and the Hon. Geoffrey Bollinger."

Than a successful revenge nothing is sweeter in life. Hector Strong was not the man to spare anyone who had done him an injury. Yet I think his method of revenging himself upon Lady Dorothy savoured of the diabolical. He printed a photograph of her in The Daily Picture Gallery. It was headed "The Beautiful Lady Dorothy Neal."

THE COLLECTOR

When Peter Plimsoll, the Glue King, died, his parting advice to his sons to stick to the business was followed only by John, the elder. Adrian, the younger, had a soul above adhesion. He disposed of his share in the concern and settled down to follow the life of a gentleman of taste and culture and (more particularly) patron of the arts. He began in a modest way to collect ink-pots. His range at first was catholic, and it was not until he had acquired a hundred and forty-seven ink-pots of various designs that he decided to make a speciality of historic ones. This decision was hastened by the discovery that one of Queen Elizabeth's inkstands—supposed (by the owner) to be the identical one with whose aid she wrote her last letter to Raleigh—was about to be put on the market. At some expense Adrian obtained an introduction, through a third party, to the owner; at more expense the owner obtained, through the same gentleman, an introduction to Adrian; and in less than a month the great Elizabeth Ink-pot was safely established in Adrian's house. It was the beginning of the "Plimsoll Collection."

This was twenty years ago. Let us to-day take a walk through the galleries of Mr. Adrian Plimsoll's charming residence, which, as the world knows, overlooks the park. Any friend of mine is always welcome at Number Fifteen. We will start with the North Gallery; I fear that I shall only have time to point out a few of the choicest gems.

This is a Pontesiori sword of the thirteenth century—the only example of the master's art without any notches.

On the left is a Capricci comfit-box. If you have never heard of Capricci, you oughtn't to come to a house like this.

Here we have before us the historic de Montigny topaz. Ask your little boy to tell you about it.

In the East Gallery, of course, the chief treasure is the Santo di Santo amulet, described so minutely in his Vindiciæ Veritatis by John of Flanders. The original MS. of this book is in the South Gallery. You must glance at it when we get there. It will save you the trouble of ordering a copy from your library; they would be sure to keep you waiting....

With some such words as these I lead my friends round Number Fifteen. The many treasures in the private parts of the house I may not show, of course; the bathroom, for instance, in which hangs the finest collection of portraits of philatelists that Europe can boast. You must spend a night with Adrian to be admitted to their company; and, as one of the elect, I can assure you that nothing can be more stimulating on a winter's morning than to catch the eye of Frisby Dranger, F.Ph.S., behind the taps as your head first emerges from the icy waters.

Adrian Plimsoll sat at breakfast, sipping his hot water and crumbling a dry biscuit. A light was in his eye, a flush upon his pallid countenance. He had just heard from a trusty agent that the Scutori breast-plate had been seen in Devonshire. His car was ready to take him to the station.

But alas! a disappointment awaited him. On close examination the breast-plate turned out to be a common Risoldo of inferior working. Adrian left the house in disgust and started on his seven-mile walk back to the station. To complete his misery a sudden storm came on. Cursing alternately his agent and Risoldo, he made his way to a cottage and asked for shelter.

An old woman greeted him civilly and bade him come in.

"If I may just wait till the storm is over," said Adrian, and he sat down in her parlour and looked appraisingly (as was his habit) round the room. The grandfather clock in the corner was genuine, but he was beyond grandfather clocks. There was nothing else of any value: three china dogs and some odd trinkets on the chimney-piece; a print or two——

Stay! What was that behind the youngest dog?

"May I look at that old bracelet?" he asked, his voice trembling a little; and without waiting for permission he walked over and took up the circle of tarnished metal in his hands. As he examined it his colour came and went, his heart seemed to stop beating. With a tremendous effort he composed himself and returned to his chair.

It was the Emperor's Bracelet!

Of course you know the history of this most famous of all bracelets. Made by Spurius Quintus of Rome in 47 B.C., it was given by Cæsar to Cleopatra, who tried without success to dissolve it in vinegar. Returning to Rome by way of Antony, it was worn at a minor conflagration by Nero, after which it was lost sight of for many centuries. It was eventually heard of during the reign of Canute (or Knut, as his admirers called him); and John is known to have lost it in the Wash, whence it was recovered a century afterwards. It must have travelled thence to France, for it was seen once in the possession of Louis XI; and from there to Spain, for Philip the Handsome presented it to Joanna on her wedding day. Columbus took it to America, but fortunately brought it back again; Peter the Great threw it at an indifferent musician; on one of its later visits to England Pope wrote a couplet to it. And the most astonishing thing in its whole history was that now for more than a hundred years it had vanished completely. To turn up again in a little Devonshire cottage! Verily, truth is stranger than fiction.

"That's rather a curious bracelet of yours," said Adrian casually. "My—er—wife has one just like it, which she asked me to match. Is it an old friend, or would you care to sell it?"

"My mother gave it me," said the old woman, "and she had it from hers. I don't know no further than that. I didn't mean to sell it, but——"

"Quite right," said Adrian, "and, after all, I can easily get another."

"But I won't say a bit of money wouldn't be useful. What would you think a fair price, sir? Five shillings?"

Adrian's heart jumped. To get the Emperor's bracelet for five shillings!

But the spirit of the collector rose up strong within him. He laughed kindly.

"My good woman," he said, "they turn out bracelets like that in Birmingham at two shillings apiece. And quite new. I'll give you tenpence."

"Make it one-and-sixpence," she pleaded. "Times are hard."

Adrian reflected. He was not, strictly speaking, impoverished. He could afford one-and-sixpence.

"One-and-tuppence," he said.

"No, no, one-and-sixpence," she repeated obstinately.

Adrian reflected again. After all, he could always sell it for ten thousand pounds, if the worst came to the worst.

"Well, well," he sighed. "One-and-sixpence let it be."

He counted out the money carefully. Then, putting the precious bracelet in his pocket, he rose to go.

Adrian has no relations living now. When he dies he proposes to leave the Plimsoll Collection to the nation, having—as far as he can foresee—no particular use for it in the next world. This is really very generous of him, and no doubt, when the time comes, the papers will say so. But it is a pity that he cannot be appreciated properly in his lifetime. Personally I should like to see him knighted.

THE ADVENTURER

Lionel Norwood, from his earliest days, had been marked out for a life of crime. When quite a child he was discovered by his nurse killing flies on the window-pane. This was before the character of the house-fly had become a matter of common talk among scientists, and Lionel (like all great men, a little before his time) had pleaded hygiene in vain. He was smacked hastily and bundled off to a preparatory school, where his aptitude for smuggling sweets would have lost him many a half-holiday had not his services been required at outside-left in the hockey eleven. With some difficulty he managed to pass into Eton, and three years later—with, one would imagine, still more difficulty—managed to get superannuated. At Cambridge he went down-hill rapidly. He would think nothing of smoking a cigar in academical costume, and on at least one occasion he drove a dogcart on Sunday. No wonder that he was requested, early in his second year, to give up his struggle with the Little-go and betake himself back to London.

London is always glad to welcome such people as Lionel Norwood. In no other city is it so simple for a man of easy conscience to earn a living by his wits. If Lionel ever had any scruples (which, after a perusal of the above account of his early days, it may be permitted one to doubt) they were removed by an accident to his solicitor, who was run over in the Argentine on the very day that he arrived there with what was left of Lionel's money. Reduced suddenly to poverty, Norwood had no choice but to enter upon a life of crime.

Except, perhaps, that he used slightly less hair-oil than most, he seemed just the ordinary man about town as he sat in his dressing-gown one fine summer morning and smoked a cigarette.

His rooms were furnished quietly and in the best of taste. No signs of his nefarious profession showed themselves to the casual visitor. The appealing letters from the Princess whom he was blackmailing, the wire apparatus which shot the two of spades down his sleeve during the coon-can nights at the club, the thimble and pea with which he had performed the three-card trick so successfully at Epsom last week—all these were hidden away from the common gaze. It was a young gentleman of fashion who lounged in his chair and toyed with a priceless straight-cut.

There was a tap at the door, and Masters, his confidential valet, came in.

"Well," said Lionel, "have you looked through the post?"

"Yes, sir," said the man. "There's the usual cheque from Her Highness, a request for more time from the lady in Tite Street with twopence to pay on the envelope, and banknotes from the Professor as expected. The young gentleman of Hill Street has gone abroad suddenly, sir."

"Ah!" said Lionel, with a sudden frown. "I suppose you'd better cross him off our list, Masters."

"Yes, sir. I had ventured to do so, sir. I think that's all, except that Mr. Snooks is glad to accept your kind invitation to dinner and bridge to-night. Will you wear the hair-spring coat, sir, or the metal clip?"

Lionel made no answer. He sat plunged in thought. When he spoke it was about another matter.

"Masters," he said, "I have found out Lord Fairlie's secret at last. I shall go to see him this afternoon."

"Yes, sir. Will you wear your revolver, sir, as it's a first call?"

"I think so. If this comes off, Masters, it will make our fortune."

"I hope so, I'm sure, sir." Masters placed the whisky within reach and left the room silently.

Alone, Lionel picked up his paper and turned to the Agony Column.

As everybody knows, the Agony Column of a daily paper is not actually so domestic as it seems. When "Mother" apparently says to "Floss," "Come home at once. Father gone away for week. Bert and Sid longing to see you," what is really happening is that Barney Hoker is telling Jud Batson to meet him outside the Duke of Westminster's little place at 3 a.m. precisely on Tuesday morning, not forgetting to bring his jemmy and a dark lantern with him. And Floss's announcement next day, "Coming home with George," is Jud's way of saying that he will turn up all right, and half thinks of bringing his automatic pistol with him too, in case of accidents.

In this language—which, of course, takes some little learning—Lionel Norwood had long been an expert. The advertisement which he was now reading was unusually elaborate:

"Lost, in a taxi between Baker Street and Shepherd's Bush, a gold-mounted umbrella with initials 'J. P.' on it. If Ellen will return to her father immediately all will be forgiven. White spot on foreleg. Mother very anxious and desires to return thanks for kind enquiries. Answers to the name of Ponto. Bis dat qui cito dat."

What did it mean? For Lionel it had no secrets. He was reading the revelation by one of his agents of the skeleton in Lord Fairlie's cupboard!

Lord Fairlie was one of the most distinguished members of the Cabinet. His vein of high seriousness, his lofty demeanour, the sincerity of his manner endeared him not only to his own party, but even (astounding as it may seem) to a few high-minded men upon the other side, who admitted, in moments of expansion which they probably regretted afterwards, that he might, after all, be as devoted to his country as they were. For years now his life had been without blemish. It was impossible to believe that even in his youth he could have sown any wild oats; terrible to think that these wild oats might now be coming home to roost.

"What do you require of me?" he said courteously to Lionel, as the latter was shown into his study.

Lionel went to the point at once.

"I am here, my lord," he said, "on business. In the course of my ordinary avocations"—the parliamentary atmosphere seemed to be affecting his language—"I ascertained a certain secret in your past life which, if it were revealed, might conceivably have a not undamaging effect upon your career. For my silence in this matter I must demand a sum of fifty thousand pounds."

Lord Fairlie had grown paler and paler as this speech proceeded.

"What have you discovered?" he whispered. Alas! he knew only too well what the damning answer would be.

"Twenty years ago," said Lionel, "you wrote a humorous book."

Lord Fairlie gave a strangled cry. His keen mind recognized in a flash what a hold this knowledge would give his enemies. Shafts of Folly, his book had been called. Already he saw the leading articles of the future:—

"We confess ourselves somewhat at a loss to know whether Lord Fairlie's speech at Plymouth yesterday was intended as a supplement to his earlier work, Shafts of Folly, or as a serious offering to a nation impatient of levity in such a crisis...."

"The Cabinet's jester, in whom twenty years ago the country lost an excellent clown without gaining a statesman, was in great form last night...."

"Lord Fairlie has amused us in the past with his clever little parodies; he may amuse us in the future; but as a statesman we can only view him with disgust...."

"Well?" said Lionel at last. "I think your lordship is wise enough to understand. The discovery of a sense of humour in a man of your eminence——"

But Lord Fairlie was already writing out the cheque.

THE EXPLORER

As the evening wore on—and one young man after another asked Jocelyn Montrevor if she were going to Ascot, what? or to Henley, what? or what?—she wondered more and more if this were all that life would ever hold for her. Would she never meet a man, a real man who had done something? These boys around her were very pleasant, she admitted to herself; very useful indeed, she added, as one approached her with some refreshment; but they were only boys.

"Here you are," said Freddy, handing her an ice in three colours. "I've had it made specially cold for you. They only had the green, pink, and yellow jerseys left; I hope you don't mind. The green part is arsenic, I believe. If you don't want the wafer I'll take it home and put it between the sashes of my bedroom window. The rattling kept me awake all last night. That's why I'm looking so ill, by the way."

Jocelyn smiled kindly and went on with her ice.

"That reminds me," Freddy went on, "we've got a nut here to-night. The genuine thing. None of your society Barcelonas or suburban Filberts. One of the real Cob family; the driving-from-the-sixth-tee, inset-on-the-right, and New-Year's-message-to-the-country touch. In short, a celebrity."

"Who?" asked Jocelyn eagerly. Perhaps here was a man.

"Worrall Brice, the explorer. Don't say you haven't heard of him or Aunt Alice will cry."

Heard of him? Of course she had heard of him. Who hadn't?

Worrall Brice's adventures in distant parts of the empire would have filled a book—had, in fact, already filled three. A glance at his flat in St. James's Street gave you some idea of the adventures he had been through. Here were the polished spurs of his companion in the famous ride through Australia from south to north—all that had been left by the cannibals of the Wogga-Wogga River after their banquet. Here was the poisoned arrow which, by the merciful intervention of Providence, just missed Worrall and pierced the heart of one of his black attendants, the post-mortem happily revealing the presence of a new and interesting poison. Here, again, was the rope with which he was hanged by mistake as a spy in South America—a mistake which would certainly have had fatal results if he had not had the presence of mind to hold his breath during the performance. In yet another corner you might see his favourite mascot—a tooth of the shark which bit him off the coast of China. Spears, knives, and guns lined the walls; every inch of the floor was covered by skins. His flat was typical of the man—a man who had done things.

"Introduce him to me," commanded Jocelyn. "Where is he?"

She looked up suddenly and saw him entering the ball-room. He was of commanding height and his face was the face of a man who has been exposed to the forces of Nature. The wind, the waves, the sun, the mosquito had set their mark upon him. Down one side of his cheek was a newly healed scar, a scratch from a hippopotamus in its last death-struggle. A legacy from a bison seared his brow.

He walked with the soft easy tread of the python, or the Pathan, or some animal with a "pth" in it. Probably I mean the panther. He bore himself confidently, and his mouth was a trap from which no superfluous word escaped. He was the strong silent man of Jocelyn's dreams.

"Mr. Worrall Brice, Miss Montrevor," said Freddy, and left them.

Worrall Brice bowed and stood beside her with folded arms, his gaze fixed above her head.

"I shall not expect you to dance," said Jocelyn, with a confidential smile which implied that he and she were above such frivolities. As a matter of fact, he could have taught her the Wogga-Wogga one-step, the Bimbo, the Kiyi, the Ju-bu, the Head-hunter's

Hug, and many other cannibalistic steps which, later on, were to become the rage of London and the basis of a revue.

"I have often imagined you, as you kept watch over your camp," she went on, "and I have seemed myself to hear the savages and lions roaring outside the circle of fire, what time in the swamps the crocodiles were barking."

"Yes," he said.

"It must be a wonderful life."

"Yes."

"If I were a man I should want to lead such a life; to get away from all this," and she waved her hand round the room, "back to Nature. To know that I could not eat until I had first killed my dinner; that I could not live unless I slew the enemy! That must be fine!"

"Yes," said Worrall.

"I cannot get Freddy to see it. He is quite content to have shot a few grouse ... and once to have wounded a beater. There must be more in life than that."

"Yes."

"I suppose I am elemental. Beneath the veneer of civilization I am a savage. To wake up with the war-cry of the enemy in my ears, to sleep with the—er—barking of the crocodile in my dreams, that is life!"

Worrall Brice tugged at his moustache and gazed into space over her head. Then he spoke.

"Crocodiles don't bark," he said.

Jocelyn looked at him in astonishment. "But in your book, Through Trackless Paths!" she cried. "I know it almost by heart. It was you who taught me. What are the beautiful words? 'On the banks of the sleepy river two great crocodiles were barking.'"

"Not 'barking,'" said Worrall. "'Basking.' It was a misprint."

"Oh!" said Jocelyn. She had a moment's awful memory of all the occasions when she had insisted that crocodiles barked. There had been a particularly fierce argument with Meta Richards, who had refused to weigh even the printed word of Worrall Brice against the silence of the Reptile House on her last visit to the Zoo.

"Well," smiled Jocelyn, "you must teach me about these things. Will you come and see me?"

"Yes," said Worrall. He rather liked to stand and gaze into the distance while pretty women talked to him. And Jocelyn was very pretty.

"We live in South Kensington. Come on Sunday, won't you? 99 Peele Crescent."

"Yes," said Worrall.

195

On Sunday Jocelyn waited eagerly for him in the drawing-room of Peele Crescent. Her father was asleep in the library, her mother was dead; so she would have the great man to herself for an afternoon. Later she would have him for always, for she meant to marry him. And when they were married she was not so sure that they would live with the noise of the crocodile barking or coughing, or whatever it did, in their ears. She saw herself in that little house in Green Street with the noise of motor-horns and taxi-whistles to soothe her to sleep.

Yet what a man he was! What had he said to her? She went over all his words.... They were not many.

At six o'clock she was still waiting in the drawing-room at Peele Crescent....

At six-thirty Worrall Brice had got as far as Peele Place....

At six-forty-five he found himself in Radcliffe Square again....

At seven o'clock, just as he was giving himself up for lost, he met a taxi and returned to St. James's Street. He was a great traveller, but South Kensington had been too much for him.

Next week he went back unmarried to the jungle. It was the narrowest escape he had had.

www.ingramcontent.com/pod-product-compliance
Lightning Source LLC
Chambersburg PA
CBHW020433180626
46812CB00003B/1208